Echoes of the Past

Maggie Ford was born in the East End of London but at the age of six she moved to Essex, where she lived for the rest of her life. After the death of her first husband, when she was only 26, she went to work as a legal secretary until she remarried in 1968. She had a son and two daughters, all married; her second husband died in 1984. She wrote short stories from the early 1970s, also writing under the name Elizabeth Lord, and continued to publish books up to her death at the age of 92 in 2020.

Maggie
FORD
Echoes of the Past

CANELO

First published in Great Britain in 2001 by Severn House Publishers LTD

This edition published in the United Kingdom in 2022 by

Canelo
Unit 9, 5th Floor
Cargo Works, 1–2 Hatfields
London, SE1 9PG
United Kingdom

A CIP catalogue record for this book is available from the British Library.

Print ISBN 978 1 80032 803 7
Ebook ISBN 978 1 80032 440 4

Originally published as *Winter Wine* by Elizabeth Lord

Look for more great books at www.canelo.co

Printed and bound in Great Britain by Clays Ltd, Elcograf S.p.A.

1

For my three children, Janet, John and Clare

Part One

1953–1957

One

On this damp November morning, the gaze of those leaving the crematorium followed the elegant figure of Marjory Lett, the second wife of the deceased, Henry Lett. With her was Hugh, his son by his first marriage, Grace Lett having died five years earlier.

Neither appeared too saddened by the loss of a husband and father. Rather their step was light as they went towards the limousine returning them to Swift House, Henry and Marjory's home. And why not? This drearier part of inheriting a fortune was over. Now they could sit back and enjoy the family business, left for them to carry on. Yet there was a snag, and by now everyone knew it.

As one of the deceased's friends, a fellow restaurateur, here to pay his respects, said to a companion: "Pity about that restaurant. They say she never had any interest in it. I expect she'll sell it now for what she can get."

"It's not what it once was," returned the other man. "Been going downhill since 1947. Poor old Henry never did learn to move with the times. Place has become too damned old-fashioned."

"Lost heart a long time ago," said the first. "He fought so hard to keep it going. As you say, she was no help. Only after one thing – his money."

3

The other agreed. "Now she can sit back and reap the rewards of those three years, eh? Bit of a gold-digger if you ask me. But he couldn't see it."

The first man nodded, making towards his Rolls beside which his chauffeur stood ready to open the passenger door. "My opinion is, if it hadn't been for that Goodridge fellow, that manager of his, it wouldn't have lasted this long. Carried him most of the time. The man deserved to have set up his own restaurant. Should have. In competition to Letts. But some are too loyal for their own good."

"Maybe he will now that it's gone to the wife and that feckless son of Henry's," put in the first man. "Budding Shakespearean actor or something, so I hear. With that sort taking over, the place won't last six months. Poor old Henry – he deserved better."

The chauffeur opening the car door for him, he slipped into the seat and, as the door closed, wound down the window to pop his head out.

"Mark my words, Bob, I give that restaurant six months."

Bob nodded his agreement and, as the Rolls glided off, went to find his own car.

On the further side of the slowly dispersing group, Victoria Hurshell, the only surviving sister of the deceased, clung to her husband's arm in a manner more possessive than loving. With her daughter Sheila close behind, eyes still red from grieving a much-loved uncle, she too let her gaze follow the progress of the woman in the expensive black outfit, high-heeled shoes and tiny veiled hat.

"So there she goes." Victoria's tone was an acidic hiss as the widow let herself be helped by her stepson into the leading Daimler taking them back to Swift House and a

4

sumptuous funeral spread. Prepared by top-class caterers it lay awaiting fifty or more guests as well as the immediate mourners, Henry Lett having been much respected.

"Off to enjoy the fruits of her bereavement," continued Victoria with a stiff smile to those around her while allowing her husband to conduct her towards the second of the five limousines provided by the funeral directors.

Keeping her voice low, she spoke rapidly as always. "I always said that woman knew what she was about, taking up with a man who'd already had a couple of heart attacks."

"Mummy," said Sheila in a cautious but accusing tone. "She didn't *take up* with Uncle Henry. You make it sound as though they'd been having a sordid affair. They married legitimately and he was happy with that. He was so lonely after Aunt Grace died."

Her mother paused to turn on her. "I still say she caught him on the rebound after Grace died. She knew it was only a matter of time before he popped off too and everything came to her. His own fault – refused to give up smoking. Saying cigars were safer than cigarettes, the fool! And what a fool he was to be taken in by her anyway. She knew what she was doing. Didn't I say that from the very beginning, Harold? What woman takes up with a man twenty years her senior if not for his money?"

"She herself wasn't exactly a chicken," reminded Harold, anxious to get into the car out of the drizzle. "Thirty-three, for God's sake, when she married your brother. You talk of Henry as though he was an old man. He wasn't an old man. Fifty-five isn't old. I'm fifty-nine, and I don't feel old."

With that he ducked his head angrily into the waiting car, the door held open by its chauffeur, leaving his wife and daughter to be helped in by the man, Victoria's sarcastic, "Thank you!" directed more at Harold than him.

Those left to their own speculations about Marjory Lett, now being driven off with her nice little windfall from three years of marriage to a sick man, were having a field day. They dawdled to their conveyances, reluctant to get back to the gathering at Swift House where they might not so easily be able to express their various observations in the hearing of others.

The only two people apparently not touched by all this were Edwin Lett, nephew of the deceased, and Helen Goodridge, daughter of the dead man's restaurant manager, William. Their eyes for each other alone, they lingered, oblivious to the drizzle that was beginning to come down harder.

Watching them as the last vehicle came alongside, William Goodridge's features softened. Helen was his only daughter. Mary, his wife, killed in an air raid during the war, had not borne any other surviving children.

Theirs had been a strange marriage – arranged almost. By Henry Lett himself. But Will never cared to think about that.

Recalling it even now after all these years carried a sense of unreality. He had obliged a request and reaped a grand reward because of it, and it still pricked his conscience. Yet he had loved Mary. He had brought up her child as if she'd been his own, in fact over the years often forgot to think of Helen as anything but his own.

His tender regard of the two young people with their fair heads close together faded. About to step into the car, he paused, his progress arrested by the implications that last thought conjured up. Edwin and Helen were cousins. Nothing wrong in that even if they were one day to be united in marriage. What did matter was that Helen was unaware of it. He'd never found the courage to tell her who her true father had been.

He should never have told Edwin in the pub that day, not thinking, but if Edwin were to tell her now, he dreaded to think what a shock it would be to her. What if she were to turn on him for keeping it from her? Should he tell her now, today, before it was too late? But he could visualise those wide grey eyes filling with pain and condemnation of him for springing this on her after all her years believing him to be her real father. Better to have a word with Edwin when they got back to Swift House, if it wasn't too late – warn him against saying anything to Helen just yet. "I'd prefer to tell her myself," he would say, "so I would be glad if you were to say nothing to her for the time being."

He was angry with himself in allowing his judgement that day in the pub to be clouded by thoughts of those two, married, eventually returning Letts to its past magnificence. It had gone through his mind that young Edwin had money left to him by his father Geoffrey Lett, Henry's brother, and Helen had that substantial trust fund which Henry Lett as her natural father had made for her many years ago coming to her next year.

Swept away on a wave of enthusiasm, his mind's eye had resurrected Letts as it had once been, before the war, the hub of society, the rich and famous pouring through its doors. No longer did the rich and famous haunt it. But he wanted to see it great again, and those two young people had been the means of its salvation. After having talked a load of tommyrot to Edwin following the reading of the will about what could be done about the restaurant if

Edwin had a mind to get involved, he'd been encouraged when he'd seen Edwin's eyes light up at the sight of Helen.

In all the world only three people had known the truth about Helen: he, her mother and Henry. Then he had to go and tell Edwin. The boy was obviously already in love with her and she with him, and if he wasn't careful it could all get out of hand where Helen was concerned. That was the last thing he wanted.

Gnawing at his lip, William Goodridge climbed into the car, aware that he had been holding up four others of Henry Lett's restaurant staff. The door with its darkened window closed with a solid thud, obliterating his view of the young couple strolling as if they had all the time in the world towards the third limousine still patiently waiting to depart the now vacated crematorium portico, already beginning to fill with another funeral party awaiting the arrival of the star player.

November was a popular if dismal month for deaths.

–

It seemed to Edwin ages since he'd taken Helen to that party, but it was only a week ago. Wrong, perhaps, attending a party so soon after the demise of Uncle Henry, but it had been arranged for weeks and Uncle Henry's death had been so sudden, taking everyone by surprise. Anyway, it had been a quiet sort of party, a few drinks in a friend's house with a few other friends, none of whom had any dealings with his family. And it had been the excuse he'd needed to ask Helen out without making it too obvious a date.

Helen had looked stunning when he picked her up to take her there. In a New Look tight-waisted, flare-skirted dress, her fair hair brushed out to curl loosely on her shoulders, and just the right amount of make-up showing up her hazel eyes, she'd taken his breath away. She had mixed with everyone so easily that as they had crowded around her, admiring her, one hopeful remarked that if Edwin had any thought of giving her up, he'd be more than pleased to step into the breach.

"Not if you gave me a million quid," Edwin answered proudly. Indeed, he had felt proud of her, as though she'd been his girl for years, and knew he'd done the right thing asking her to go there with him. Better than being alone, at a loss about what to say to each other, the date ruined before it had begun, she wary of him and he self-conscious and stammering, making an idiot of himself.

He had been out with plenty of girls before, but none like Helen. Going to a place full of other people had broken any ice there might have been. Afterwards he had driven her home to her door and they *had* been alone together, but by then they had grown more at ease in each other's presence. And she had let him kiss her.

He hadn't been able to ask her out again with all the funeral arrangements, Aunt Victoria presiding of course, but expecting him to help, Hugh practically useless if not disinterested and Marjory Lett, the widow, not so much too bereaved to assist as stating quite openly and without a tear that it was a chore she'd rather not have to do.

"I need some time to myself so that I can consider seriously what to do about my future," she'd said somewhat off-handedly, and even Hugh had been taken aback by the cold nature of the statement.

"Of course I felt it, the old man going like he did," he said to Edwin. "But it wasn't as if he and I were that close, me not exactly living under the same roof. Only saw him occasionally. She saw him every day. I know they had separate bedrooms – she led her own life – but it's a bit heartless, don't you think? She's not missing him at all. And everyone knows it."

To that, Edwin kept his own counsel and said nothing. He'd had other things to think about, such as when he was going to ask Helen out again.

Sitting in silence next to her as the Daimler took them back to Swift House, his mind alighted briefly on them being cousins though now wasn't the time to mention it. Besides, it wasn't important.

At Swift House, they soon became separated, Helen spending most of the time with her father who seemed to Edwin to prefer her by his side, perhaps because she knew no one. For himself, he readily took part in the general conversation, knowing everyone, though the laughter, encouraged by their hostess's lively tones tinkling out above the buzz and making no one feel they must be solemn any more, made it seem as if Henry Lett had in fact never passed away.

To Edwin it felt like sacrilege. Most after-funeral gatherings invariably did brighten up, maybe helping take the bereaved's mind off the loss, if only temporarily. But Marjory's brightness jarred on his nerves. It was as though she saw herself freed of some sort of chain and was making no secret of it. Even Hugh, grown increasingly independent of his father, was more affected than she – but then, blood had to be thicker than water.

"What are you going to do now?" asked Edwin.

Hugh looked up from a whisky and soda and lifted his shoulders in a don't-know attitude. Edwin strove to enlighten him.

"Are you going back to acting or have you given any more thought to what's going to happen about the business?"

"What's there to think about?" returned Hugh, taking a large gulp of his drink. He was already a little drunk. "Up to Marjory really. As for me, I'm not particularly anxious to give up my career and play waiter. That's what it boils down to. If Marjory wants to sell the place for what it brings, that suits me. Puts a bit of money in the old pocket to help me get somewhere in my profession. The place has become run down. It's not all that much to speak of these days."

"It was once."

"Once. But it isn't now. Trying to make it what it once was would be a monumental uphill struggle, old man. Marjory has the controlling interest and she's keen to sell; not much point me hanging on to my shares. We've had a few long chats about it and have finally come to an agreement."

Edwin felt the anger rise up in him.

"To let it go to some third-rate chain of restaurants with no knowledge of what a fine history it has and caring even less!"

More than ever he wanted to get his hands on the place. After everything Mr Goodridge had told him the day following the reading of his uncle's will, he'd been gripped by enthusiasm for the idea of buying Marjory out. Still unsure whether there'd be enough in his own inheritance from his father to match what they were looking for, even boosted by a sizeable bank loan, he could almost visualise her putting up the stakes to wring the last penny out of him. Old-fashioned and no longer patronised by the best people though it was, Letts was still a restaurant that gave good account of itself and could still command a good price.

Edwin had heard that when his grandfather had died there had been the self-same feelings of uncertainty in the two sons as he had now, but they had pulled it out of the doldrums into which it had floated following the old man's demise. And if they could do it, so could he.

But there had been two of them: his father and his uncle – he'd be doing this on his own. It was daunting. Even though William Goodridge had boosted his enthusiasm and could still help him over the rough bits, he was no longer a young man and his own enthusiasm would wane with age.

All in all it was something of a Sisyphean task he was contemplating taking on. Would it be worth all that effort, all the money needed for it? He would have to mortgage himself up to the hilt. Perhaps he should think again.

He kept to the far side of the gathering, well away from the restaurant manager. If he got into Goodridge's clutches again he'd be persuaded all over again, and lose sight of straight thinking once more. Yet if the place were to go…

Unbidden and without warning, in the way the mind has of winging back to the past of its own accord, Edwin's dredged up the memory of the time of his parents' death.

They'd been killed by a doodlebug, a flying bomb, a V1 rocket, it didn't matter what they called it. It had landed on a restaurant in Piccadilly where they'd gone to eat. Brought home from college, he had been gently told by Uncle Henry, with Aunt Grace sobbing quietly in the background so that his uncle had had to turn round to look warmingly at her from time to time while explaining things in a faltering, roundabout way until finally coming to the point. But having already guessed what his uncle had been trying to tell him, Edwin had found his uncle's tactics made the news harder rather than easier to bear.

For the first time in his young life he was made aware how swiftly people can be cut from life – there one minute, gone the next, annihilated, no longer existing, the world going on without them as if they had never been. That was how it had seemed to him at that moment. Even now he couldn't think hów he'd got through those first months, his recollection of that time failing him to some extent.

He did know that Uncle Henry and Aunt Grace had taken charge of him, perhaps mistakenly saying that he need not go back to college. What exactly he did do over those months was not there in his brain as though it meant to erase the pain.

But the day he learned that he'd lost both parents in the blink of an eye stood out to the last detail in his memory: how people had come and cuddled him, sobbed over him, crooning over him, saying, "Oh, you poor dear!" as if that helped. He could recall standing alone for a few brief minutes during a lull in the commiserations in the middle of the huge drawing room at Tilse Hall, his parents' home in High Ongar, the room looking more vast than he had ever realised. He remembered staring at his reflection in the big gilt-framed mirror over the marble fireplace and wondering why he wasn't crying like everyone else was. That pale, drawn, teenage face had stared back as if to say, Who are you? He remembered Beryl, their young house-maid, coming in for something – he didn't know what – and, seeing him, her already reddened eyes had filled up again as she gabbled, "I'm so sorry, Master Edwin, I didn't mean…" Then, blubbering, she had rushed out.

They had never let him view the bodies – too young, they'd said. He'd been sixteen, old enough, but they wouldn't let him. Uncle Henry had gone in his stead and forever after became grim-faced whenever the death of his brother was mentioned.

Not being allowed to see his parents rather than helping had raised all sorts of pictures in his mind. The war had not been kind to the young – talk of people blown apart, buried under tons of rubble, burned to death, did not escape young ears – and what he saw in his mind was his parents' broken, unrecognisable bodies, their lovely faces torn and rent. He had suffered nightmares, still indelibly etched in his brain to this day, while his waking life around that time remained clouded as though it had never existed.

Everything had gone to Edwin, being their only child: their money, possessions, the house with all its contents and their shares in Letts, though Uncle Henry as the main shareholder in the family had still retained the controlling interest.

As for himself, a wealthy young man, he had grown up with no interest in the family business. Life stretched ahead of him, and to block out what it had done to him, he took advantage of what its future had to offer a young man of means. He left college, despite Uncle Henry's frowns, and did not go on to university. But his grades had been high and when called up for National Service after the war, he'd gone in as a junior officer as a matter of course. Stationed in Germany, he'd had a good time, lots of girls, plenty of booze, great mates. When he'd come out of that, he continued to seek the high life, bought the flat he had now, held parties there, had plenty of friends, his pick of the girls, but somehow it had all gone stale.

There is only so much one can enjoy before that happens. One can weary even of eating caviar at every meal.

He often wondered if his parents had ever felt like that, gallivanting all over the place as they had, gambling, spending money, always away somewhere. He had grown up hardly seeing them for much more than a few weeks at a time. Perhaps it was that which had affected him so on their death, the feeling of lost opportunities, of some sort of lurking void.

For a while he had aped them, but it was forced, and he began to realise that he wasn't like his wayward father – that deep inside him slept a more thoughtful character. It had often sent him downhill into a pit of misery. But he'd always had a base when the doldrums hit – his Uncle Henry and Aunt Grace in that big rambling house of theirs, so different from his parents' ultra-modern home in High Ongar which he couldn't bear going near. Under John Creasy, the manager in charge, it was well looked after. Now it would have to be sold off if he listened to William Goodridge.

Edwin felt no pangs at the thought of seeing it go. It would be a weight off his back, sitting there in the countryside glowering accusingly at him for ignoring it all these years.

Eventually Aunt Grace died, of cancer. Uncle Henry had sat with her for weeks in that private clinic, never leaving her side, was inconsolable after she went. But three years later he'd remarried. Now he too was dead. Things always moved on, and now it seemed it was his own turn to knuckle down and take on the responsibility of the family business no one else seemed to want, all only too eager to be rid of it.

Edwin felt anger against them all rise inside him, like gall in his throat. Across the room full of people he saw Goodridge gazing at him as though reading his thoughts. As their eyes met, Edwin was dismayed to see him leave those he'd been with to shoulder his way across the room towards him. Edwin tightened his lips. The man was bent yet again on persuading him into taking on the challenge Letts held out.

"Would you mind if I had a word with you in private?" he began, and what could Edwin do but nod assent, suspecting the worst? But it was not about the restaurant after all.

"I have a great favour to ask of you," he said, having guided him to the open but deserted front porch. "Do you recall my telling you about Helen's mother?" he embarked, hurrying on before Edwin could affirm it, "and that I'm not her real father – that your Uncle Henry was?"

Again he gave his listener no time to reply. "You did realise it makes you cousins? But that's not important. What is important is that I need to know if you've said anything to her about it."

"I've not mentioned it," said Edwin, mystified. "Being as we were with other people while we were together I never thought to say. Why? Should I have?"

Goodridge bit his lip. The older face smoothed a little as though in thankfulness. "This is the favour I have to ask. I would be obliged if you didn't mention the fact at all. You see, I've never told her that I wasn't her real father. I've kept putting it off and now, at this late stage in her life, I find it excruciatingly difficult to embark on it. I know I should have told her at an early age, but to tell the girl who thought she was your daughter that her real father didn't want his good name and his marriage messed up and so had me bring her up in secret as her father, that would have destroyed her. Do you see what I'm getting at?"

Edwin did not reply. Yes, he saw only too clearly. This man was a coward through and through. He'd lived a lie all his life and now he wanted Edwin himself to further that lie.

"You can't hurt her now." The plea cut through his thoughts. "It has to come through me. I shall tell her. But please, not you. Please, say nothing."

Dismally, Edwin nodded. "I have to go now," he said. "I've had enough of this charade they call a funeral gathering." He didn't want to be around this man who was virtually making hell of a promising heaven with Helen.

Two

Across the restaurant, Edwin caught a glimpse of William Goodridge and swore under his breath.

Certain of it being the restaurant manager's day off, he had come here with the intention of seeing the place through different eyes, without Goodridge's influence, but the best laid plans, as they say... There was nowhere to hide, and to walk out would in itself attract the man's attention. All he could do was sit here and hope for the best. All he wanted to do was form his own opinion of the place, make up his own mind about it.

Over the years he had seldom ventured here. Before his uncle's death he'd been having a good time. Having done his National Service, and found it quite cushy really being a lieutenant, he'd had every intention of enjoying life to the full with friends of his own social standing, going to parties, having a good time with plenty of girlfriends. He'd hardly been near the family business. But the good life had worn a little thin of late anyway, and the thought that he must one day knuckle down and do something had begun to nag at him. Goodridge's suggestion that he at least try to pull Letts up by its bootlaces was tempting, he had to admit. Tempting but frightening. So here he was looking the place over through the eyes of a customer.

Goodridge hadn't seen him yet, the place being just over half full this lunchtime. Office people mostly, enjoying their hour's break. Once, according to Goodridge, it would have been full to overflowing, customers of notability rubbing shoulders with their own sort. Now it held white-collar workers.

Edwin's reverie was cut short. Goodridge had caught sight of him, was coming over. The tall figure in the dark jacket possessed the somewhat intimidating bearing of a man in control of an entire restaurant and all who worked under its roof, its smooth working assured under an eye that missed nothing. An almost imperceptible nod or lift of the chin sternly commanded one or another waiter to hasten himself, be more attentive or to mind himself in what he was doing.

"Mr Lett, we don't often see you here."

Edwin offered the man a smile. Still the precise formality despite his being so young, just twenty-five, a mere boy to William Goodridge who must be approaching sixty. All so different to the informality of the pub when he had spoken of the good old days of Letts. Perhaps it was because he was here in the restaurant rather than that pub. Edwin decided to keep to the formality this man had set.

"I thought I'd cast an eye over the place," he began. "After all you told me about it, I feel I've stayed away too long. I've had a lot of social catching up to do since doing my National Service."

The attempted joke fell flat; the other man's lips hardly twitched. Still being bloody formal, making him uncomfortable. Suddenly any interest in resurrecting this place fell away. What was the point? Drop the whole thing.

"May I ask, Mr Lett, if you've had any more thoughts on approaching your uncle's widow and son about this place?"

Why he should feel irritated, Edwin wasn't sure. "No, not yet," he replied curtly, huffy as a young girl. The man was being pushy.

"You should get cracking, Mr Lett," said Goodridge. "I've heard that Mrs Lett will be talking to some people on Monday or Tuesday. Doesn't give you much time, if you're still of a mind to buy her out."

Was he "of a mind"? He wasn't sure. Uncertainty must have shown in his face as Goodridge said, "Don't order yet, Mr Lett. I'd like you to come with me. I've something I want to show you."

He was already on his way, compelling Edwin to get up and follow him across the restaurant and up the curved flight of carpeted stairs to the mezzanine level, its gleaming circular dance floor at the moment deserted. One glance at the outdated art deco chandeliers, the glittering gilt cocktail bar, the surrounding plum-coloured carpet and the scattering of spindle-legged tables and chairs, and Edwin was instantly reminded of a film set straight out of the thirties. This was its problem: nothing had moved forward, all had become stuck in the decade prior to the war, his uncle loath to change anything.

But why? There had to be a reason. To all accounts he'd been quite a go-getter in the twenties, his brother Geoffrey, Edwin's father, much less interested in Letts except to spend its profits, if Goodridge was to be believed.

The man had pulled no punches in telling him of his father – had told it as it was, no inflexion or emphasis of any sort on the memories he had raked up from the past in that pub some ten days ago, and everything he'd said had been utterly believable.

Edwin, a little taken aback by Goodridge's frankness about his parents, still retained a sneaking suspicion that he had held back more than he had told. It would have taken weeks, would have filled a whole book, and any memory related instantly off the cuff can never be that complete. No doubt a lot of it had been more forgotten than left out. The man perhaps could be forgiven.

He was led on across the dance floor to a door exactly matching the surrounding decor. This Goodridge opened and, stepping through, Edwin found himself conducted along a dingy passage, up more stairs to another door that led to an office, then across that and through a glass door into a smaller room, a private office. There Goodridge went, pulling open the drawer of a wooden filing cabinet on the far side of the room and taking out a brown leather photograph album.

"Here," he said. Laying it on the desk he opened it. "Come and look."

Lying inside the leaves were photographs. "Taken of the restaurant in its heyday," he enlightened Edwin. "From the 1920s onwards. Mr Henry liked to take photos of it all. See what you make of them."

Obligingly Edwin bent over them, scrutinising each one as he was shown it. One took his attention so that he stayed Goodridge's hand in the turning over of the next leaf. He didn't see the smile on the other man's face as he let the page remain.

Faded to sepia, the photo was an enlargement of a group of revellers, clustered close together for the snap to be taken. Behind them people were seated, every table occupied. All around were Christmas decorations that even in this faded photo looked as though they still moved, still glittered in the bright light of a myriad chandeliers. For a moment or two Edwin felt he could almost hear the raucous din of a dance band, the echoing murmur of voices, felt he could even hear the tune – "I'll See You In My Dreams"?

Why that song? The more he stared, the more he was drawn into the picture, as though becoming part of the excitement. His blood had begun to run like a river approaching a cataract. His face had become hot as though he had been drinking, his breath grown sharper. In his mind the people were actually moving, laughing, responding to the photographer's commands to "smile and say cheese!"

Edwin looked up quickly, realising his lips too had formed around the word, and experienced a small shock to discover the office in which he stood all still and quiet. He found himself looking at Goodridge, his own eyes, he was certain, glowing from the experience he'd had.

Goodridge was looking intently at him, smiling, the older face creased with satisfaction. "You see what I mean," he stated simply.

Slowly Edwin nodded, then straightened his back, found it stiff from the posture he'd adopted to stare at the photo. Not only that, the scene was still with him and so was a desire, so strong that he could almost taste it.

"I'm going to do it, Mr Goodridge. I'll go and see her this afternoon."

"First," warned Goodridge, his face now grown serious and businesslike, "look in on your bank manager and find out how much he would lend you on top of your own finances for such an enterprise. I cannot see him refusing you, Mr Lett. You are one of the family. Your credit will always hold good."

"I wonder," mused Edwin as the album was put lovingly away. He could still see the photo as though it had taken up permanent residence in his brain. "The place isn't worth half of what it once was."

"Don't be too sure, lad." Informality dropped away from Goodridge; it was like a father talking to his son. "Once an outsider is interested in developing it the value will rise soon enough. Mrs Lett and your cousin are eager to get rid of it and take what they can before it loses any more of its value. That catering firm they are meeting may be keen to snap up it up before word does get around and up goes the value. On the other hand they might delay making a decision to scare your aunt into lowering the price even more. I don't think she or your cousin have much idea of business. They just want to take the money and have out. Though Lord knows, your aunt as his wife has Mr Henry's entire estate other than what he bequeathed in his will."

Edwin stared at him. One thing he hated was Marjory Lett being called his aunt. She was a money-grabber, leaping into the shoes of his real aunt hardly was the woman cold in her grave – or that was how he saw it. The other thing he hated was being told what to do as if he hadn't any savvy of his own.

"Whichever way," Goodridge went on, "if you're serious about giving this place a go, you've got to move fast, lad."

It seemed this man was practically taking over, making decisions for him. Edwin felt angry. "I'll make my own choice," he said.

Goodridge held his gaze. "I know you will. And it'll be the right one, I'm sure."

In all this he'd not once mentioned the conversation about Helen.

Edwin had come away not sure whether to be angry at being so spoken to, as though he were a boy, or chastened by superior knowledge. He did know that things were becoming urgent and that should he decide to buy Marjory out, he needed to confront her with an offer that would top rather than match the one being quoted. William Goodridge, who seemed to have an ear permanently to every inch of the ground and had no doubt been talking to Hugh, had told him what the present offer for the majority share in Letts was. He'd also warned that, in his experience, any assurance that might be given during negotiations to include the family name with that of the new management or guarantee that the staff would keep their jobs would be all eyewash.

"I've seen it before," Goodridge had said. "Hardly are signatures dry than promises are neatly side-stepped under the excuse of streamlining the business. It'll be the last you'll ever see of Letts Oyster Restaurant, lad."

Edwin went to see his bank manager immediately. He came away quietly elated, the promise of a sizeable loan ringing in his ears. His father's country house, Tilse Hall in Epping, Edwin's own since losing his parents but seldom visited, would be collateral. Yes, he could do this thing. If only he felt a little easier about what he was letting himself in for.

This venture would leave him pretty well strapped. No matter what, he'd keep his flat in Mayfair, bought with money his father had left him – he would need a place to live if things went wrong. But everything else would be tied up in the expansive loan his bank manager Mr Shawcross was arranging on the back of his shares in the business, on Tilse Hall. Its farm still required a manager, as it had done when his parents had been off elsewhere, mainly in the South of France, spending Lett's profits in casinos. He'd heard how Uncle Henry would often settle his father's debts; Geoffrey had even at one time sold some of his percentage in Letts back to his brother, leaving his son fewer shares in the business than he would have had even though a decent living still came from the farm.

The loan had been given on the back too of all he had in savings, the restaurant itself if he went ahead with it, and above all on the family name. The family name went a long way. But if Letts failed now to make profits, he'd lose everything. Not a nice thought.

Driving out of London towards Essex and Swift House, he wondered more and more what the hell he thought he was doing. How would Marjory receive him? Though he could hardly see her sending him packing, not with what he was offering. She couldn't care less who took over the restaurant so long as she could have done with it, hard cash in her hand instead.

Still, it was daunting. He wished Goodridge was with him. An older man to back him up. But that would have been silly – a mere restaurant manager poking his nose in, as she'd see it. Could turn her off any deal. No, best this was done alone and the sooner it was over the happier he'd be.

To push the invasion of negative thoughts from his mind, he turned it instead to Helen and immediately felt better. He had asked if he could take her out tonight, and she had said yes. When he'd asked where she would fancy going, she'd said, "I'd like to go to the pictures, if that's all right."

Of course it was all right. Not one for high living, her father had brought her up modestly, all credit to him. Edwin liked her simple ways – yet she had such bearing, fine enough to match that of any girl fresh out of a Swiss finishing school. Helen dazzled him. Tonight would be the fourth time they would have seen each other and she dazzled him.

Thinking of her Edwin reached Swift House in no time at all.

The door set in a sleek stone-pillared portico was opened to him by a young girl. For a second or two she peered at him as though he were a stranger, her round face tightening in readiness to challenge his right to be here. Then she saw his car drawn up on the drive at the same time as he said, "I'm Edwin Lett, the late Mr Lett's nephew." Her round face relaxed in a beaming smile.

"Oh, I didn't know. If you want to see Mrs Lett, you'd best come in. She's on her own."

"Is Mr Hugh not here?"

"No, he's off acting. Winchester, I think. Doing rehearsals or something."

Yes, Hugh had mentioned it at the funeral though, with his mind on Helen and on the exuberant funeral gathering, Edwin hadn't been listening much. He seldom he met Hugh without having to hear all about his acting career. Hugh, exuberant, took centre stage.

Now he was due to rehearse with some quite major company, *Much Ado About Nothing*, Edwin thought he had said. Hugh enjoyed the lighter role, saw it as much more suited to his convivial personality, seeing himself also as a high flier like his Uncle Geoffrey.

Edwin could remember his father never being there for him, he and his mother gallivanting off here, there and everywhere, having fun, sometimes losing, sometimes winning at the tables, usually abroad. Until the war, when Geoffrey had gone in with the rest. He and Mother had been having fun that night in Piccadilly, Major Geoffrey Lett on leave, when the doodlebug came down.

He'd been told the next day. The both of them killed outright. It had been ironic really. Geoffrey had been stationed in England throughout almost the whole war, maybe having pulled a few strings – Edwin never knew if he had or not. He'd been involved in the D–Day landings, of course, but after having been one of those who'd landed, he'd met his end on home ground hardly a mile from where he should have been that particular night giving Uncle Henry a helping hand in an extremely busy restaurant.

Like his Uncle Geoffrey, Hugh enjoyed his gambling too. No doubt selling his shares would help boost that hobby. Other than that, Hugh was a likeable guy. In fact, as cousins, he and Hugh got on very well and Edwin felt a surge of disappointment at his being away. This business included him, though whoever Marjory sold out to, he would go along with it. With no axe to grind he had no interest in the problems Letts had, needed only to be rid of it so that he could go on acting, foreseeing himself as famous one day.

The young girl was leading the way across the familiar square hall. "Mrs Lett is in the drawing-room," she announced, ready to conduct him on into the long narrower hall that led off it.

He stopped her. "That's all right, I know where the drawing-room is."

The round face became alarmed. "I have to announce you, Mr Lett. It's part of me job."

Edwin gave in, smiling, and allowed her to do her job. Somewhere on the second floor a vacuum cleaner droned. This place had just four staff, someone who still did the cooking and housekeeping, this girl, another who probably did the cleaning, and a gardener/chauffeur. Not like when his grandmother had lived here way back before the war – a woman who ruled the roost, being bowed and scraped to by a butler, housekeeper, maids, cook, skivvy, gardeners, stablemen and lots more that Edwin couldn't even think of – the inferior classes. The war had swept all that away.

The girl knocked on the drawing-room door and, getting a reply, went in with Edwin following, but paused so sharply that he nearly fell over her.

"Mr Edwin's here to see you, Mrs Lett." With that she stood back to let him continue in, taking herself off down the rest of the corridor.

Marjory Lett had been sitting in an easy chair reading. She stood up, her beautiful face welcoming, her red lips parting in a smile. Yet the clear blue eyes retained a naturally calculating glow, her voice cool.

"Edwin. How nice to see you. What brings you here?"

"I'm sorry," he began. "I should have telephoned before coming." He should have. Why hadn't he? In his haste he'd overlooked that she might need prior warning. Yet if he had warned her… "I've come on a small bit of business which I hope you might find interesting."

Marjory Lett allowed herself to blink, just the once, the calculating gleam returning to hold him in its gaze. The only problem in speaking to this woman who'd taken his Aunt Grace's place was not that she was older than he by a mere ten years, or an assumed aunt, but facing that cool stare. He fought the feeling of discomfort and ploughed straight in.

"It's about selling your controlling share in the restaurant."

"Would you like some tea, Edwin?" she interrupted him. Sitting down, she indicated the sofa that stood sideways to the old-fashioned fireplace in which incongruously glowed an electric fire. "Do have a seat, dear."

She had addressed him as though he were a teenager. But he sat.

"It is really nice of you to drop by, you know. And to come such a way from London. But, of course, you drove. I plan to sell this place too, you know. Too large and empty since your uncle went. I shall move back to London. So much more doing there."

"What about Hugh?" he heard himself ask, for the moment completely distracted from his errand.

"Hugh? He's never here, is he? I don't think he cares to rattle around in this place all on his own either. I know he can hold decent parties here. But then, there are so many other places to do that. We had a talk about it, and he agreed that London was a far better place to be."

With Marjory's powers of persuasion, no doubt. The same method that had got Uncle Henry to lose interest in the restaurant: a fluttering of eyelids, that wide, blue, compulsive stare, those full lips stubbornly thinning.

"The place is outdated," she continued in a chatty vein. "Draughty. It costs the earth to heat and it's a bore having to employ staff to keep it running. A modem flat in London, a woman popping in two or three times a week, and so many places to eat out, would be so much simpler and streamlined."

Edwin could feel his hackles rising. "Uncle Henry loved this place."

"No, I don't think he did all that much. He was far happier, he told me, in that penthouse of his above the restaurant than here. The place gave me the shudders the

29

moment he showed it me. His first… your aunt… died there, you know. The moment I saw the place I actually got the shivers. That's why we came here to live more or less permanently. It was the one thing he did insist on even though I tried hard to convince him that being in an entirely different flat in London would have been far more convenient with a lot more social life."

So in a roundabout way she'd scotched her copybook. How she must have suffered tucked away in this Essex backwater, precluded from the high life a woman of her type craved, and not purely for love of Henry – a sacrifice to keep him sweet rather than happy. Edwin hid a grim smile. But she was having her own back now, ridding herself of every trace of this marriage to Henry Lett, putting even his home up for sale.

True, Edwin had never found it that cosy when he visited – which had not been very often, he had to admit – but to realise that this might be the last he'd ever see of it… Nostalgia perhaps, but still, the last of his uncle's memory, the last of what was part of the Lett family, was being torn down. Marjory was destroying everything.

"About what I came here for—" he began, but was again interrupted.

"Oh, we must have some tea. I'm dying of thirst. Or would you prefer something stronger?"

"Tea would be fine," he said. It was far too early for "something stronger".

He waited while she got up and went to the door. The days of ringing for servants had gone long ago. The sound of vacuuming had ceased. He sat fuming as Marjory called out, "Carol?"

From somewhere came a faint reply.

"Could you bring us some tea and a few sandwiches and cake?"

Again came the distant response, this time a longer one.

Marjory's tone grew resigned. "Very well, Carol." She came back into the room and sat down again.

"She has to make it yet. Says it will take her fifteen minutes to do sandwiches and tea, though I expect that'll be more like twenty. But I'm sure you will be staying a bit longer than that. It's nice of you to call. I've not seen a great deal of the family since your uncle died. A few friends have been here, but it is a bit of a nuisance for them to come all the way from London."

He needed to get off his chest what he had come to say. He needed to be firm, polite but firm. Steeling himself, he launched straight in.

"The reason for my being here is in regard to a meeting I understand you are going to have next week with people offering to buy us out. What I want to say is, if you're willing, I can match their offer. Keep it in the family."

She was staring at him. "Where did you hear what the offer was, or that I even intended to sell? Did Hugh tell you?"

"I haven't heard from Hugh."

"Then who did?"

"Does it matter? I just want to say that I can match what these people are offering you."

"How?"

"That doesn't matter either. Just that I can."

She had become faintly flustered, like someone playing for time. "I've virtually promised them, Edwin. I can't go back on a promise."

"Yes you can. This is business. A mere verbal promise? You've not signed on any dotted line. What've you got to lose by taking my offer?"

Marjory had regained control over herself. "It isn't very good business if you're intending only to match the going price."

He glowered. "Should that be any skin off your nose, Marjory? Unless you've a special point in not wanting it to stay in the family. What difference would it make to you whether it does or doesn't? You'll get your money."

He saw her smile. Sweet. Yes, sweet as a meadowful of flowers, all held behind barbed wire.

"Edwin, dear. I'm businesswoman enough to know you'll be only too willing to top their offer to get what you want." *And you intend to get what you want – play us off against each other, sit back and watch the bidding go up.* He wished someone else was here with him. Why hadn't he thought of bringing his lawyer along? Already he was sinking out of his depth. Callow. The way he felt at this moment, would he ever have the wit to run a large restaurant?

Uncle Henry had. And he'd been only twenty-two.

Edwin recalled hearing how the place had gone down alarmingly after his grandfather's death, having to be brought up again by sheer hard graft. But Father had been there to help. And there was the difference. Who did he have? Mr Goodridge, an already ageing man. It was useless. Awareness of the uselessness of it tightening his lips, he made to get up. It was then that he saw Marjory frowning at him.

"All right," she said suddenly, almost in alarm. "How much?"

She had misinterpreted his expression, read into it a decision to back out, saw herself losing a good chance, for who could say if the first party might even at this stage withdraw? At least here she had this bird in hand, and she was prepared to grab it before it flew off. Edwin felt his spirit rise.

The maid came bustling in with a noisy rattle of the tea trolley, looking pleased with herself at having brought it quicker than she'd promised. But, seeing her employer wave her away, her jaw dropped several inches and, turning the conveyance round, she rattled out the way she'd come, all in one unbroken, rather huffy operation. Marjory hadn't once taken her eyes off Edwin.

"How much?" she demanded again.

Three

He'd come away from Swift House triumphant. Having upped the asking price by a mere fraction of what the other party had been prepared to meet, he had expelled any doubts Marjory might have had. It had been precious little to sacrifice, for when his solicitor made further enquiries it transpired that the other party's offer had been their top one.

All along he'd had this nagging feeling that Marjory had already pushed them to their absolute limit and his suspicion had paid off. Later he heard through his solicitor's dependable grapevine that when she'd asked them to meet what he had been prepared to give her, they had shaken their heads, gathered their papers and had withdrawn without ceremony, saying that even a place like Letts wasn't worth fighting over. But he already guessed what was in their mind. They had their own grapevine and had no doubt predicted that without much experience of running a restaurant, he would make a complete mess of it and have to sell and that later they'd get it at far less than this first offer of theirs. Big concerns could afford to play a waiting game.

Two weeks later the necessary papers were drawn up and signed. Benjamin Raymond, the family solicitor, lugubrious as ever and even more so about this venture, had asked if he was at all sure of what he was letting himself in for.

"Completely sure," Edwin said confidently, Mr Raymond regarding him as though he saw straight through that facade to one mass of jelly.

–

"It's done," Edwin announced in the taxi taking him and Helen to the theatre early in February. "The family business back in the family."

In the dimness of the cab, she turned to look at him. He had invited her and her father to spend Christmas and Boxing Day with him, saying he had too much on his mind to go to parties and needed time to think. It had turned out to be a lovely two days.

In these couple of months he had changed. The boy had become a man, going from the lively and easy-going person she had first met to a serious-minded one with a load on his shoulders. She was happy enough with the change; if anything it made him more attractive.

It had been so nice, the three of them in his luxury flat. It had been cosy and snug with the heavy curtains drawn against the wintry weather outside. There had been plenty of good food despite Edwin having sold his family home and now borrowing heavily from the bank to regain control of Letts. She only hoped his Aunt Vicky was appreciative of all he had done, she after all being one of the directors.

Edwin had apparently had a long argument with his cousin Hugh against following his stepmother by getting rid of his share of the business, finally persuading him to hang on to some of his shares. That alone boosted her certainty that under Edwin the restaurant would rise again.

During Christmas he'd been sweet and attentive, yet at times he was so wrapped up in his own thoughts that she wanted to share the anxiety he must be experiencing in having ploughed all he had into the venture. For a man with little knowledge of running a high-class restaurant it was a great worry and she longed to take some of the weight off him. The money from the trust her father had put aside for her would have helped considerably but she wouldn't be able to use that until next year. She had resisted the temptation to buck him up by trying to be too lively and he seemed to appreciate that. The last thing she wanted was for him to think she was trying to smother him.

"I'm sorry if I seem to have neglected you," he said now. "It's been a tough time these last couple of months. I wanted so much to see you but it's been hopeless."

So far he'd taken her to the theatre, to the cinema to see *The Robe* as she'd asked, and to a New Year party which he hadn't seemed to enjoy. Consequently neither had she and he'd brought her home only half an hour after 1954 had been heralded in.

Each date had ended with a lingering goodnight kiss at her door but when invited in for a coffee he'd declined, whether because her father had been working and he felt he might not be able to trust himself if they were alone, or because he had too much on his mind, she'd been at a loss to fathom. But those ardent kisses had to count for something.

"I think you've done wonders, Edwin," she ventured and, taking the initiative, threaded her arm through his.

She was overjoyed for him but, as he remained sombre, it was best not to be too demonstrative about it.

"I'm not so sure," he mused, turning to gaze from the taxi window at the brightly lit stores they passed. "It's a great deal I'm trying to take on."

Helen remained silent, not sure quite what to say.

"I suppose I should have taken more of an interest in the running of it," he continued. "But then I had only just turned sixteen when both my parents were killed. My Uncle Henry took over the entire running of the place. His sisters, Aunt Maud and Aunt Vicky, never had any dealings in it so long as their shares paid out each year. Their husbands had their own businesses. I may have inherited my father's share of the firm but I was too young to see any reason to bother my head with it. And of course I went into National Service for two years, mostly in Germany. I just got on with life on the interest from my father's shares and the money he left me, as well as the proceeds from the home farm. Now that's tied up as collateral for this damned great bank loan around my neck, and still I'm blowed if I know what I'm doing or even if I've done the right thing."

"Of course you've done the right thing," she tried to encourage him. Her arm tightened on his, if only to remind him that she was here.

He trained his eyes on the brilliant dazzle of Piccadilly Circus. "I wish I had your faith. Now I've had more time to think about what I've done, it's a bit overwhelming."

"You'll be all right," she said confidently. "It's in your blood. I know it is. My father will be there helping you. If you still wish to keep him on."

Edwin turned to look sharply at her. "Of course I wish to keep him on. He's important to me. You both are."

She didn't reply to that last part, but was suddenly reassured. "He knows the place from top to bottom," she said hastily, "its workings and its problems. With him there you can't go wrong, Edwin."

One hand came up to cover hers. The touch was tender. "I hope so," he said quietly. "I'll need all the help I can get."

Tender though the touch was, it was firm and sent a thrill of pleasure through Helen, for the moment making her feel more certain of his feelings for her. Even so, she tried not to respond too much to it, lest he withdraw his hand. Instead she said, "It's in his interest to see it succeed. He has his own few shares."

"It's in everyone's interest," said Edwin. "I've given a lot, all I've got. When everyone else was only too willing to pull out, your father was the only one who believed in it. Nor do I want that woman Uncle Henry married smirking from a distance, or have Hugh or Aunt Vicky coming back at me to taunt me that didn't they say I had to be mad. It just *has* to succeed."

The emphasis on that one small word said so much more than all the others put together. Yes she knew what he had given, and felt only contempt for those who had been all too ready to sell out, especially the woman who had married his uncle, proving that it was only his wealth she'd been after by making off with all she could get hardly a month after his death.

Like him, Helen wanted to see Marjory's face as she saw the restaurant rise again like a phoenix, becoming again one of the best in London, and realised her mistake in allowing it to go out of her hands. Edwin had spoken volumes when, prior to going off to conclude the business deal, he said he hoped never to have to set eyes on her again. "I remember on the day she married my uncle," he said, "she told me I could call her Aunt Marjory. I never did. Aunt, indeed! She'd never take the place of my real aunt."

Helen only faintly recalled his Aunt Grace, Henry Lett's first wife. She remembered the woman as being a sweet-natured person, though Edwin had once let slip that he had always thought her oddly cool towards his uncle and could never understand why because he had been a loving man. Well, his aunt could live on in his memory. Marjory Lett with her new money would fade away, no doubt seek some other well-heeled man to marry.

"I know you'll make it succeed," Helen said with absolute conviction, and as the taxi slowed to negotiate the heavy traffic going towards Leicester Square and the Wyndham Theatre he took her hand in a strong grip.

"Helen, I've known you only a short while but you're one of the very few loyal people I know. It makes me feel good knowing that you have faith in me and I know I could do anything if I had you beside me. Helen, will you marry me?"

The question, bursting out like that, took away her breath for an instant. Lost for words, she stared at him, mouth agape. He appeared to realise that he had sprung this on her far too suddenly. He gave a little laugh.

"I'm sorry, Helen, I don't know why I said that the way I did."

She found her tongue. "You mean you didn't want to say that."

He looked full of remorse. "I didn't intend it to come out the way it sounded. All I know is that if I'd stopped to rehearse it, I'd never have been able to get up the courage.

Honestly, Helen, I didn't intend to spring it on you like that. But I do want to marry you."

"Why?"

"I'm in love with you."

She was staring at him. "You can't be. We hardly know each other."

How could he be in love with her in such a short space of time? They'd met in November. This was February – three months later. He didn't truly know her. She didn't really know him. And here he was proposing marriage. They needed more time together. This was far too hasty. Was he merely looking for a convenient prop to boost him in the venture that she could see was terrifying him? She'd told him about the money she'd soon be getting from that trust. That had to be it, even though he didn't seem to be the kind of person to use her that way.

"How long does it take to fall in love?" he queried, frustration beginning to sound in his tone. The taxi had drawn up outside the theatre but he appeared unaware of it. "You must know I'm in love with you."

"I don't." Anger was beginning to mount up inside her. She pulled her hand away from his. "Sometimes you seem more occupied with your restaurant than me."

"That's not true."

"This where yer wanted, chum?" cut in the cabby, having reached back to slide open the glass partition. "Was Wyndham's, weren't it?"

Distracted, Edwin shot him a glare. "What?"

"This where yer wanted ter go?"

"Yes, this is it. But could you possibly take us around the block again?"

"If yer say so," came the resigned reply.

In the driving mirror, Helen could see the middle-aged man's lips twitch into a grin. Why did it make her feel even more annoyed? Edwin had turned back to her, had taken her hand again. She made to withdraw it but then let it lie limply beneath his.

"What d'you say, then, Helen?" he asked. "Will you say yes?"

"We hardly know each other," she said in reply. "And you're wealthy. I'm not in your class."

"Now that's stupid!"

The cab was going very slowly. She felt irritated by the driver, quite obviously ready to cooperate to the full with his male passenger's wishes. It was all the same to him where he went, and he might get an extra-large tip for this. She could imagine the thought ticking over in his brain just as the meter was doing at this moment. In fact he wasn't only taking them around the block but left down another street, making a meal of it.

"It's not stupid," she said. "I keep remembering that my mother was once married to your father."

"What's that got to do with it? If you're suggesting that has anything to do with us, it doesn't. They divorced and he married my mother."

"My mother had a daughter by him." Helen couldn't help a tremor in her voice. It seemed their families were too closely linked for Edwin to be asking her to marry him, yet common sense told her she was being foolish.

"Who died at eighteen months," he bit back.

"Yes, my father mentioned it to me, years ago."

"He mentioned it to me too, though I knew. He told me a lot after my uncle died, maybe too much, I don't know. Maybe it would have been better to have kept some of the things to himself."

The words sounded bitter. Her father had said that he'd had doubts at the way he had tried to entice Edwin into thinking seriously about acquiring the restaurant, that he might have laid it on too thick. She wondered if some of it had come as a shock, hence the bitter ring to his tone.

She herself knew little beyond that her mother had once been married to Geoffrey Lett. The Lett family meant nothing to her. Until now.

"What did my father tell you?" she asked.

He shook his head. "Too much to go into now. Some things I knew already and some that I didn't, and I've a feeling there was a lot he left out, though of course I've no idea what. What really matters is how you feel about me."

He broke off to glance out of the cab window and, seeing its direction, pulled himself together with a visible lift of his shoulders before turning back to her.

"Look, Helen," he said. "We'll be outside the theatre soon. If you can't give me an answer yet, all I need to say now is that I love you and I want to marry you. Why not think it over at least?"

She needed time for it all to sink in. Deep inside her she had hoped something would come of their being together, but the suddenness of his proposal shook her. It lacked gentleness, was out of character, not like the Edwin she'd come to know. Nor was she one to bend to demands, her father telling her often enough that she was her mother's daughter, and this was what Edwin's proposal had been, a demand.

"A woman of determination," her mother had been described as being. "Never given to allowing herself to be browbeaten no matter what life threw at her."

42

There were times Helen wondered what life had really thrown at her mother, but Dad had never said even though she had asked once or twice. He'd merely smile secretively and say, "She was a woman and a half, was your mother."

Helen brought her mind back to Edwin as the taxi pulled up once more outside the brilliantly lit theatre. "You'll have to give me a little time, Edwin," she told him. "I can't deal with this right now. I do care for you." She didn't dare say the word love, though that was playing such a strong part in her heart that it was strangling her. But she felt she needed to trust him a little more as well. No girl should be railroaded into saying yes. "But I need to think," she finished. "You do understand?"

He seemed to collapse a little. "Of course," he said, opening the cab door and helping her out before paying the fare with a larger than usual tip.

"Thanks, chum," she heard him murmur to the driver, as though the drive around the block had helped solve a lot of problems for him. Perhaps he was hoping for her reply to be soon. She too wanted to give it soon, but that depended. What she needed was his full attention and to know that she didn't play second fiddle to his work. Wasn't that what all girls wanted?

Four

Helen watched her father getting ready for another day in the restaurant, already in the dark attire required of a restaurant manager. He ought to have had a restaurant of his own by now, but had harboured no ambitions in that direction.

"I've seen the problems and heartaches that can go with having one's own business. Soul-destroying, that's what it is," he would tell her. "Like this, I can come home at night and put it all behind me. With a business, no matter what it is, you'll take it to bed with you and wake up with it in the morning, take it away with you at weekends and *if you* ever give yourself a holiday, you take it on that too. Not for me, poppet. Let someone else do the worrying at the end of the day."

"But you do worry, Daddy," she had told him so many times. "You do bring it home with you. I've watched you. And all for someone else's benefit."

His reply would be an indulgent smile, accentuating those increasing wrinkles around his eyes and mouth, and a hand tousling her head. These days he didn't touch her hair any more, respecting her wish to keep it tidy, but his response to her pleas never changed. Most likely he was extremely happy in what he did and saw no reason to spoil it.

He was beginning to hurry himself, pouring out a final mug of the coffee she had made for their breakfast before setting off.

She too had to be off soon. She worked very near by, in the accounts department of a Regent Street department store. But there was still time.

"What do you really think of Edwin Lett?" she asked, putting their used cereal bowls in the sink and coming back to the table for the mugs, her father still drinking his.

"Edwin? Why do you ask, poppet?" He paused over what was left of his coffee and leaned forward slightly, a little playfully, to gaze into her face. "Has he upset you?"

Helen shook her head, but somewhat unconvincingly. "We've been going out together for five months now. But lately he seems to have cooled off."

"He has his hands full with the restaurant," said her father, draining his mug. "Can't be going off here, there and everywhere like normal chaps."

"He's become so serious and sombre these days. He was so light-hearted when we first met."

"That's what I mean, poppet. He has a lot on his mind."

"You know I told you he asked me to marry him, that February in the taxi taking us to a theatre."

"And you came home very much at odds with the world. I would have thought you'd be pleased, flattered. I know I was."

"No, you weren't," she shot at him. "You had a look on your face as if you were as unsure about it as me, but you wouldn't say why. Anyway, if you were thinking it was far too soon for him to say things like that, I agree with you."

"I suppose I was thinking something like that. That was probably why I looked so worried." He put down his cup and glanced at his watch. "I must be off."

"Before you go, Daddy, what I want to know is do you think he still feels the same about me? He's never asked me again and it's been three months since he did. Perhaps he's changed his mind."

Even as she said it, she was conscious of a lowering sensation inside her chest, her heart grown heavy.

"He still takes you out and about," pointed out her father. "If he didn't like you he wouldn't do that." His expression grew briefly mischievous. "Do you want me to ask him?"

Helen pushed the weight aside to gaze at her father in horror. "No!"

He laughed and made to pat the crown of her head, then remembered that she'd only just done her hair, the short, fair waves combed tidily back from her face just so, and withdrew the hand to touch her cheek instead.

"I didn't think you'd want me to do that. But he does still take you out, poppet. I gather you're seeing him this evening."

"To the cinema," she supplied. "To see *From Here To Eternity*."

"That's supposed to be a good film. Well, there you are then. He's still interested in you. Probably biding his time as you asked. I suppose he did somewhat jump the gun in February. We men are like that. Can't wait."

Again he laughed, and bending to kiss her on the cheek, said, "Don't be too impatient. And have a nice evening, poppet. I expect you'll be home and in bed before I get in. Most likely Mr Edwin will have a look in at the restaurant after he's brought you home."

Her father had adopted the more formal address in speaking of Edwin, it having to do with business, but became casual again almost immediately. "Friday night's always a late night. I expect we'll be there until the small hours, as usual. The place has begun to look up tremendously these last few months, thank God. See you, poppet."

Picking up the empty mugs as he left, Helen deposited them in the sink with the cereal bowls and spoons and, turning on the hot tap, she squeezed a drop of washing-up liquid into the water. Thoughtfully she rinsed the few things, putting them on the draining board to dry themselves. When she came home at lunchtime she'd put them away.

Daddy was right, Letts had begun to look up. Maybe it was the worry of making a go of the place that had made Edwin withdrawn of late, but he had warned her that night in the taxi going to the theatre that he was having doubts about how much he'd taken on.

Many times since then she'd regretted the way she had reacted to his proposal, for in truth she had lost her heart to him. In fact she'd already lost it on their second meeting in November, even breaking things off with Alan Rees whom she'd been going out with for nearly a year. He too had dropped vague hints about getting engaged some time in the spring, but fortunately she had not given him any answer.

She had always had plenty of boyfriends and had once actually got engaged, to a Richard Stevens, but had broken that off on discovering that while with her he had also gone out several times with one of her friends. For a while it had hurt but she'd got over it. She'd been nineteen. As for other boys, none mattered: they came and went, even some of their names escaping her now. Then Edwin had come along and she'd found herself in danger of falling in love with him. In love perhaps for the first time in her life. Yet despite having been with him for five months she still didn't truly know what really went on in his mind. Having blurted out in February that he wanted to marry her, he'd never asked her again. But whatever was in his mind, she was not prepared to ask. She needed to be one hundred per cent sure of the man she would finally marry without having to beg.

Her mother had thought she had been a hundred per cent certain, so she gathered from Daddy, when she married Edwin's father. At that time a mere kitchen hand, an employee of his, she'd been carried away by his high standing, and what girl's head wouldn't have been turned by the attentions of Geoffrey Lett, who to all account had been handsome and debonair and adventurous? And she had come unstuck.

Helen did not want the same fate. Yet she was in love with Edwin. And the thought came into her head as she dried her hands and went to get ready for work, What if he never asks me again? She would get on with her life, of course. She had that determination – her mother's determination, as her father had said many a time – but inwardly it would destroy her.

"Oh, don't be so damned dramatic!" she burst out in irritation to the empty kitchen. Destroy her! No man would ever achieve that. But her heart ached with questions and doubts as she left the flat to take herself off to work.

–

The place was taking up all his time lately. All he wanted to do was to see Helen, yet this place laid first claim on him every time. It was only common sense to realise that if he wanted it to thrive he must put every effort into it, give it all the time it demanded, be seen by the customers, the old valuable patrons slowly coming back, saying how much he looked like Henry Lett in his heyday, though far younger of course.

"It's looking good, don't you think, Mr Lett?"

William Goodridge moved alongside him as he leaned his elbows on the balcony rail to gaze down at the crowded restaurant. On the same level as them, people were dancing to a foxtrot, doing that slow manoeuvring step suitable for small, crowded dance floors. Others sat up at the bar with its new chromium plating, maple surfaces and uncluttered glass mirrors. They sat on leggy bar stools upholstered delft blue and cerise with fine gold lines, as were the chairs clustered around the low maple tables – the colour scheme he'd chosen to run throughout the whole restaurant.

"Not bad at all," he answered, and remained with forearms leaning on the chromium rail while Goodridge moved off to take himself down the small curving flight of cerise and blue carpeted staircase to the main restaurant, the man moving with great dignity that made one proud of the whole place.

Looking down, Edwin saw the restaurant manager position himself in a far corner of the lower restaurant where he could see all the staff and be sure they were applying themselves as was expected of them. Nothing escaped his eagle eye and his staff knew it, each station working smoothly as a team, customers fully satisfied.

Watching him, Edwin wondered what he would have done without him, in a way felt as though he were still being carried by him, but grateful. Goodridge was right, the place was doing well. Halfway through the year already and at last Edwin felt he was able to breathe again.

As he said to Goodridge, fast becoming his adviser and confidant in nearly all things, there being no one else to turn to, "Amazing how fast the money's going. I just hope I can pay it all back."

"You will, Mr Edwin," was the man's reassuring response.

Even so, he'd got through sums of money on modernisation, though modernisation only up to a point – it was no good completely obliterating the well-loved character that had made the place what it was. It had to be money well spent and was necessary, as was stuff like advertising. Done tastefully, no blare of trumpets to cheapen it, it had done wonders.

He had taken on new staff at slightly higher wages to get the best. Letts had always been known for its top-quality waiter service and of course its fine cuisine. He had a top-class head chef, Ericson, ruling over equally fine sous-chefs and supportive kitchen staff. He had installed modem equipment to replace that from earlier years which the war had prevented being renewed. Then there was the everyday outlay – general maintenance, wages, entertainment, provisions necessary to place quality menus and choice wines before a customer if the name of Letts was to survive. But all nibbling into, or more like devouring, the extensive bank loan.

The bank was already looking for its returns but for the time being it was better not to say too much to the rest of the family. Shrunken these days, it consisted of Hugh, Aunt Victoria, her husband and children and himself. (His late Aunt Maud's husband and children had moved to Canada.) Marjory Lett gone, Hugh and Victoria had finally decided to hang on to their shares, trusting him but still with a say in the business though they seldom showed themselves.

Occasionally Hugh put in an appearance, checking up on him, Edwin felt. Aunt Victoria merely sent occasional letters full of demands rather than requests on how things were progressing.

"I'm almost tempted at times," he remarked to Goodridge, "to tell her to get stuck into some of the business herself and realise what it entails."

The only shareholder not family was Goodridge, the only one he felt secure in consulting, knowing he'd get an honest, unbiased answer.

Edwin thanked God for William Goodridge. Without him he'd have been entirely alone to take the flak if things went wrong. A hundred things could go right, but if one thing didn't, Hugh and Victoria would be sure to be on him like a ton of bricks, scared their share in the place might suffer. He had a warm feeling that Goodridge would never be like that.

At the moment, thank God, things were beginning to show a profit, allowing him to keep up repayments on the interest without much pain. But it meant keeping his nose to the grindstone twenty hours a day, more or less, enticing the regular valued and more distinguished customer.

"I'm getting to be more like my uncle every day," he told Goodridge. "They say he could be a bit too solemn at times."

"At times one has to be slightly serious. Life's not all tinsel and glamour and, if I may say so, Mr Edwin, gambling."

"At times I wish I was more like my father," Edwin countered the reference to his father's shortcomings. "More adventurous, more devil may care."

"Wouldn't be good for the firm for you to be too head-strong," came the reply. "Though between them your father and uncle did make a good team."

"At least my father made customers laugh," put in Edwin, faintly defiant despite that modifying remark. Goodridge was being a bit too honest for his peace of mind. Older, wiser, beside him Edwin knew he was a mere boy even at twenty-six, still green to the blows that running a business could deal, yet he had to trust the man and certainly needed his guidance. "It was that which brought customers in," Edwin persisted, trying to overcome this slight sense of rebellion, more because that struck him as the attitude of a boy, not a man.

"There's more to it than just making them laugh," said Goodridge.

"But it helps. I think they preferred my father to my uncle."

"They certainly enjoyed a laugh with him, Mr Edwin, but they trusted your uncle, knew that whatever they told Mr Henry in confidence would go no further than his ears."

"I know. But my father lightened the place up. That must count for something."

"Oh, it did, Mr Edwin."

"Then perhaps that's what I need. To be a bit more light-hearted."

But he now knew whom he resembled. It came to haunt him every time he thought of that conversation. He might strive to be like his father, but sobriety was a trait he'd inherited from his uncle and nothing he did would change that. He would just have to make the best of it. Henry Lett had been popular, for all his sober ways; but oh, to have inherited a bit of his father's debonair light-heartedness, the sort of nature that revealed itself in Hugh, making Edwin almost jealous of his cousin.

He'd been light-hearted enough when he'd taken on this venture, but five months later saw him growing more and more – what was it? Stuffy? Stodgy? Laden down by the weight of what he'd taken on? He was certainly no longer happy-go-lucky. His social life was suffering, and would Helen put up with that for much longer? He didn't think so.

It was this that stopped him referring to marriage again, regretting the hasty way he'd proposed. He should have been more sure of the future before leaping in as he had. What if she had to put up with this for the rest of her life if she did marry him? Maybe she already realised it and that was why she had grown colder towards him lately. Maybe he'd lost her already. Maybe he'd left it too late to ask her again. But this he did not confide to Goodridge.

–

The dinner things could wait. Let them soak awhile until the baked grease had eased off the pots and pans. Then she would go back and finish the job.

Helen went into the lounge where her father sat reading his *Evening Standard*. Picking up the magazine she'd bought this morning on her way to work, she sat down in an easy chair and opened it up three or four pages in. But she didn't read. Tilting her head, she glanced at her father.

"Daddy, what *do* you make of Edwin?"

As he looked up she saw a mixture of enquiry and vague impatience in his brown eyes. It was Monday evening and he was enjoying a few hours off at home in his flat. The restaurant was usually quiet this first working day of the week, people doing the same as he – taking it easy. But it wouldn't be long before he grew restless. Around nine he would put down his paper, mumble that he would just pop along to Letts to make sure his assistant manager was coping OK, then return home around ten. The restaurant was a mere couple of minutes' brisk walk from the flat, though these days his walk wasn't quite so brisk as it had once been.

Fifty-eight wasn't a great age and he was still upright and sprightly, not an ounce of fat on his gaunt frame, nor all that much grey among the brown hair. Helen felt immense pride looking at her father, yet the years were beginning to tell just a little bit. Maybe for him the walk to Letts would be more like four minutes now.

"What do I make of Edwin?" he echoed her question.

"Not as a boss or a restaurateur. As a person."

Her father was scrutinising her closely, his expression now filled with concern for her. He was obviously coming to realise how worried she felt.

"This isn't the first time you've asked me that, Helen. What do you want me to say, poppet? He's a very likeable young man."

She fiddled with the magazine. "Yes, but I wondered what you think of him, personally. Does he ever mention me to you?"

The concern had not diminished. "I don't think he would judge it correct to talk about you during business hours."

Her father was hedging. "But does he ever give you the impression that he misses me when we're not together?"

William put his newspaper down on his lap and leaned back in his easy chair. "Helen, my dear, I can't be inside his head. When we're at work we talk about work and little else. What's bothering you, poppet?"

"Nothing." She said it far too quickly. "It's just that we don't see as much of each other as we did a few months ago."

"He still takes you out."

"Once a week." Her voice took on an angry note. "If he's not bogged down with his blessed restaurant."

"He's working hard trying to make a go of it," excused William.

"He's always working hard. He should have made a go of it by now. Seven months since that proposal of his — if it was a proposal."

William gave her a severe look. "A restaurant's not a job with an end product, Helen. You don't just complete one job then sit back to wait for the next, and while you're waiting take time off. A restaurant never stops. It goes on from day to day, from week to week, from year to year."

"I know. But does he still want to marry me or not? He's never so much as whispered it to me since that time in February. As far as I'm concerned, Daddy, if he has changed his mind, I don't see why I should hang around waiting for him. In fact there's a young man I often see at lunchtime who has asked if I'd go out with him."

"Then why don't you, Helen?"

It was an open challenge, and it confused her. Her father had seemed so keen at one time that she and Edwin should get together, and now this. As she fell silent, he gave a low cough, deep in his throat, and lifted his newspaper to begin reading again. At odds with herself, Helen stood up and hurried out to the kitchen to deal with the washing-up and vent her confusion on the undeserving pots and pans.

It occurred to her as she washed up noisily that Edwin wasn't turning out to be the ideal man she'd imagined. His cousin Hugh was so much more lively. She had only ever met him once, at the restaurant when she had been with Edwin. Taller than his cousin and good-looking to the extreme, she had to admit that he'd turned her head for a moment – but only for a moment. His bearing had immediately proclaimed him to be a bit too charming, a bit too cocksure, perhaps a bit of a womaniser, perhaps not to be trusted with someone's heart. She had turned back to Edwin and had noticed the vast difference between them, and, yes, she much preferred Edwin. She would always be able to trust Edwin, give him a lasting place in her heart. But the way things looked at the moment, did she still hold a place in his?

Five

"I'll tell you one thing, old man – if you don't ask her soon, you're going to lose her. Hopefully to me!"

Panic welled up in Edwin. Hugh had popped in on one of his rare visits, though they were lately becoming less rare. Edwin realised he'd been labouring under two misconceptions about Hugh's increasing visits: one being that Hugh, acting in some Shakespearean play at a small London theatre nearby, was taking the advantage of being able to look in more often; and the other, that he was genuinely taking more interest in the restaurant.

Not so in either case. It had become apparent that the source of Hugh's interest was Helen. From the first Edwin should have been warned by the way Hugh's grey eyes twinkled on being introduced to her. Since then his visits had grown more frequent. Worse, he'd begun to ask questions then make comments as he was doing at this moment, high-flown thespian rhetoric giving way to a breeziness that had always got under Edwin's skin.

"Quite a smasher, your Helen," he was saying blithely. "I say you're a lucky devil. But if you don't realise it and get off your miserable arse and marry her soon, you'll find me hot on your heels ready to step in."

He gave a low chuckle as Edwin continued to glare, and changed the subject, to Edwin's mind deliberately trying to emphasise his earlier comments.

"So, Edwin, old thing, how's business coming along?" he breezed.

By the time he left, having taken a look around the kitchens, exchanged the odd word with a few waiters as well as William Goodridge and gone up to the office to examine a few files, then into the penthouse his father had once used, all as though he were sole owner of Letts, Edwin was wishing him miles away. More to the point, he needed to keep Hugh away from Helen – without letting his cousin know how closely they were related. If Hugh found out about her it would only be a matter of time before she too found out about herself. He knew Hugh only too well – never one to keep his mouth shut, and warning him would be betraying Goodridge's trust.

With Christmas a few weeks off, the restaurant with its hands full taking bookings by the score, every cover filled daily, nightly, with people often being turned away disappointed, it was hard for Edwin to get to Helen.

Money was rolling in and it should have felt good. But every iota of his time was being taken up, and although Helen said she understood he could see her getting short of patience. What if Hugh pounced first? The result would be disastrous.

It would be a year come February since he made that impulsive proposal. If he wanted to save her from Hugh, he'd have to spring it on her as he'd done once before. But this time it had to be right, the right place, the right atmosphere or she could say no, again, and add to the complications. The odd half-hour would not be enough to create the conditions needed for so important a question as asking her to give her hand to him in marriage.

Then there was the engagement ring. He could have surprised her with it. That was how his flamboyant cousin would have gone about it. But he had a feeling that Helen would want to choose her own, carefully and with great deliberation – a protracted and solemn ritual for every girl. Helen was not one to treat having surprises sprung on her lightly, as he'd learned to his cost early this year. The last thing he needed was Hugh leaping in.

He knew his cousin – girls flocked around him like silly birds. He had the looks and the manner that could make any girl flip. He took pleasure in loving 'em and leaving 'em when he'd had his fill. Edwin could take no chances of having Helen drift into Hugh's clutches and have her world collapse about her.

–

It was Tuesday – not usually a busy day of the week, but tonight a party had booked a table, a titled person planning to entertain several distinguished American guests before taking them on to a theatre.

"I do apologise for the short notice," he had told the receptionist who had taken the booking that morning. "But I don't expect you'll be overbooked on a Tuesday. My people have to be back in the States well before the weekend to commence filming. They tell me it'll cost them big bucks if they delay. So I wonder, can Letts accommodate us at short notice?"

Of course Letts could accommodate them. Edwin put off his Tuesday arrangement to see Helen. He usually saw her on that day; normally it was quiet and the restaurant able to afford his absence.

Trouble was, and he cursed himself for it now, he had cried off last Tuesday as well, that night being a little more busy too, there being only three weeks left to Christmas. He hoped Helen would understand.

Next week, come what may, he would put work to one side despite the mounting Christmas rush. He would get tickets for a show, afterwards take her to supper, not in his own restaurant, but somewhere like the Dorchester or even the Ritz, booking a secluded table. Having been stood up two weeks running she deserved somewhere really special, would need to be appeased.

Over a good wine, he would renew his proposal, suggest a Christmas engagement – surely that would delight her. They would go together for her to choose the ring. After that they would set a date for the wedding. All this, of course, would have to be done sensitively, discreetly, gently, respectful of her feelings.

Hastily he telephoned her at lunchtime at her workplace to make his excuses for this evening, his heart in his mouth. There was silence at the other end of the phone as his voice died away.

"You still there, Helen?"

"Yes." Her tone was sharp. She was disappointed. She was angry. He had let her down. What did he expect?

"Please understand, darling. I know you're upset. I'm upset too. I was really looking forward to tonight because I had something extra special to tell you. But it looks as if it might have to wait until next week."

"If there is a next week!"

Terse. He must tread carefully. "Helen, I've said I'm sorry, and I really am. But I can't let these people down. They expect me to be there. Uncle Henry never let himself be absent when someone special was coming in."

"But you're not your Uncle Henry, Edwin."

"No, but I am trying to do the job as he would have done it."

He too was becoming angry, irked by her disparagement of his efforts to be like the man who had spent his whole life turning Letts into a special place. Well, he was going to make it great again. His uncle would have been proud. But Helen didn't see that.

"I'm sorry you feel like that, Helen," he went on. "I was going to make it up to you next week, but if you feel like this about it, I shan't bother."

"Don't then!" came her response. The phone went dead.

–

By Saturday afternoon Edwin had calmed. Tuesday evening had gone well. His distinguished party had said that they'd enjoyed every minute of their time at Letts. The host had congratulated him, said that he could not have had better service or more excellent food and wine anywhere else in London and that he'd make certain to patronise Letts whenever he came to London – words to warm Edwin's heart and take away the sting of Helen putting the phone down on him like she had.

He hadn't heard from her, nor had he contacted her. Pride. But he'd ring her tonight. By now, like him, she would have calmed, and come hell or high water he was prepared to drop everything and take her out somewhere really nice.

He was making sure everything was in place for the usual Saturday rush when he glanced up from discussing Chef's extensive and varied menu for the evening to find Hugh lounging in the doorway to the kitchen.

Acknowledging him briefly, Edwin hurried through the remains of the menu before going over to him, his welcome a jovial quip. "Come to give me a hand?"

Hugh smirked. "Not likely. Thought I'd pop in for a bite before going on to the theatre. Meeting a young lady there."

Edwin led his cousin into the restaurant proper, one arm about his shoulders. "No doubt someone I don't know. I've never known anyone like you for having so many different women. Don't you get tired? Amazing how you can ever afford it all on a mere actor's pay."

"Oh, I don't do so badly," returned Hugh. "I'm beginning to reap good notices and there's always plenty of stage-door hangers-on. But you'll know this young lady all right."

"I will?"

"Absolutely. Helen Goodridge." He was still grinning amiably despite Edwin pulling up sharply to stare at him, Edwin's friendly embrace falling from his cousin's shoulders. "As you seem so intent on letting her down time after time, old man, I thought it only decent to give her a bit of a break."

"You can't do that!" Edwin burst out.

Hugh's expression didn't change. "Now why ever not?"

"Because—"

Edwin fell silent. How could he say what he knew about Helen, that Uncle Henry being her natural father made them half-siblings? Hugh would be shocked rigid. And Edwin knew his cousin well – wouldn't put it past him to say something to Helen, whether by accident or design. Hugh had a nasty streak in him as well as a thoughtless one, and Helen could get hurt beyond measure in the realisation that William Goodridge had never told her about her real father. It was a terrible situation Edwin found himself in.

"I phoned her yesterday," Hugh was saying. "Just on the off-chance, to see how she was. She told me you've been too busy of late with this place to give much thought to her."

Dread squirmed inside Edwin. "What the devil are you up to, Hugh?"

"Nothing, old chap," answered Hugh in all innocence. "She's been stewing at home evening after evening waiting for you to find a tiny niche to fit her in. A girl can't go on being let down."

Edwin was becoming aware that they were in the hearing of people coming in through the entrance. "I'm not discussing this here," he hissed savagely. "We'll go upstairs to my office."

"There's nothing to discuss, old chap," said Hugh, his tone still lively. "I offered myself and, unlike you, I never let a girl down. And certainly not one like her. Only a fool would let a girl like Helen Goodridge slip through his fingers."

"Leave her alone, Hugh."

He might as well have been talking to himself as Hugh continued in a blithe and easy tone, "I said I'd take her to a theatre and afterwards for a nice meal… Don't worry, old man, we won't come here to upset you."

Edwin kept his own voice down, though it grated harshly. "I said leave her alone!"

"I don't think so, old boy."

"I've already proposed to her." It was the only excuse he could find to give. "I asked her to marry me last February."

"And she appears to have turned you down, judging by the amount of water that seems to have flowed under your bridge."

"She needs time to think about it."

"If she has to think about it this long," said Hugh in a flippant tone, "my advice to you is don't get too excited. It sounds to me as though she still has a pretty free hand to choose whoever she prefers the most."

"We'll see whom she prefers," was all Edwin could find to say. He hated the subterfuge, but Hugh must never know the truth. No one must know. It was strictly between himself and Will Goodridge and always would be. So long as he could keep Hugh from knowing as well as keeping him away from Helen in that respect, she would be safe.

"As you wish," Hugh dismissed his threat. "Well, I'll have a bite then be off."

Left alone, Edwin stood in the body of the restaurant, a few afternoon customers looking for a pot of tea and cake passing him by, mostly ignoring him – the regulars would come in later. His eyes were on his cousin going to a table in a far corner. He saw him summon one of the waiters with the lift of a hand that was as near as damn it to arrogant self-satisfaction, and seethed. It was more than evident that every gesture Hugh made, even summoning the waiter, was being done to taunt him.

William Goodridge was descending the central carpeted stairway and, to combat the anger inside him, Edwin went over to him.

"William, I'm going out."

"Right now, Mr Lett?" William gave him an enquiring look of scrutiny that bordered on reproof and which, in his present mood, annoyed Edwin.

"Is there a problem, William?" He said it too sharply. It was always hard to have a go at someone who, though his employee, could very soon be his father-in-law also.

He moderated his tone. "You remember I did mention I wouldn't be here this evening?"

"I do, Mr Lett." Still formal, but a knowing twinkle had stolen into his eyes. "I merely wondered that she might be a little unprepared for you this early. Unless there's something you have to say to her that can't wait."

Edwin chose to ignore the hint. There had been many these past couple of months and he wondered if Helen had anything to do with them.

"It's just that things being quiet at the moment I thought I'd take the opportunity to have a bit of time to myself before calling on Helen. I'll be back here around eleven thirty or so."

These days there were now regulars lingering into the small hours, as in the old days. It was increasingly evident that his presence was being sought by them, just as his uncle's had been. That little exchange of backchat; that chance to share a laugh or a confidence with the proprietor himself, feel privileged enough to address him by his first name, all went a long way to building a restaurant's reputation, perhaps even more than its fine cuisine did.

It was good to know he had inherited his uncle's trait for attracting confidences even though he sometimes wished himself more flamboyant, as his father had been. He couldn't crack jokes as Geoffrey had with his favourites or be nonchalant and easy of nature. But Uncle Henry had always been the one to whom regulars turned rather than his father. He must settle for that and be content.

He returned his mind to his restaurant manager in time to catch the studied look William was giving the figure in the far corner. Nothing escaped William's eyes. Edwin immediately found himself excusing his cousin's presence.

"He's beginning to pop in more often these days."

"Yes, so I notice," said William. "Makes one wonder why."

Edwin couldn't help but pick up the connotation in the remark.

"Probably because he's nearby at the moment," he said off-handedly, but his restaurant manager's expression at that excuse didn't go unnoticed. William Goodridge often seemed to possess a sixth, even a seventh sense that could not be ignored or answered. Had he already guessed what Hugh was up to? Was he endeavouring to warn Edwin about Hugh's motives?

"Well, I'm off then," said Edwin sharply, and hurried away to avoid any more loaded inferences from William. Nevertheless he would take them on board. The man was seldom wrong in anything he said and he needed to get to Helen well before Hugh did.

Edwin's exit did not go unobserved. Hugh sat over his pot of tea and angel cake, his eyes bearing a look of amusement. Edwin *was* in a tizzy. But though he had only been teasing his cousin, he felt quite serious about Helen, so the amusement didn't quite extend to laughter.

He stirred his tea and wondered if he ought not to have been so quick on the draw. What if Helen decided to ditch him and go off with Edwin? Damn it! Perhaps he should go after him. He could picture the look on Edwin's face as he turned up right behind him just as he was getting somewhere with her.

"It don't do, old man," he murmured to his cup of tea, "to be too cocksure of a girl, even your own girl." Edwin was a bloody fool, assuming he could leave her for days on end before showing his face. Even so he should make sure.

Finishing his rapidly cooling tea and enjoying the last of the angel cake, he strolled off in the wake of his cousin. He'd been a little too leisurely, however, for by the time he reached Helen's home his ring on the doorbell reaped no response.

Hugh shrugged in his nonchalant way. There would always be another time, knowing his work-mad cousin and the time he took to get around to doing the things that really mattered, such as making a girl happy.

Six

To Edwin's intense relief Helen was home from work.

Pressing the doorbell of her flat he hadn't expected a reply, had been prepared to wait around for ages until she appeared.

For a second she gazed at him like someone faced by a stranger. He knew she'd expected it to be Hugh standing here and a surge of anger swept through him. His bright grin was forced.

"Sorry I didn't get in touch earlier, Helen. I've been bogged down at work."

The look had disappeared, replaced by one of vague confusion, but he ignored it, letting the words tumble out. "I thought I'd pop round rather than phone, surprise you. Wondered if you'd like to go out this evening. I know it's early and you've probably only just got home from work, but if I'd stayed at the restaurant much longer I would probably have been caught up with something or other, and I'd rather see you."

He'd hoped this last statement would work. It didn't. She continued to stare at him, her lips having compressed themselves together a little, though the expression didn't mar her pretty face. He could see her hands flexing a little and there was a slight frown on her face. A far more abject apology from him was being called for here.

"Helen, I know I been neglecting you lately, but—"

Now she found her voice. "Yes, Edwin, you have. I've been wondering very seriously lately whether we should be getting on with our separate lives – if you know what I mean."

He certainly did know what she meant and his heart missed a beat.

"No, don't talk like that, please! I know I've been remiss of late, but I want to make it up to you." Any minute now Hugh would be on his tail, he could feel it in his bones. His tone took on a note of panic despite his trying to keep it even. He tried to smile again. It felt like a grimace.

"Can't we go out somewhere this evening?"

She took in a small breath and seemed to pull back from him. "I'm already going out this evening, Edwin."

He kept his smile going. "On your own?"

"No, with a friend."

"Girlfriend?" No girlfriend – he already knew who it was. "Someone from work?"

"Not from work."

He made himself laugh light-heartedly. It sounded abrasively loud. "It's not a boyfriend, is it?"

"As a matter of fact—"

"Don't!" His voice burst out despite his attempts to stay calm. "Helen, don't go out with him. I'm so sorry. I realise how much I need to be with you. Please, Helen, can't we start again? I'll do anything. I won't ever leave you alone again. Just… let's go out this evening. There's so much I want to say to you, make up for the way I've been just lately. It's…"

No, he must not make excuses, mustn't say the name 'Letts' and spoil that gradual relaxing of her face muscles to something more tolerant of him.

"I should have phoned you before chasing round here. Look, can I come in, Helen? I feel such a twerp standing here at your door trying to tell you how much I love you."

She stood her ground, though there was the faintest trace of a smile. "So how much do you love me, Edwin?"

"Enough to ask you to be my wife. I know I asked you once before, but I was jumping the gun then. I'm not now. I'm deadly serious, Helen. Look, let me come in. I can't stand here like this."

Now she stood back. He was in; she was closing the door, leading the way into the lounge and saying over her shoulder, "Won't you be missed at the restaurant?" She had to get in that last little dig but instead of being annoyed, he felt humble. He had been totally in the wrong.

"From now on," he said with all sincerity, "you come first. I mean that, Helen," he went on as she turned to face him. "I feel it can run itself a bit more and I intend to devote all my time to you."

Her laugh was a lovely tingling sound to his ears. "Now that's going over the top, Edwin." She was shrewd like her father, picked up on things hardly had they been dropped.

"Well," he blustered, "I know I have to keep the place on its toes if I want to have something to offer you when we're married."

She sat down on the sofa, looking up at him. "You haven't yet asked me to marry you exactly."

He came and sat next to her, taking her hand. "Then I'm asking you now. Will you marry me?"

Helen stood up suddenly, pulling her hand away from his. "You know what I'd like to do this evening? I'd like to go dancing."

"Where?" He wanted so much to bring her back to his earlier question but all he could say was, "Where?"

"You choose," she said quickly. "Surprise me."

"And what about what I've just asked you?"

"I'll answer you when we come home," she said.

—

They'd gone to the Hammersmith Palais. He'd wanted to take her somewhere exclusive, but despite wanting him to surprise her, Helen had suggested Hammersmith, an odd choice. "Wouldn't you prefer somewhere nearer?" he'd asked, but she had shaken her head.

"I've never been there. I'd like to see what it's like."

To argue would have undone all his efforts. But it had been good, the vast hall echoing to the sound of a big band and the shuffling of a hundred pairs of feet as couples did slow waltzes under dimmed lighting and racing coloured flecks from the slowly revolving ball in the middle of the ceiling, fast quicksteps with the lights on full, seductive foxtrots and tangos and occasional jitterbugs, as the buzz of chatter and laughter, the heady scent of perfume and hair oil mingled with the smell of floor wax and dusty drapes.

Helen was so light in his arms – an accomplished dancer, as was he. But there were many accomplished dancers here and no one took any notice of them. He had danced with her often but tonight was particularly wonderful and they stayed on the floor until their feet ached.

Around eleven, Helen bent down as they sat at a table and eased a foot out of one shoe. "I think I've just about had enough," she sighed. "Maybe we ought to go home now." He was happy with that until she added as he helped her on with her coat, "Besides, I expect you'll have to get back to the restaurant to show yourself. You usually do."

"Not tonight," said Edwin, huffily, following her out where pavements, wet from a recent downpour, reflected street lighting and electric signs as brilliantly as a river. It was still raining slightly, but they hurried for his car, glad to be in the dry.

He'd hoped she would snuggle up to him as he drove, but she stayed stiffly in the passenger seat, saying little but that she'd enjoyed the evening. Not once during the whole evening had she referred to his question of marriage, but then she had told him to wait until they got home. It had marred his own joy at being with her, his mind constantly running back to it. Now she was home, what would her reply be?

At the bottom of her flat, she asked, "Are you coming up for a nightcap, Edwin?"

Of course he was coming up. He wanted his answer. He nodded without speaking. Waiting until they'd got into the lounge, he said, "Well?"

"Well what?" she queried.

"About me asking you to marry me. Will you?"

She was taking off her hat, gloves and coat, dropping them across the back of one of the armchairs and laying her handbag beside them. "I'll get coffee," she said, making for the kitchen, but paused in the lounge doorway, turning round to look at him. "Or do you prefer a proper drink?"

He was near his wits' end, standing there still in his overcoat and trilby. "I don't want anything, Helen. I want your answer."

"To what?"

72

"The question I asked you before we went out."

"Which was?"

"Helen, stop playing games. Will you marry me?"

"You'll have to ask me properly."

"Damn it!"

She was smiling. "That's not the way, Edwin."

"Well, what d'you want me to do, for God's sake?"

Helen came slowly back into the room. "I think you know what," she said.

The next second he'd grabbed her in his arms, holding her so tight that she had to take a full breath so as not to be crushed.

"Edwin!"

"Marry me, Helen. Darling, say you will. I'll look after you, work for you, make you happy. I'll love you to my dying day. Helen, please say yes."

"Yes," she said.

"What?"

"I said yes. I will marry you, Edwin."

It was all too simple. "Do you love me – enough to say that?"

For a reply, she pushed him away a little with her elbows, leaning herself back against him, her lips raised to his. The kiss seemed to go on forever. At one time she eased her lips away from his sufficiently to whisper, "Does this answer your question, Edwin, my love?"

It did. He became lost in yet another kiss, his head spinning with the knowledge that he had asked her to marry him and she had said yes.

–

It was one thirty. He had forgotten all about getting back to the restaurant. They had made love, on the sofa, a spontaneous thing that neither of them had expected to happen, and had lain there wrapped in bliss in each other's arms, he slowly drifting off to sleep. Suddenly he came awake with a start, realising that he was still here.

"God! What's the time?" he'd burst out.

Helen, who'd remained awake, gently and repeatedly smoothing a hand over his hair, shifted her body a little to glance at the clock over the electric fireplace. Then she too shot upright.

"Oh Lord! It's well past one in the morning. My father could be home at any time."

If Edwin knew anything about Letts these days, he knew it was becoming very much as he'd been told it used to be before the war, remaining open until any time between midnight and two or three o'clock. With Christmas approaching rapidly, people were given to eating and socialising more and more, well into the early hours. It got later as they neared the festive season. Yet this could have been one of the quieter evenings.

"I've got to go," he said, and there began a race to dress, to obliterate all traces of anything suspicious, he already making up excuses for William for not having gone back to Letts after seeing Helen home.

Even as he left the flat he could see in his mind's eye the scepticism on Goodridge's face, though whether laced with amusement or disapproval he didn't know. Disapproval would be more likely. Helen's father would see nothing amusing in what they had been up to, even if marriage was in the offing. He was of the old-fashioned sort and protective of his only daughter, and to him things like that did not happen to girls like her before marriage.

Edwin hurried through a persistent drizzle to his car, got in and revved away, relieved not to see Goodridge turning into the short mews. But then, unable to resist the temptation, he drove the short distance to Letts. It was still lit up. Customers were still in there. He should be attending them. But to make an entrance at one thirty in the morning… again he visualised that questioning look on Goodridge's face. Yet if the place was that busy perhaps he should go in – make some excuse for being so late, delayed… by what? Not a thing came into his head as he pulled well down the alley next to the restaurant.

For a long time he sat there, thinking, the window wound down for some fresh air. Emanating through the closed door to the kitchen came the muted sounds of the last few pots and pans being noisily put away. He just hoped no one would come out and notice his Ford Zephyr and go carrying back tales to Goodridge. He'd bought this car new four months ago, before that putting up with a second-hand 1949 car that would never have been noticed. Until then, lack of money, all ploughed into getting this place back on its feet, had prevented extravagance. Now he thought about it. The place was doing wonderfully well coming up to Christmas; he felt it would continue, and by next year he'd be able to buy an even better vehicle – a Citroen perhaps. He might even get Helen behind the wheel of a car, an easy-to-handle Morris Minor perhaps.

A sudden hubbub in the street disrupted his thoughts. People were beginning to turn out, a chattering group passing the top of the alley and making towards a large car that had just drawn up, then another group, as noisy as the first. Edwin's watch showed the time to be almost two.

After a while he got out and walked towards the road. It was quiet now. Only a few lights were on in the restaurant, with the staff clearing up. In the rain everywhere smelled damp. The stale odour of refuse from the alley mixed with the lingering aroma of cooked food, coffee and faint perfume hanging in the air. Some time later the restaurant lights began to go out one by one. Edwin moved back into the shadowy alley-way as the home-going kitchen staff, then the waiters emerged. Finally, with the place in total darkness, the tall, spare figure of William Goodridge appeared, turning left to walk the short distance home, his stride long and supple despite his fifty-eight years.

Would he find Helen still in turmoil? She'd been agitated when he'd left her, her pretty face creased with self-reproach, saying that they should never have let themselves be so carried away. His comforting arm about her and his words of love had helped soothe her, but only temporarily, he knew, for as soon as he'd left, those pangs of conscience would attack her anew, rather as they were attacking him now. He just hoped, as he waited for Goodridge to disappear before letting himself into the restaurant to go up to the penthouse where he now lived, that Helen's face would not give her away to her ever-discerning father; hoped that she might have the sense to be in bed by the time he got home. By morning she would have had more chance to compose herself.

But what bothered him more, as he let himself in, was that while making love there had been a total blindness to the possible consequence of what he was doing, with no thought to anything but his need of her and, he'd assumed, her need of him, selfish bastard that he was. Yet Helen had been as consenting as he.

The thought was still with him as he mounted the stairs to the penthouse that had once been his uncle's. Edwin had sold his flat by St James's Park when he'd needed more money to help pay back the bank. With people crying out for places to live, he'd been very pleased with the good price it had brought.

The penthouse greeted him coldly. He would have to make it cosy again, ready for Helen. So far he had never asked her up here, knowing not only that she would refuse, aware that here things might happen, but that he had become ashamed to let her see it. Until now, he hadn't much bothered with it, seeing it merely as somewhere to lay his head after a long day's work. Now, of course, it was imperative to make it as nice and cosy as he could. He would buy a television and a small modem corner bar to replace the old-fashioned pre-war one; buy new furniture; install a shower in the bathroom, which he'd have retiled; have the rest of the place redecorated – new drapes, new carpet, lots of side lamps – the idea quite excited him for a moment as he turned on the sitting-room light, until he thought again of the fateful question that had been bugging him: what if he'd got Helen pregnant?

–

For some while after Edwin left, Helen sat on the sofa where they had so recently made love with the feeling that she could hardly face herself. She didn't feel cheapened, her love for Edwin was strong and overpowering even now, but it was hard not to wonder if he had seen her as easy. Surely he didn't.

After a while she got up and began moving about the flat, doing little unnecessary tasks, unable to bring herself to go to bed. It was too suggestive of what they had been doing. Edwin had asked her to marry him and she had consented but that didn't excuse what they had done.

Slowly she got into her nightdress and came to sit on the sofa again. Edwin had said that he'd be here tomorrow morning to ask her father for her hand in marriage – all so outdated, but he had meant every word of it. She tried to feel consoled by that but it wasn't working. All she could think of was how she could have allowed herself to be so carried away. And what would they do if Dad said no? She could hardly see Edwin flying in the face of his refusal and demanding that she elope with him. But if Edwin did ask her to do so, could she? The thought of hurting her father like that was utterly abhorrent.

Another, less weighty thought struck her as she finally decided that she must try to sink her thoughts in sleep: that it seemed ludicrous for her father, an employee of Letts – without question its most respected member of staff, but an employee nevertheless – having to be virtually beseeched by Edwin, his boss and half his age, to look kindly on him. In this, Edwin was behaving like a subservient.

Hearing her father's key in the lock, Helen threw the room a hasty glance to make sure that all was as it should be, that there was no sign of what she and Edwin had been up to – although she had already checked the second Edwin had departed – and fled to her room, diving into bed and pulling the covers up to her chin.

She didn't reply as her father softly called out to her. Laying very still, trying to regulate her breathing as though asleep, she heard him creep into her room to drop a light kiss on her forehead with a whispered, 'Goodnight, poppet,' that he didn't expect her to hear. Tiptoeing out, he closed the door gently behind him.

Left in darkness, her eyes wide open, part of her still shrank from what she and Edwin had done. But the other part of her experienced a deep flow of warmth spreading slowly through her body, and she knew she would love Edwin until the end of her life.

That alone should have lulled her to sleep. It didn't. The thing preventing sleep was the memory of having made love without any protection, so suddenly had it happened. In the midst of her joy she had thought of it too late and was now being kept awake by a useless exercise of counting the days to her next cycle. She had heard somewhere that certain times of the month were safe but had no idea when they occurred. As if that would make any difference now. It wasn't even possible to still the heavy thumping of her heart with the consolation that if something had happened, at least Edwin had asked her to marry him and they could always bring the wedding forward.

With this going round and round in her mind she made a concerted effort to sleep, squeezing her eyelids tightly together, but it was useless – she was never going to be able to sleep this night.

When next her eyelids opened again it was to the broad daylight of a sunny Sunday morning, her father already in the kitchen, setting about making breakfast if the sound of a boiling kettle and the frying pan being laid on the cooker was anything to go by.

Soon, to the appetising aroma of frying bacon, Helen ran a bath, sank into it and washed her hair. Refreshed, she wrapped herself in a dressing-gown and went into the kitchen. The night was past. A few hours' sleep had made a lot of difference and now she could face her father without having to avert her eyes from his. If something had happened, Edwin would see her all right.

-

79

He arrived around eleven o'clock. To Helen it had seemed a lifetime waiting. Hearing the doorbell, it was she who rushed to answer it, her father holding back deliberately and leaving her to go.

She'd already had told him over breakfast that Edwin was coming and that he had something to ask him.

"Sounds important," he'd said, and she had leapt on the conjecture.

"Oh, it is – very important. But I don't want to say anything until he comes."

Her father had nodded sagaciously and got on with his eating and scanning his *Sunday Times*. His nod said quite plainly that he had guessed what Edwin was coming here for. The one thing it didn't reveal was whether he intended to approve or not. Helen felt a surge of hostility towards him, something she had never before known, but was immediately angry with herself. William was the dearest of fathers.

Thoughts of elopement kept racing through her mind as she tried to eat her own breakfast, an almost impossible feat. Finally she gave up to clear the table, energetically washing up and stacking away just so as to push that eventuality and any subsequent adverse thoughts from her mind.

In the same vein she tidied, dusted, made the beds, folded clothes and sorted out already tidy drawers and cupboards, unable to sit down or rest. By the time Edwin arrived, she was dressed and groomed and felt as though she had done a whole day's manual labour.

Her father was the epitome of politeness. "We're just about to make coffee, Mr Lett, if you'd care for a cup," he said, behaving exactly like an employee speaking to his boss. Helen cringed inwardly and leapt to the rescue.

"Dad, Edwin has something he wants to ask you. I'll make the coffee while you two talk."

Again she cringed as Dad, half bowing, indicated for Edwin to be seated, as though they were in the restaurant instead of her father's own home, he the master here. She hurried off to the kitchen but left its door ajar so as to hear what went on and be on hand if needed. But with the kettle having been boiled ten minutes ago, it almost immediately began making a devil of a din, reducing whatever she was trying to overhear to a mere mumble.

Helen felt her hackles rise. Why was she being consigned to a kitchen while they discussed her? This was 1954, not 1900 – the days when women's lives were managed for them were long gone.

In a fit of offended pique, she turned off the kettle and strode back into the lounge to stand over the two men, who both looked up in surprise.

"Well?" she demanded of Edwin, her hands on her hips. "Have you asked him yet?"

Edwin half smiled, then, reading her steady gaze, dropped his own. "Not yet."

"Then I will." Her lips thinning, she turned immediately to her father. "Daddy, Edwin and I want to get married."

Her father was not as easy to outstare. "I thought that was what he'd come to ask, but it's an awkward thing for a young man."

"Maybe it is," snapped Helen. "It's also old-fashioned and quite silly. So I've come in to sort it out. It's simple enough. I want Edwin and me to get married. All we're asking, Dad, is do you mind?"

William knew he should have been prepared for this. He'd always tried to bring her up as he thought a girl should be, not too pushy, obedient but not subservient, not submissive but willing to be guided. But Helen had often shown herself to be her mother's daughter. She showed it now and for a second it was like looking at Mary. A wave of trepidation passed through him, partly the nagging awareness that Helen was Mary's daughter but not his. The other was that it might already be too late to reverse things. These two seemed in too much of a rush to get married for his liking.

"Not straight away?" Concern already ringing in his tone, he silently admonished himself. Surely he wasn't thinking she and Edwin had been up to something and she might be... he could not form that hovering word.

Helen's determined lips had begun to relax. He'd been wrong to even dare think what he had been thinking. As for his other worry, he knew too late that those three words of his had innocently been tantamount to giving permission as Helen broke into a huge smile and bent forward to kiss his cheek.

"No, not straight away, Daddy." Her voice was teasing. It also revealed relief and happiness. "We could make it some time in the spring or maybe early summer."

He couldn't return her smile. The moment loomed before him that now should be the time to confront her with who her true father was. Why in God's name had he left it so long to tell her? If he didn't speak now, it would be too late. Leaving it and leaving it would only cause her more pain and bitter disappointment. She must be told and he must face the fading of joy on that face he cherished so much. Edwin already knew his secret of course, but he didn't care about Edwin, only about how much it would hurt his daughter being told at this late stage in her life. But it had to be done.

He opened his mouth to speak but, seeing her ecstatic expression, his courage melted. All he could do was to gaze up, straight-faced, into her happy face.

Edwin had risen to stand beside her, his face too wreathed in smiles. "We'll need to do a great deal of planning for it, Mr Goodridge. I want us to have the best wedding ever, and a wonderful honeymoon somewhere really special. I can't thank you enough, Mr Goodridge. I shall take care of her."

He sounded so young, so immature. No longer was he acting as William's employer; Edwin was looking on him as his benefactor, a man to please and to thank for allowing his daughter into his care. He was the boy, and William the man who had given his decision.

So as not to be left looking up at the pair, William also rose, standing taller than either of them. "Let me know when you've set a date. I shall need to know how long I have to set aside enough funds for all this."

"Oh, no, Mr Goodridge, I should be able to take care of everything."

"No doubt you can," said William severely. "But Helen is my daughter and it's my prerogative to provide for her special day."

He knew he wouldn't be able to match what Edwin probably had in mind, but he would no doubt eventually capitulate and let them go ahead with whatever they had planned, merely putting in what he could towards it. It was odd to imagine being father-in-law to his employer.

What did worry him was Edwin being aware that he was Helen's cousin; worse, that she had no inkling of it. How long before Edwin let slip to her? If that did happen he would at least be free of the weight of it, but did it matter who told her? It would still send her world crashing about her to know that she had for so long been kept in the dark.

It had to be his responsibility, no one else's. But until then, he must trust Edwin to keep his promise. How could he have let it go on for so long? He should have told her when she had been eighteen and he had mentioned that trust coming her way when she reached twenty-five. He should have told her then, but he'd let her believe it to be what he had put away for her at birth.

There had been a nasty moment when in her happy surprise she'd expressed amazement that he could afford to have put aside all that much. Even then, completely lacking courage, he'd laughed it off as something he'd done when he had come into a bit of money and considered it better to put into a trust for her. Overwhelmed by such kindness, she had flung herself into his arms in love and gratitude, while inwardly he'd cringed, feeling a physical stab of pain at his bold-faced lie. He should have explained then. But he hadn't.

Now, he wondered, would they all come to suffer because of his crass cowardice? Dear God, he hoped not.

It was a sober, thoughtful man who offered the couple a benign smile.

Seven

All week Helen had half expected to see Hugh come rushing round asking her out. She hadn't relished the task of telling him about her engagement to Edwin, but there'd been no sign of him. When Edwin told her that the London play he'd been in had finished and he had gone off to Stratford-upon-Avon rehearsing with the RSC, of which he had become a member, mostly in very small parts though he saw it as an honour to be with them, she was glad and relieved.

Edwin, however, had come visiting every other evening – something of a huge turn-around after what she had viewed as his earlier neglect of her. Now, she happily put all that behind her, even more so when he arrived the following Saturday morning, fulfilling his promise of taking her to choose the engagement ring.

"Come on, darling," he said as she let him in, his tone as excited as she felt. "Hurry up and get your hat and coat. Snuggle up nice and warm. It's freezing out there."

In fact it was blowing half a gale, not a day to be out in but, tripping off on his arm to his car, her head bent against a wind that instantly caused her eyes to water, Helen's whole body glowed warm.

They bought the ring in Hatton Garden, the place to find the best gems. Letts was doing very nicely after Edwin's initial struggles. He was seeing a profit and his commitments to the bank were decreasing by the month. "You and I will start to live very comfortably from now on," he'd told her in triumph, his mind racing on. "In time we'll be able to buy ourselves a lovely house out of London and hang on to my flat for when we're in town."

His words had brought a tingle of joy though sometimes it didn't seem real and she still had to pinch herself that this had all happened to her. Other times she felt a low feeling of panic in the pit of her stomach that it was all too good to be true, that something could happen to wreck it all. Her earlier fears about falling pregnant had been unfounded. Even so, to let herself be carried away by too much excitement could be tempting fate.

Perhaps that was why she felt no conceit or self-satisfaction in being chosen by someone like Edwin, who showed the promise of becoming as wealthy and well-known as his uncle and his father had been. She felt none now as in a small exclusive jewellers she slipped one of the rings from a black velvet tray of flashing diamonds on to her finger. It had taken her eye the moment she saw it, being slightly smaller and neater than the rest, which had struck her as far too ostentatious for a girl such as her. The solitaire, however, was still so huge as to not only take away her breath but almost frighten her.

"Is that the one you like?" asked Edwin, seeing her eyes shine as she extended her hand for a better view, twisting it this way and that for the shop lighting on this dull December afternoon to catch the brilliant facets and fling the sparkle back into both their faces.

The proprietor beamed. "It sits well on madam's hand, sir. Not too large for such delicate fingers."

Helen felt herself balk instantly. "Darling, it's much too expensive. I don't want you to spend so much. Can't we find something a little less—" She broke off, not daring to utter the word "expensive".

She felt the proprietor's eyes turn questioningly towards her and her innards curled. He'd already noted her as not the type of customer he was used to seeing here. She had sensed it immediately they had entered, in fact had felt it in quite a few shops they had visited. This man's glance only confirmed it more even though his beaming smile had faltered not once.

Edwin came instantly to the rescue without knowing it. "If you want it, then have it," he said simply.

He could have added, "Darling, I can afford it, and it's for a very special person who I love deeply." But she read all that in his eyes and he had no need to enlarge on what he'd said. She also knew that he wasn't about to belittle her before the shop owner with an excess of persuasion to make her even more ill at ease than she already was, and her love for him swelled in the knowledge that he could be so sensitive to her feelings.

She took a deep breath and lifted her head, more in defiance of the proprietor's air of superiority than any decisiveness.

"Darling, it's lovely."

"And you're happy with it?"

Again she took a deep breath. "Yes," she managed, relieved to have it over and done with.

They celebrated the event with dinner, not at Edwin's own restaurant but at Claridge's where, in a small but light-hearted ceremony, he took the ring from its box, asking again if she would marry him and, with her saying yes, she joining in with the lightly contrived formality, he slipped it gently and reverently on to her engagement finger, then leaned forward in full view of everyone and slowly kissed her. Later they would seal their engagement more positively.

-

Several evenings later, Helen opened the door after an urgent double ring on the bell to find Hugh standing there. She looked back at him, somewhat bemused. He was the last person she had expected to see and in fact had forgotten all about him.

There was a huge grin on his lean and handsome face. "Come to apologise for not calling on you sooner. Thing is, I've been up in Stratford-on-Avon, rehearsing."

"Yes, Edwin told me," she answered, unsure whether to ask him in now.

After all, he would be her cousin-in-law come next year – Edwin was talking of an autumn wedding. On the other hand, the slanted grin and the roguish gleam in his eyes said that he probably wasn't yet aware of her and Edwin's engagement and was anticipating his chances with her.

"He did?" A touch of chagrin had stolen into his voice. Obviously he was thinking his cousin had stolen a march on him and intended to rectify it. "When was this?"

"Last week." When we got engaged, she wanted to say, but found herself needing to withhold that news, not wanting to cause him upset too suddenly. The anticipation in his expression told her to explain in a more gentle way, perhaps a bit later.

She noticed that he was holding an elaborate bouquet of yellow and bronze chrysanthemums and a small box wrapped in Christmas paper. Seeing her gaze travel down towards them, he thrust the bouquet at her.

"Peace offering," he announced, then, as she automatically accepted it, taken off guard by the force with which it had been offered, he held out the small box to her. "A little something wishing you a happy Christmas."

"Hugh, you shouldn't!" was all she could gasp, everything telling her that she must not accept the present whatever it was. Yet it looked churlish to refuse now that she was to become part of the family.

He still stood there smiling. "Well, open it, Helen," he demanded as she reluctantly took the package from him.

Now she must behave sociably. She stepped back. "Won't you come in, Hugh? This is very nice of you to call and give me a Christmas present."

"Is that all?" he asked, following her into the lounge. "That it's very nice of me – so formal. Don't I even get a kiss?"

She turned to him, forcing a smile and, leaning forward, pecked his cheek. His eyes widened as he accepted it and his expectant grin froze a little, but he recovered himself immediately. "Don't you want to see what I've bought you?" he persisted and, to placate him, she rapidly ripped off the gold and green paper to expose a small, square, blue felt box.

With her heart in her mouth she guessed at its contents before even opening it. And yes, it was a ring, a band of diamonds and rubies. Hastily, she grasped the initiative.

"Oh, it's a dress ring! How lovely. But I can't accept anything so expensive." She was gushing foolishly. "I haven't anything for you yet."

There was no need to look up at him to see his expression as he said, "If you want it as a dress ring of course it's not too much to give someone like you. I was hoping you'd like it."

89

He was staring at her left hand, for the first time noticing the ring on the third finger. Why he hadn't seen it before was a surprise, it sitting there sparkling like a flashlight. But perhaps he'd been too occupied with his own hopes.

"So when did that happen?" His tone had become hard and, glancing down at her hand, Helen had difficulty in looking back at him.

"Last Saturday," she managed.

"Bit sudden, wasn't it?" His eyes had narrowed and his tone was one of unhealthy enquiry. Helen balked at what she felt he was implying. All she wanted now was to see him, his flowers and his ring go.

"Yes, it was a bit sudden," she snapped. "Not that it's any business of yours, Hugh, but Edwin quite took me by surprise too." That would settle any unsavoury questions lurking in his brain. "He asked me to marry him a fortnight ago and I accepted. We'll probably get married next autumn." Further proof for any nasty minds that all was above board.

Hugh was smiling that one-sided smile of his, loaded with derision for all that it added to his good looks.

"You can't want to marry him. All he ever thinks about is that damned restaurant of his. Yes, he might be all attention at this moment but it won't last. He'll be back to standing you up because he's wrapped up in work and you'll find yourself left waiting in the wings. Is that the kind of life you want, Helen? A lively, great-looking girl like you, there's so much this world could give you."

"I've never noticed," she broke in, angry.

"Because you've never gone looking."

"I don't want to *go looking*! I'm content to be what I am."

"How do you know what you are unless you look? For instance, have you ever been abroad to see other sights, other lives? Geoffrey, my uncle, knew how to enjoy himself and that's what I intend to do: travel, go abroad, do things. And I could take you with me, show you all the wonders you've never dreamed existed outside of books."

She refused to be baited. "I expect Edwin will be just as capable of showing me all those wonders, as you put it."

He remained quite unruffled. "Don't bet your bottom dollar on it, darling. My bet is that it'll take a blast of dynamite to prise him away from that restaurant now he has his clutches on it. I think you may be in for a rude awakening, my dear."

Helen could feel herself getting rattled. He was as smooth as ever, and as charming. There was something about Hugh that stirred a woman. It wasn't just that he was so good-looking; there was something in his manner – that despite her annoyance with him fascinated her, and no doubt plenty of other women too – something of the prowling wolf that was never quite hidden by that flashing smile, that roguish gleam in his eyes, that debonair bearing.

"I'm afraid," he was saying, "your Edwin takes after my father, a stick-in-the-mud. Now I take after his father, my Uncle Geoffrey. Nothing stood in his way. Odd how often one resembles one's father's brother rather than one's father." Obviously Hugh modelled himself on Geoffrey Lett, admired him. Helen had heard tales from her father on the man's spendthrift ways, how, in borrowing for his pleasures, his gambling, he'd nearly bankrupted the business. She had heard a little of how the sober Henry had taken the brunt of his brother's gambling debts on his own shoulders and had had to settle them time and time again.

Looking at Hugh it was as though she were seeing the man she had heard tales about. But she also realised how much Edwin was like his Uncle Henry, and out of the two it would be the stable, dependable one she would always prefer. Hugh might excite her, though she tried not to admit it at this moment, but for all his charm and handsome looks, it was Edwin she wanted. She hated the way Hugh stirred up something inside her, forcing her to fight the attraction he had over her.

Putting the feeling from her, she stood before him – she hadn't even asked him to sit down – and lifted her hazel eyes to look squarely into his blue ones, hoping hers did not betray what he was doing to her.

"Hugh, it was good of you to come calling and to give me flowers. But I think the ring is much too much, and as I suspect it wasn't exactly meant to be a Christmas present, without wanting to hurt your feelings I think you should take it back."

It had turned out quite a speech, and reading in his expression that he thought so too, she had a fight to quell the sense of embarrassment it caused her. She pushed past him, going to the open lounge door. "I am truly sorry, Hugh, and I do appreciate how you feel, but I think you'd best go now." She was trying to put it as nicely as she could, but her heart was beating heavily and she knew that were he to turn awkward, she wouldn't be able to stand up to him. With that thought she realised it was herself she was frightened of, not him.

"Please, Hugh," she begged. "Please go."

For a second he hesitated, almost as though he'd read her mind, making her squirm even more. Then he moved past her, managing to brush her body as he did so. He seemed well aware of the tingle the touch created inside her as he smiled down at her. Then he had moved on past her to the hall and the front door, which he himself opened.

"You know, Helen, you're making a huge mistake. I know your mind is made up, but I think you'll come to regret marrying Edwin. When you do, I expect I'll still be around to pick up the pieces."

It was only after he had gone that she realised she still held the ring he had given her.

–

Leaning over the balcony's gleaming brass balustrade, Edwin gazed down with satisfaction at the throng below. Friday, Christmas Eve, and the place was buzzing. Outside was chilly but in here all was bright, cosy, lively. Christmas decorations had been strung across the ceiling and walls. A large Christmas tree with flickering fairy lights and small gaily coloured parcels had been placed at the top of the marble stairs by the entrance. A smaller one hung with glass baubles was at the foot of the wide, blue-carpeted steps down to the dining room. Holly and ivy had been wound around the two lines of pillars each side of the large dining area, so that the whole, along with the chatter from those eating, presented a happy and festive air.

Behind him was the bar and small circular dance floor on the mezzanine level, where more voices babbled above the number, "Fly Me To The Moon", being played by the four-piece band hired for the evening. Edwin took it all in and felt utterly content. Since taking over here, he'd done a great job of making this place work.

A polite cough behind him made him turn. William Goodridge had come up in his quiet manner, unnoticed.

Edwin smiled. "What is it, Will?"

He was finding it rather awkward to address a man who was to be his father-in-law. Debating what to do about it, he was coming to the conclusion that the only sensible thing to do would be to invite him on to the board of directors; it would be so much easier speaking to him as an equal rather than an employee. But first he must gain the consent of the rest of the family. How easy would that be? None of them as yet had any inkling of his and Helen's engagement. He'd tell his Aunt Victoria when the family gathered here on Boxing Day. Victoria had expressed a desire for them all to get together then for a family lunch, closing Letts itself to the public and opening up in the evening.

"Mainly to have a little chat about how business is coming along and discuss anything we might need to," she had said. "Being that this is the restaurant's first year under more or less new management, for all Edwin here is our own family."

Taking a cue from the somewhat dominating Victoria who, as the surviving sister of Henry Lett, felt herself in charge of affairs if not of the business itself – a woman very much like her own mother in that respect - everyone had been in wholehearted agreement. Anyway, a sumptuous free dinner was itself an attraction, Edwin thought with an uncharitable grin.

Only Hugh had not replied to the invitation. Edwin hadn't set eyes on him for ages, not since he'd mentioned rehearsals in Stratford-upon-Avon. Hugh's silence struck him as irritating though not surprising. His cousin ploughed his own furrow, usually only showing up if in need of something. Staying away was most likely a sign of doing OK. Hugh being what he was, Edwin suspected he'd not have much objection to Goodridge being voted on to the board. It all depended on what Aunt Victoria had to say about it. Whatever her opinion, Edwin strongly felt that Goodridge could hardly remain as his employee and at the same time become his father-in-law.

"Everything seems to be going very well this evening, Mr Edwin."

"Yes, it does," Edwin replied to William's comment. Now was the time to broach the subject that was in his mind.

"While you're here, William," he began, "I've something I want to say. I think you should drop the 'Mr' and just call me Edwin."

Goodridge's expression, usually so impassive, was a picture to behold. "Not during business hours, Mr Edwin. We could never have that."

It was almost as if he were being reprimanded. Edwin looked at him at length, held the brown eyes with a steady gaze. The happy sounds of the restaurant in full swing receded.

"Listen. When you become my father-in-law, it's going to be very awkward to call you William or Goodridge. In fact, even now I feel uncomfortable considering the way things stand with us. Before long I will have to address you, rightly, as Father."

"But not here, sir."

Edwin winced. "Please, don't call me sir. That's even worse. *I* should be calling *you* sir."

"You can't do that, Mr Edwin."

"Then what do you suggest?"

Not a muscle of William's features moved. "That I leave your employ. I would prefer to continue working here. This place is my life. It's all I have ever known in my working life. I came here as a young man from the war and I am not yet of retiring age, but if it becomes awkward for you, Mr Edwin, I had best leave."

"And do what?" challenged Edwin.

There was still no expression. "I have no idea, sir."

Consternation had taken hold. This man was his right hand; without him Edwin knew he'd never have got this place back to almost what it had once been. There was still some way to go. Without Goodridge, Edwin could see himself as a man clinging to a waterlogged raft in the middle of the ocean. He needed this man, needed his smooth, efficient running of things, holding everything together when it got a bit hectic, his calming advice when he himself was at his wits' end, his very presence reassuring. He couldn't let him go. He capitulated. What was in a name, after all?

"I don't want you to leave." It sounded like pleading. "I don't think I could manage without you. But I can't continue being your boss, Will. I've been thinking. I want you to come into the business. We will get a really good man in to take over your job, but you will stand alongside me."

For a while Goodridge said nothing. He stood, taller than Edwin, gazing around the lively restaurant, taking his time. Finally, he said, "Your family would never stand for it."

"I'll make them," burst out Edwin. "We're meeting here on Boxing Day, the whole family. I will raise it then."

"I think not, Mr Edwin," said Goodridge. "It's very sad, but I can see no way out but for me to leave. It's not only the manner in which we address each other. You and I know what our relationship is. The problem is, so will all the staff in time, and that would make for very unhappy working conditions. But don't worry, Mr Edwin, I shall not go away. I will be there, in my own flat, if you need any advice from me."

"But you won't be here when a crisis arises."

He felt Goodridge's eyes bore into his. "Isn't it about time you faced up to the fact that all of us must stand alone in the end? Your uncle did. So did your father, for all his ways. We are but little people, Edwin. The world dictates to us and all we can do is hope we do our best. Some try to manipulate it and think they do a good job, but in the end it just goes on without us. The world isn't going to wait for you. I'm not saying take what you can and run. I'm saying work with what you're offered – in your case learning to stand on your own and not rely on others. We all have to finally learn to come to terms with what life has in store for us and face it, alone. Work hard at it, have faith in your own abilities and – what is it they say – nail your colours to the mast. You have Helen to work for now. This is your restaurant. Be your own man, Edwin. You'll manage well enough and make it what it was destined to be."

"What will you do?" repeated Edwin as the long speech ended.

"I'll find something."

"I intend to make sure you'll be absolutely comfortable, Will. And I still intend to speak to my family, no matter what you say. You deserve some recognition of what you've done for this place and I'm going to make sure you get it."

He heard the determination ringing in his own voice, but even if he hadn't, it reflected in the older man's eyes, and at that precise moment he knew he could stand alone, that he had indeed become his own man. Goodridge would live to be proud of him.

Eight

Time was going so quickly, her mind taken up with her fast approaching wedding day. Already the end of April. Everything else merely skimmed over the surface of her mind – talk of a grand new motorway, the newspaper strike, Churchill resigning, Anthony Eden taking over as prime minister.

What did concern Helen was not the preparations for her September wedding, but the wedding dress, still to be chosen, and here lay a nagging question. If what she suspected was correct it wouldn't even fit by the time she walked down the aisle, carrying all before her as the saying went.

Last month she hadn't come on. She'd put it down to nerves even though a little devil in her head kept saying something else. She and Edwin had always played it safe after that first mad moment last November. And when nothing happened as a result, Helen felt she could breathe again. So when, after so long being careful, another mad moment had came over them in February – the weather terrible with thick snow and ice even in the capital, she relenting to going with Edwin up to his warm, cosy penthouse – she'd felt confident that as she hadn't fallen that first unprotected time, she wouldn't this time. But she must have. This month's period hadn't arrived either.

Low-spirited, she huddled up to the electric fire she had put on in the living room, feeling cold from the inside out despite a balmy April evening that held promise of a fine summer to come. Beside her, Edwin held her hand protectively, as if that could help. He was as worried as her. This was to be a society-type wedding, newspapers, cameras, the history of Letts and its young owner emblazoned over inside pages not too far from the main headlines.

"If my reckoning is correct," she whispered, "I'll be seven months. I shall look like a galleon under full sail." It sounded like a joke, but didn't feel like one. "Everyone talking, pointing, smirking, I can't go through with it, Edwin."

He took in a deep, alarmed breath. "You mean you don't want to marry me?"

"Of course I want to marry you. But September – darling, we can't wait until September."

He was staring into the two glowing bars of the four-bar electric fire, not looking at her. She too stared at them, her face flushed and hot from their dry radiation. She and Edwin were alone, her father at the restaurant, having agreed to retirement next month with a more than generous pension suggested by Edwin.

"Darling, we're going to have to bring the date forward." She was still whispering, feeling oddly loath to have the whole room hear her voice.

"It's all more or less arranged," said Edwin, inadequately, causing a small stab of anger to rise up inside her. She turned to face him.

"Oh yes, we must go ahead as planned. Doesn't matter about me being the laughing stock of the century."

"I didn't mean that."

"Then why say it? Surely we can cancel things, bring the date forward and no one will argue. God, Edwin, you're laying out enough on this wedding; I'm sure the caterers and the people doing the venue, and everyone else, can bend a little, considering the money they'll be making."

He met her angry hazel eyes, his own filled with wretched indecision. "But are you really sure you're pregnant? If we do all this and then you—"

Her voice interrupting him rang out loudly enough for all the neighbourhood to hear. "For God's sake, Edwin, I should know! I'm the one who's pregnant. I'm always as regular as clockwork. It has to be that."

"I'm sorry," he said. "Then we've got to do some thinking before it's too late." Now he was beginning to be decisive. With that new attitude he put his arm around her shoulders and drew her to him, in charge now.

"First thing in the morning I'll start sorting things out. Don't worry yourself, darling. It'll all be done. We'll bring the wedding forward to June. You'll only be four months if you are—" He paused, then hurried on lest she had noticed the error. "You won't be showing enough for people to notice and you could have your dress designed to help disguise anything."

Again he paused, this time to regard her with something like fear. "Unless you had it in mind to do something about it."

"No!" She knew what he meant. "Did you?" she challenged.

"No, not if you want it. I just see it as a symbol of our love, Helen. I would have been devastated if you'd said you wanted to get rid of it. I don't really mind what people say. It's ours and we'll cherish it."

His arm about her tightened, bringing her even closer until their lips almost met. "Now I'm getting used to it, my lovely darling, I've realised it's what I want. One of the things I want. I want you for my wife and I want our baby. So don't fret any more. I'll sort it all out."

With that their lips met, and with nothing to lose they made love, free of constriction, in front of the blazing electric bars that seemed hardly needed now, and it was the best yet, Helen thought as she gave herself up to him.

–

"I don't know what's the matter with Hugh. I've still not heard from him and it's only one week to the wedding. I can't understand it."

Edwin had sent out all the revised invitations to family and friends, his excuse for bringing it forward that September had seemed the wrong month for weddings, that June was preferable. He'd apologised for any inconvenience, requesting replies from those still wanting to come. Everyone had replied, agreeing innocently to his choice, with the exception of Hugh, who not only hadn't responded to either invitation but had blatantly ignored Edwin's request that he be best man.

"Perhaps he's moved," said Helen. "Theatre people do move around."

"He's in touch with the rest of the family," said Edwin. "Aunt Victoria told me when I saw her last month. He *had* moved, so maybe he didn't get our first invitation. But he knew from the family we were getting married and that I wanted him as my best man. She gave me an address in Birmingham so I wrote there, but not a damned peep! I can't think what's got into him. We've never been all that close, but I don't know what I've done to him to make him ignore me like this."

Helen kept silent. Edwin was perplexed but deep down she felt she knew the reason. Hugh had taken that episode at Christmas much more to heart than she'd thought. She still had his ring somewhere at the back of a drawer. Had it been given in the spirit of a Christmas present she'd have shown it to Edwin, exclaiming how generous his cousin was, but they'd both known there had been more to it than that. But surely he must know that with the wedding a week away there was no hope for him and that he had to accept the fact with good grace and honour her special day. She was angry, even as she smiled comfortingly at Edwin and said, "We'll hear from him soon."

-

In the flat upstairs over the restaurant, the phone rang.

Edwin, getting ready for church on his big day and still hurting from his cousin's continued silence, a friend named Gordon Greaves whom he'd known for years having stepped into the breach as best man, irritably answered its harsh summons.

"Yes?" he blasted while Gordon stepped away from him to fiddle with the double white carnations to go into the buttonholes.

"Edwin, old man!" an animated voice blared in his ear. "Sorry I've not been in touch earlier. So much is happening. Listen, I've landed a part in *Mother Courage* – Theatre Royal, Stratford. Not on Avon – East London. I want you to come and see it. I'm in London at the moment."

"Hugh, it's my wedding day," Edwin reminded him.

There came a moment of silence, then, "Yes, I know, old man. I should have replied to your invitation, I know. But it completely slipped my mind. But I'd love to come and see you married. I'm just round the corner at the moment, and I'll be at the church to witness it all."

"I asked you to be my best man, Hugh. Can you imagine how I'm feeling, you not responding in any way?"

"I know. I'm sorry, old man. I can't apologise enough. But I had my reasons. Listen, we'll be there, God's honour!"

"We?"

"Glenda and I. Oh, I didn't tell you. Glenda is an actress. Pretty good one too. Glenda Dearing. Well, she and I have got engaged. I should have told you, old man, but there. I'll introduce her to you at the church. She's a real cracker! Anyway, see you in church, Edwin. Best of luck!"

"Hugh!" burst out Edwin, but the line had already gone dead.

–

Circulating among the hundred or so guests attending the reception, Helen was tired but happy. It had gone really splendidly. Not one hitch. It had been a great relief to see Hugh turn up out of the blue, a woman on his arm whom he declared to be his fiancée. As tall and slim as any model, and as stunning as any film actress, she clung to him as though fearing he might vanish.

"We hope to follow you in a few months from now," he said brightly, "but it'll probably be in a registry office – neither of us are particularly fond of all that hoo-ha church stuff." And he'd invited them, as already mentioned to Edwin on the phone, to see him and Glenda at the Theatre Royal.

"Show you what I'm made of." He'd winked at Helen, a little too suggestively for her liking, ending with, "Acting-wise, that is."

Left wondering if he really fancied the girl he said he was going to marry, and made a little uncomfortable by the way his wink had brought a funny feeling to her stomach, Helen shrugged it off and congratulated herself that her wedding dress had been a total winner, all things considered.

It seemed her slim figure was the type that wasn't going to show her condition for ages. No one would have cottoned on to her pregnancy, though she had striven to choose a suitable dress, much to the consternation of the saleswoman in the exclusive boutique Edwin had made her go to. "Wouldn't madam prefer something more clinging?" she had enquired, as though her customer's choice of the billowy, lacy creation was an affront to her personally. "With such a lovely figure it seems a pity to hide it." But Helen had been adamant.

She'd also chosen her going-away outfit with care. In pale grey silk, the coat was long and loose, leaving one still able to visualise the slim figure inside it.

"By the time the baby's born," she said to Edwin after they had departed for their honeymoon in the Channel Islands, "people will have forgotten when our marriage was."

"By then who'll care?" he replied flippantly, his arm around her in the chauffeur-driven car taking them to Southampton for the boat they would catch. It was to be a simple honeymoon. In accordance with her wishes, he had played down the wedding, with no publicity they could help though one or two news reporters had turned up – Letts had become popular enough again for its young owner to be worth a small column in the society pages.

"I wonder what I will have," murmured Helen as she snuggled a little closer to Edwin.

She hoped it would be a girl, but guessed Edwin would wish for a boy, to carry on the business. He was obsessed with his business. Even being absent from it on this week's honeymoon, Helen suspected, tore at him, but she smiled indulgently.

She'd bidden a tearful goodbye to her father, saying she'd visit him immediately they came back. How would it be for him, on his own from now on? For the time being she and Edwin would live in the penthouse. He did intend for them to get a house. "But a really nice one," he said. "I need to take my time."

Edwin was one to do just that, steady, reliable, but so thorough she sometimes thought of a snail – getting there, even if he was a little slow about it. These past months she had noticed it even more. Again she smiled. She had a good husband here.

She'd thought Dad was exacting and deliberate enough, but Edwin beat him hands down. Fortunately he and Edwin had grown more at ease with each other. Edwin had told her of his initial awkwardness, not sure what to call him. Now that they'd settled for first names, it meant that her father no longer felt the need to leave Letts. She was glad and relieved. What would he have done with nothing to work for? Letts was his life.

Edwin too was thinking about William. A week before the wedding he had made another attempt to try to get the family to allow his future father-in-law into the business.

"After all," he told his Aunt Victoria at her home, her husband Harold and her daughter Sheila, minor shareholders, also present, "we owe it to him. Without him I'd never have brought that place back to life. It's thriving and all thanks to him."

Hugh should have been here. Edwin hadn't bought all his shares off him. Yet he was showing his worth by not even bothering to reply or be present. Edwin glowered around the dining-room table at the remaining three.

His aunt had been aghast by Edwin's suggestion – aghast and abrupt. "You want an outsider brought in? This is a family business, and it should remain so. No, Edwin, quite out of the question." She was so like her own mother, his grandmother, whom he'd heard had been a veritable matriarch of the Edwardian type. Aunt Victoria either took after her or aimed to be like her. But it cut no ice with him and he'd glared back at her.

"Are you enjoying this year's profits, Aunt?" He didn't wait for her reply. "It's not my doing. It's William Goodridge's doing. He holds it together. I'm still learning. He deserves some recognition."

"Then promise him a substantial retirement pension," came the retort.

"I want more than that. And anyway, he should have a say in the business. Uncle Henry gave him a few shares years ago, and you agreed to that."

"Because we were railroaded into it," put in Harold, leaning forward to emphasise the point. "He pushed until we finally gave in – saying the amount was too negligible to argue about."

"As I'm saying now," Edwin pointed out. "He still has those few shares."

"It was very remiss of Henry to have made so much of the man. But, no, I won't have this Goodridge coming to family board meetings putting in his say. Tell him that we thank him very much for all he has done in the past, and let it go at that."

"Thank him!" Edwin had retorted. "You should be going down on your knees in gratitude to him."

But in the end he had come away with no agreement reached. Now though, it didn't matter so much. William was staying on, as restaurant manager and his adviser and friend, as he'd once been to Uncle Henry, and he seemed content enough with that – maybe even relieved at not being included in family meetings, aware that he would always be considered an outsider.

Nine

"Edwin! Darling! I think it's started."

Edwin awoke from a deep sleep to the sound of Helen's voice and of her hand shaking him by the shoulder. For a moment he could not think where he was, what time of day or night it could be.

"You've got to get up, darling!" Helen's frightened voice broke through his befuddled senses. "I think the baby's coming. What's the time?"

Now he was fully awake, ripped into consciousness in the way an animal is when presented with a fight or flight situation. He sat bolt upright in bed, his mind alert. He shot a glance at the bedside clock.

"Three thirty. It's all right, sweet. Don't get in a stew. Just take it gently. Leave it all to me. Get dressed if you can. I'll ring the hospital."

With that he was out of bed making for the telephone, yelping as his little toe collided with the splayed leg of the dressing-table on which the phone sat. Ordinarily he'd have roared in fury at the sudden pain, but he gritted his teeth as he lifted the phone and dialled the number, all the while rubbing vigorously at the tender toe.

Before long, Helen having hastily dressed, not at all properly, between pauses fraught with little moans, they were in the ambulance. Once in the hospital, all signs of birth pangs dying away, she lay in a bed, as comfortable as its hard mattress would allow, smiling guiltily at the nurses and excusing herself to Edwin at jolting him out from sleep for what must have been a false alarm, he being assured that his wife was in good hands and he could go home, leaving her here, that she was dilated so she should stay.

Labour started in earnest around seven o' clock that evening. Edwin was summoned back to the hospital but banished to the waiting room, while Helen and the attendant nurses finally brought the baby – "You have a beautiful little girl," she was told – into the world at around seven the following morning. In need of "only a couple of stitches" after twelve hours, she was a little shocked to be told that it was a relatively quick and easy birth for a first baby. Tired but elated, she was able to make her face up and do her hair in preparation for Edwin, who looked more exhausted than she did.

"I've never smoked so much in all my life," he told her, and she felt quite proud of having got through the birth without too much fuss while he still showed signs of his suffering. She felt strong and in charge and it was a good feeling.

"How do you feel," she asked, "at having a daughter?"

Edwin grinned and pressed her hand between his. "I'm the proudest man in the world. And I'm so proud of you darling. You've been marvellous. And you look marvellous."

A nurse was trundling the crib into the ward, positioning it beside the bed and folding back the shawl for the father's inspection of the tiny scrap.

"She is quite beautiful, don't you think?" she enquired as Edwin peered.

"She looks a bit red and screwed up," was his doubtful response.

The nurse indulgently clicked her tongue, half laughing. "I don't know. You men!" She swished away, leaving the happy parents to it.

"What do you really think of her?" asked Helen.

"I think she's perfect," Edwin said. "Is she?"

Helen sighed contentedly. "She is. The doctor and nurses are all very pleased with her." She looked into Edwin's eyes. "We are so lucky, my love."

–

"We've decided to call her Angela, because she looks like a little angel," Helen told her father when he visited. "Edwin wanted to call her Carol, being as it was so near Christmas, but I said there was three weeks to go to Christmas and he was being a bit previous. So we've settled on Angela, but already he's started calling her Angel."

William laughed. He could afford to laugh. The secret worry he'd had for months about the issue of first cousins possibly being flawed no longer had substance. He could even chide himself for his fears. Better still, there was now no point in upsetting Helen with the truth as to her real father – it was all water under the bridge.

Now all he need do was forget it. He was a grandfather in the eyes of all but himself, and the mind has an odd way of deluding itself. He didn't care.

Leaning carefully over the hospital crib he dropped a fond kiss on the tiny warm head. That touch had an immediate and magical effect on him, all earlier doubt receding, leaving him filled with belief that this was indeed his own flesh and blood. Why spoil it?

But his brain hardly acknowledged the question, cast aside in his joy of this tiny being, in the joy of seeing how his daughter's face glowed, and the obvious awe his son-in-law possessed in having become a father.

–

"She's such a placid child," said Helen to Edwin's Aunt Victoria. "We're so lucky."

Seated on a sofa at Aunt Victoria's home, Helen gazed down at the little five-month-old Angela lying quietly in her arms. It was Aunt Victoria's husband's sixtieth birthday, the fifteenth of May 1956, and she had given a little party to celebrate. The weather being beautiful it had been held outside in Victoria's extensive garden, but as it turned chilly towards late afternoon the gathering had migrated indoors.

Victoria leaned over a little to peer down at the child and cooed, "You are quite a beauty, aren't you?" in her normal strident tones. The wide blue eyes stared back, unresponsive.

"Can she see all right?" asked Victoria in her straight-forward manner, never a believer in pulling her punches, much less seeing why they might cause offence. This was one of those moments.

"Of course she can see all right," Helen shot back, wishing she could get up from the sofa and move away. But there were no more seats to be had. As well as the family, Aunt Victoria had invited a mass of friends from her church, including the vicar. There were in fact several people standing – Edwin for one, at the moment in deep conversation with his Uncle Harold – and Helen didn't much care to go and stand so pointedly at her husband's elbow.

"Perhaps it's her hearing," Aunt Victoria went on. She moved a finger before the child's face. The blue eyes automatically followed it. Aunt Victoria clicked her tongue. "Could it be, then, that she didn't hear me? When that maid dropped her tray a while ago with such a clatter, it made us all jump. But this little one took no notice whatsoever. Have you had her hearing properly checked, my dear?"

Helen drew in a silent, aggravated breath. "The doctors say she is perfect. There is nothing at all wrong with her. In fact they're very pleased. Would you excuse me, Aunt, I need to have a word with Edwin."

Glad to escape, she hurried over to him. He was free now, his uncle having fallen into conversation with someone else. She touched his arm and he turned to look at her.

"Are you all right, darling?" His expression was immediately one of concern and she knew then that consternation Was showing on her face. Pooh-pooh his Aunt Victoria's observations though she might, a seed had been sown that was hard to dislodge. She tried to smile.

"I'm fine. Just a bit tired, that's all. It's getting late, Edwin, and I think we ought to get Angela home. We agreed she should have a regular bedtime from the start. I don't want to break it now."

"I'll get our things," he said readily. Moments later they were saying goodbye to everyone, thanking Aunt Victoria for inviting them and hoping she liked her present of an original watercolour for her drawing room. The drive home would only take three-quarters of an hour, ample time for Angela to be put to bed just half an hour later than her set bedtime.

All the way home, Helen could hear Aunt Victoria's words. "*Have you had her hearing properly checked?*" She felt angry. How dare the woman presume to hint that she wasn't a good enough mother to care about her daughter's welfare? Yet had she checked it? She had taken one doctor's word for it. What if he *had* missed something?

She said nothing to Edwin even when he remarked how quiet she was, merely telling him she felt tired, which he accepted well enough.

—

Helen's cheeks were wet. It had taken her another two months to bring herself to relay Aunt Victoria's suspicion to Edwin.

He'd taken it grimly and had then grown angry, as she had done earlier, repeating her own thoughts that his aunt presumed too much and insisting that they above anyone should know about their own child's well-being. Finally he'd become thoughtful and agreed that it might be worth getting a second opinion. "Just to put our minds at rest."

Emerging from the Harley Street clinic into brilliant July sunshine, Helen sniffed back her tears, letting the warm summer breeze dry her cheeks as she gazed down at the child in her arms.

Edwin held the car door open for her to get into the back seat with Angela. "It never feels safe, you sitting in the front with her," he always insisted. "If I had to pull up sharp, you could be thrown forward and she could be hurt. Both of you could be hurt."

Now Angela was hurt, or rather impaired. All their care and attention, their love and protection, and neither of them had seen it. The doctor had been most meticulous; peering into the ears with instruments, he had been hard put to do as good a job as he would wish with Angela persisting in squirming, retaliating to the insult to her small person. Attentive from all this rough handling, when he clicked his fingers behind her head her lively eyes had seen the slightest of movements and had turned. Her mother had gained hope that it was all a false alarm; had even felt anger again towards Aunt Victoria for her interfering amateur's diagnosis.

"I can find nothing wrong," the doctor had said, raising her confidence still further that this had been a fool's errand. "But I'm going to bring in one of my colleagues for him to have a look."

It was this colleague that had pronounced the dire sentence on the child. Having allowed Angela to calm down, her mother to give her a feed in a quiet room, even banishing the father from the vicinity, the colleague quietly entered while Angela lay relaxed in her mother's arms.

"I am going to make a sharp noise," he whispered from the doorway. "It will be quite loud, but try not to jump, Mrs Lett, as it will startle her. She's a lively, attentive little girl and will probably pick it up from you. Now just stay still."

With that there came a loud snap. Helen remained quite still, her eyes on Angela who was looking contentedly at the coloured pictures on the wall opposite. Again came the ear-splitting snap. Helen saw her baby's eyes slew slightly, wondered if her own body had moved, but was sure it hadn't.

"I'm certain she heard that," she began, but a third unexpected snap brought her own automatic reaction to it. At the same time Angela struggled up in her arms to peer round to see what was going on.

The doctor came to stand in front of them. He smiled down at the child then, looking at Helen, said, "I think there is an impairment here. It seems to me that there is only partial hearing."

The look on Helen's face must have hit a soft spot and he placed his hand on her shoulder. "She is not profoundly deaf, Mrs Lett."

"How can you say she's even slightly deaf?" Helen challenged him. "You couldn't see what her reaction was. You were behind us. But I saw it."

He smiled sadly and glanced up towards the ceiling. Helen followed his gaze. There, angled just above her, was a mirror, reflecting them all in minute detail. She hadn't noticed it before, so wrapped up in calming Angela down had she been. Through it he'd been watching the baby's eyes for signs of any reaction to the noises made.

More tests had followed, intensive, harrowing, but all the comforting words in the world couldn't lessen the blow of being told that Angela had impaired hearing. Going home that day Helen found herself wondering what she could have done while her baby was in the womb to cause this thing to happen to her child. She blamed herself. There was no one else she could blame.

–

Edwin stood before his father-in-law, his expression thunderous. Since yesterday's news about Angela's affliction he'd hardly said two words to the man. Now, in the man's own flat at one in the morning, the restaurant having closed late this evening, he confronted him with the news concerning his grandchild.

Goodridge stood stunned, finally finding his voice.

"God, that's dreadful, such a shock. That poor little kid – I don't know what to say. She's so bright, so quick – I never dreamed of anything like…"

He paused, seeing the father's unrelenting glare but, taking it for grief, carried on. "I know how you must feel, Edwin."

"Do you?" came Edwin's harsh query. "How do you feel?"

"Same as you: deeply shocked, dismayed, sorry."

"For what? Her having hearing problems or the real cause of it?"

"I don't get you," William began, but he knew full well that he did. Cousins marrying – no problem legally, but could it have weakened the child's right to perfect health, a full life?

"It can't be," he went on, appalled.

"What else can you put it down to?"

"Edwin, it could happen to any child. It doesn't have to be because you and Helen—"

"There's no other explanation," Edwin cut in, his features tight.

"Are you blaming me, Edwin?"

"I'm blaming myself. And of course you. We both carry this secret and poor Helen is entirely ignorant of it. Yet she's the one who's suffering."

Alarm gripped William like some iron fist. "Don't tell her," he begged. "Not now. It'll slay her."

"We're both guilty. What if she wants more children in the future? I'm going to have to tell her. I can't keep this to myself any longer."

"No! Please!" William grabbed his arm. "You could wreak untold damage, to her, to your marriage. Edwin, think. Think before you go off half-cocked. I know you're shocked. I am too. She's my granddaughter – it doesn't matter about blood ties. I love Helen and Angela as much as if they were my own. Edwin, let it be. What good would it do spoiling what you have, what Helen has? Why destroy her?"

"Because another child could carry a similar weakness, or worse."

"How are you going to prevent it, then? Forbid her having any more children? Tell her the truth and risk your marriage breaking up? Or maybe you want to live with a woman whose mind has been damaged by what you want to tell her? You can't do that to her."

He saw Edwin's already tight lips grow even tighter. "There seems to be no answer, does there?" he said, and pulled away from William's grip. "There seems little point continuing this discussion so I'll say goodnight."

"Give it some deep thought," William called after him, "if not for mine or yours, at least for Helen's sake."

The door closed with a crash, leaving him to stew, not only that sleepless night, nursing his own sorrow for the child, but for days after when Edwin avoided him as much as possible, speaking to him only when necessary and then in terse sentences.

He deduced, however, as time went on and Helen, visiting with Angela, remained serene apart from her worry over the baby, that Edwin had said nothing after all.

-

One Sunday morning that September the phone by the bed jangled. Half asleep after a late night supervising the restaurant, a good crowd in, Edwin reached out and felt for the thing, at the same time glancing at the bedside clock. Eight fifteen – a brief prickle of irritation rippled through him.

"Hullo?"

"Edwin? It's Hugh. Hope I didn't wake you. We're in Southampton on our way to Madeira. It's just a quick call to tell you I got married yesterday and ask if you'd like to congratulate me, old man."

It was typical of Hugh to do a thing like that with not a word to anyone. "Who've you got married to?" was all Edwin could think to say.

"I told you. Introduced you to her at your wedding. Glenda Dearing. You remember."

"Yes, I remember."

"We've been shacked up together for far too long. I didn't want to lose her so I popped the question. She said yes so we got married yesterday in a registry office, last night came down to Southampton. Off on honeymoon for a week or two, then we're in Ireland where we'll be playing in Dublin: the Gate Theatre."

"I see," said Edwin. "So when will you—" It was as far as he got.

"Look, got to go. You going to congratulate me, old boy?"

"Congratulations," murmured Edwin, adding, "You could have invited us, at least told us if no one else," but he was already talking to no one.

Smiling at the receiver, he replaced it then rolled over towards his wife who, stirring, asked, "Who was that?"

"Hugh," he whispered. "Phoned to say he got married yesterday."

Instantly Helen was awake, staring up into Edwin's face. "Did you say got married?"

"That's right. Rang to ask us to congratulate him. He and his bride are off to Madeira on their honeymoon."

Quickly he related all that Hugh had told him. She listened without smiling and when he'd done, merely said, "Well, I wish him lots of happiness," in such a strange tone that Edwin frowned. But as she had turned over to recapture her sleep, he said nothing.

–

Why should she feel so strangely hurt? Hugh's life was nothing to do with her any more. She had refused him, chosen to marry Edwin. She was a wife and a mother – she had no right to feel enmity against Hugh for having gone off and got married to someone else. Yet there was a heaviness of heart that all day refused to shift. Every time she thought of him, his face was as clear in her head as though she had seen him yesterday, for all the months she'd not seen him. And with it came the same strange stirring deep inside her that she'd been conscious of the very first time she had set eyes on him.

It was an effort to face the day. Edwin was at home; the restaurant was closed on Sundays. It was an effort to behave normally, make conversation with him, smile at him. He noticed it.

"Something wrong?" he queried as she put their breakfast on the table She replied that she'd been awake part of the night with Angela teething, which was true. He asked again at lunch, however, this time more persistently.

"I'm just a bit tired, that's all." She dismissed his concern and went on eating the chicken salad she had prepared.

That night, as he kissed her before turning over to sleep, she clung on to him. "Make love to me," she begged.

"I thought you'd be too tired," he said amiably.

"No, not too tired for that. It's ages since we really made love; Angela and her teething always gets between us. Make love to me, Edwin, before she wakes up. I've given her some medicine to soothe her gums. She should sleep for a few hours."

"Well, if you feel like that," he said and took her gently in his arms.

But she needed more to take away the dull ache of Hugh having got married. Edwin, finding himself overwhelmed by her hunger, was guilty of taking full advantage of it, taking no time even to seek the protection which they had agreed was needed. Angela was too young to have a baby brother or sister yet, and with her hearing impaired as it was, she would need their full attention for some years to come. Another baby, they had agreed, would only interfere with that and wouldn't be fair on her. But that night all good intentions flew out of the window, leaving Helen wondering next morning if she had conceived.

The continuation of her periods told her that she hadn't. But just prior to Christmas the period she'd expected did not appear. Wondering if she was right in what she was thinking, she counted the months. If she were correct, the baby would be due next September. There would be nearly two years' difference between this one and Angela: ideal, she began telling herself before long, and by January she had missed another period and was already beginning to look forward to the event.

Ten

It was late February by the time Helen felt certain enough of her condition to tell Edwin, her doctor having confirmed it. She told him that same Monday evening when he came up from the restaurant.

Mondays were usually quiet around this time of year, people preferring to stay indoors during the winter, gathered round their electric fires and televisions.

"Damned television will be the death of the restaurant business," Edwin had said more than once, though he'd admitted that Easter and the approaching summer months would see the place becoming busy again.

This Monday, however, he was able to devote his time to her. She told him of her pregnancy and his reaction was one of happiness, with just a hint of relief, or so it seemed to her.

"It's just what you need, Helen, my darling. Another little one."

"Don't you mean 'we'?" she asked, her own happiness abating a little. "Just what *we* need?"

"Of course – just what we need. But it's you I'm thinking about. I'm sorry I have to leave you up here on your own so often. It's difficult at times to fill the place in the winter months, and we do need to entice our regulars as well as casuals away from the damned television taking over lately. I don't like leaving you here alone. I'd sooner be here with you. But a baby will be a companion for you as well as for Angel. And I shan't feel so guilty not being here all the time."

She nodded, understandingly. Understanding that he would not have to feel so guilty. A baby would make it all right for him. But he was right – a baby might make her feel less lonely here. Being wanted, being at someone's beck and call would give her no time to dwell on Edwin's absences, her isolation.

That had been her trouble as time had gone on, too little to do but dwell on that. Angela had never been hard work. At fifteen months she remained the placid child she'd always been. But it was a placidness that had become painful to see.

In everything else Angela was perfect; bright, happy, always smiling, people pointing her out as perfectly beautiful. She'd begun crawling earlier than normal and by nine months she was pulling herself up on to her feet by hanging on to furniture. Now she was toddling well, and her ready smile revealed the right complement of milk teeth.

In all things she was healthy. But she wasn't talking. The expected "Mama" and "Dada" had not appeared. When she wanted something she would point, make sounds, but it wasn't talking.

Helen found that speaking close to her ear would reap an instant response, but rather than be glad that Angela wasn't totally deaf, it constantly broke her heart. She had been told that an operation could be had but that it was far too soon to contemplate as yet.

Slowly, however, by speaking loudly to her, Helen could see Angela beginning to make sense of her world. But it was hard work and she had to dedicate herself to playing with her daughter more than some mothers did, comforting her more, mouthing her words carefully, making sure Angela was watching her as she did so. She was determined that her daughter would not be deprived of all the things other children took for granted, would not have to suffer being in a world where she'd be pointed out as an idiot. She was a bright child and no one was ever going to look on her as a fool.

The next morning Helen bent towards Angela, sitting in her high chair, and put the little red feeding mug on the tray as usual. Angela picked it up and put the spout to her lips.

"DRINK," Helen said slowly and loudly, repeating the word several times. Angela's grey eyes watched her from behind the cover of the mug.

Taking the mug away as she had done so many times before, Helen saw the child's face change as she was deprived of her favourite orange juice. As Angela held out her little hands to reclaim it, Helen gave it back. "DRINK," she said again. Weeks of this had always produced the same frustrating results: a wide-eyed stare, a perplexed frown, followed by a flashing smile as the mug was returned. She was sure Angela must hear her, if only in a muffled way. If she could cotton on just this once, it would be such a start.

Her heart gave a small leap as, taking the mug away and repeating the word yet again while resisting the small hands reaching out for the mug, she saw the lips begin to purse, following the movement her own lips were making. Moments later came a sound that made her almost want to burst into song. "Rrr… ing."

How tiny the voice was. How wonderful to hear – soft, high-pitched and beautiful. Helen felt as though she had climbed heights hitherto out of reach, was looking down at all the world and seeing that it was lovely.

It took another half an hour to end up with "Dwink", uttered in that adorable soft tone, and almost a further hour of repeatedly indicating herself to finally produce "Mama" from Angela. It was like a miracle. Helen could hardly wait for Edwin to come up from the restaurant to tell him. But by the time he did, weary and ready only to fall into bed, Helen and Angela were fast asleep.

–

Easter was spent quietly, on their own. There had been an invitation from Aunt Victoria but Edwin wanted to stay at home.

"I do enough socialising at the restaurant," he said, and Helen appeared quite content with that – said that she needed to keep on with Angela's tuition, now going well with Angela proving herself an even brighter child than they had imagined. Spending the weekend at someone else's home with all its distractions would set back all her hard work, she said.

He was proud of her efforts with Angel. He looked at her, so happy with her daughter, and smiled.

Helen returned the smile. "It's so good having you home, darling. I wish you could be here more often so you could take more part in sharing in the way Angel is coming along." She began to frown in an attempt to back up the admonition, mild though it was.

"I wish I could too," he responded lamely. "But I do need to be down there."

Of course she'd be happier if he stayed at home. But all the comforts she reaped, the nice clothes, the good living, a good private school for Angel one day, came only from the success he made of Letts. If only she would try to understand that, to be more content.

She never said as much but he could sense that feeling she had of him being more at home down there in his beloved restaurant than up here with her. Perhaps it was the restrictions of this penthouse meant only for two. She'd mentioned from time to time that she was bored with him always working, but whenever he'd suggested the theatre or the cinema, she'd be loath to leave Angela. Suggesting getting someone in to look after her for an evening made no difference. If she had somewhere roomier to live, she might not feel so cooped up. He'd even broached the idea of buying a house.

"Out of London," he said. "Lots of fresh air. With so many cars about these days, the London fog's full of carbon dioxide as well as smoke. It's bad for Angela. A fine big house in the suburbs, not too far from London: it would be perfect for her."

And perfect for him, thought Helen – perhaps a little unkindly, for he was thinking of Angela's welfare. But he was right. It would benefit her. The problem was that Angela saw little enough of him as it was without his having to travel to come home.

Living here, on the premises as it were, he was at least within calling distance, but moving away would isolate her even more. Helen thought of her own father. There would be no more popping in to see him; it would be a travel thing, again emphasising the sense of isolation. As for a fine big house; as Edwin put it, what did they want with a large place except to show off with it? She wasn't one for entertaining anyway.

As the weeks passed following Helen's announcement of her pregnancy, Edwin had begun to feel the insidious pricking of anxiety. That night as they lay in bed, Helen fast asleep but he wide awake, staring up at the ceiling, he spelled out his fear to himself: What if this baby should also prove to be impaired in some way? Angela's hearing difficulty didn't seem to bother her, being slight, but as she grew older would it grow more noticeable? Would she be teased or, worse, bullied by other children at school? Thank God she hadn't been born profoundly deaf, but could this next baby be afflicted even more, or by something even worse?

Sleeplessness always emphasised his worries and he had to tell himself that night, as he would for many to come, that he was being silly, that if the law allowed cousins to marry then repercussions from such close blood ties had to be rare and surely Angela's trouble was purely coincidental. Such things could happen to any child, yet it plagued him. It plagued him worse that he dare not share his fears with Helen. All he could think was that if this new baby were perfect there'd be no need to send her world crashing about her with revelations as to her real father. And he would see to it that they remained a two-child family, so side-stepping the need for her to know the truth.

Next morning he turned a serene face to her and, glancing around the penthouse, spoke again of finding a house, something really grand. In its way it helped blanket the apprehension he felt.

"This place will be far too cramped for all four of us. I'll get the ball rolling and we'll do some viewing."

"Can't it wait until better weather?" she pleaded. "Perhaps in summer?"

"You won't want to go traipsing around when you're big as a barge. We'll start now, looking for something really worth buying – lots of room and large grounds for our little Angel and her brother or sister to play in."

"Nothing too big," she pleaded.

He stared at her, stunned a little by the sharpness of her tone.

"We want something worthwhile. Something similar to Swift House, my Uncle Henry's home, where we can invite people and not have them look down their noses at it. It's a pity I had to sell my parents' house. If I'd known what a success Letts would become I'd never have let it go."

"The bank wasn't prepared to let you keep it, if I remember," said Helen, searching back into her memory of what he'd once told her. "You had to sell it to make up the money to pay back your loan." She came to where he stood by the ornate fireplace with its electric coal-effect fire. "If only that trust of mine had come to me earlier, it would have saved having to sell your family home."

His arm came around her shoulders. "I wouldn't have asked that of you, darling. It's your money, for you to do with as you please."

"It's for you too," she told him. "What's mine is yours."

"And what's yours is mine," he quipped, but she didn't laugh.

"I mean it, Edwin. If you ever need it…"

He too had sobered. His arm tightened about her. "I can afford to keep us, and quite decently, thanks to Letts. But we will need a bigger place to live and I don't want to see the children brought up in London. I'd like to go back to that area I was brought up in. High Ongar – it's lovely there. Lots of woods, lots of space." He surveyed her face. "What do you think?"

Helen felt coldness creep inside her, the cold of impending loneliness. "What am I going to do all on my own out in the country while you're here with the restaurant?"

Edwin's smile was infuriating. "You'll have the children. And we'll get domestic staff: a nanny – you'll need all the help you can get – and someone to clean and cook, and a general handyman and gardener."

"That all costs money."

She hated that indulgent smile. "Helen, I can afford it. My parents had domestic staff, a head gardener, and a farm manager when my father turned part of their grounds into an arable farm for a while during the war when home-produced food was needed. We had a butler too."

"That was then," cut in Helen. "People don't have butlers now."

"Titled people still do."

"We're not titled people, Edwin!"

His expression was impish. "You never know!"

But she couldn't return the smile. "Edwin, this is serious. I'm not sure I want to go off and live miles away. I like it here."

The impish look faded, replaced by a perplexed frown. "Why are you being so grumpy, darling?" he began. "I'm trying to do what's best for you, for us, for Angel and for the new baby when it comes, yet you're behaving as though I'm being thoroughly rotten to you."

Helen felt her chagrin fade. It was she who was being rotten. He didn't deserve this. "I'm sorry. I just feel I won't see so much of you, that's all."

Relieved he pulled her to him and held her close. "Darling, is that all? Then I'll make doubly sure to spend every bit of time I have with you and the children, I promise."

Which to her meant she'd see roughly about as much as she was seeing of him now.

–

It was a lovely house, she had to admit. He'd taken such care choosing it, had taken her out to view it, and she could have fallen in love with it had she not been plagued by the old doubts of no longer being on the doorstep so to speak. The knowledge that Edwin would no longer be able to pop upstairs to see her persisted in invading her thoughts.

The house, called Small Hill Hall, had a large garden of over an acre which meant employing someone to look after it. Being spring, the secluded walled part which had been lovingly tended by the previous owners was a delight to one who'd never before had a garden – spring bulbs in glorious bloom, flowering cherry trees, tidy crazy-paving paths weaving between masses of early flowering shrubs. Elsewhere were beautifully kept lawns for Angela to play on, and a large fish pond that Helen immediately began planning to fence in for her daughter's safety.

"And you can learn to drive," Edwin told her, encouraged by the look on her face. "Go up to London any time you like in your own car or have a chauffeur. Or there's a very good train service these days. I'll be coming home every night anyway, I'll make doubly sure of that. This being a village, you'll make friends much faster than in town. People get together more in a village."

Slowly Helen found herself being won over even though a faint anxiety regarding possible loneliness still persisted.

She'd spurned the idea of a nanny for Angela, and the baby when it arrived. But she did welcome the presence of a woman to cook and give an eye to the house in general, and who over those first few weeks in the new house proved herself a good companion. Hilda Cotterell was her name. Around forty-five, thick-set and motherly, she had a daughter, Muriel, who helped with the cleaning of the five bedrooms, three reception rooms, study, conservatory, large basement kitchen, servants' hall and pantry.

In the old days there must have been a mass of staff judging by the size of the place, but with modern appliances such an army was no longer needed. Helen was glad. She'd had ancient and alarming visions of giving orders, going through accounts, planning meals, but Hilda was of a placid nature, content at being virtually given a free hand. In fact she was almost becoming like a mother in Helen's eyes and would tut quite critically on her behalf when Edwin failed to come home some nights.

"We're going to like it here," Edwin had said as furniture was moved in after the decorators had finished. "It isn't that far out of London. Probably take me just under fifty minutes by car so I'll be here more or less all the time." It would probably take longer than that, but Helen let it go.

For the first month he'd been true to his word, except for Saturdays, when he was obliged to play host into the small hours just as his uncle had done years before. Sometimes it was Friday night as well, though while he made sure of being at home on Sunday, Helen felt she must make one or two allowances. But she missed him when he slept overnight in the penthouse, "to save coming home at three in the morning and disturbing you."

"I don't mind being disturbed," she insisted, but he'd say that with her time being so near she needed all the rest she could get without him creeping in at all hours.

So determined was he and so mindful of her peace of mind that she gave in, at least for the time being. But it wasn't going to become a habit, if she had her way; as soon as the baby was born, things would change, she'd make sure of that.

—

"Hugh!"

He stood there in the hall, eyeing her bulge as she came to greet him, she with three months to go. He grinned at her.

"Your maid let me in."

"She isn't my maid," said Helen as she came forward, smiling. "She keeps the place clean, that's all. She said you were here."

"Nice little thing," he remarked, then took her hands. "Well, how are you, Helen? You look blooming, if I may say so."

"I feel very well."

"Hope you didn't mind my barging in. Saturday morning and all."

"Not at all. I don't get many visitors. My dad once a week, and your Aunt Victoria came with her husband and Sheila to look at the house when we moved in."

"She would," he remarked as Helen led him to what was the drawing-room on one side of the wide hall, from which she'd emerged to greet him. "She must inspect everything, as if without her approval you'd drop all you're doing and start again. She's like my grandmother in that way, so I hear."

Helen's chuckle of conspiracy heartened him. He was welcome. Maybe now he'd get a foot in the door, so to speak. He desperately needed to.

Life wasn't treating him so well these days. What had started off rosy was wilting fast – his career, his marriage, and he was broke.

Yesterday he had stormed out in a rage from the Royal Court Theatre, where they'd been rehearsing for a new, somewhat controversial play. It had been a bloody good part but he knew now that he'd blown it and had cursed himself as ten sorts of fool for having lost his temper like that. The producer had been the biggest idiot, unable to make up his mind what he wanted, setting Hugh on edge over and over again until he'd exploded.

That had been the culmination of weeks of conflict. He'd been reprimanded in front of the whole cast for turning up late, even though the leading lady had turned up even later on several occasions and she hadn't been shown up in front of everyone. Turning on the tearful face, she'd had them flocking round her, giving her their sympathy over something that struck him as downright trivial. It just showed what a pretty face could do.

Even Glenda got away with it. He and Glenda had attended the audition together. She had been picked out first then, after a bit of pleading on her part, he had been too. But from the very start he'd been picked on, accused of having tantrums, of being late, of disrupting things by continually forgetting his lines. Everyone did one of those things at some time or another. Why had he been the scapegoat? It was Glenda who always redeemed him, the producer having fallen for her pretty pout and her superb figure, making Hugh squirm with jealousy.

Had it not been for the leading lady being so well known, Hugh was sure Glenda would have had her part. Glenda was such an excellent actress. She would go far, he knew, and again he was filled with jealousy that she could make it. Sometimes he wondered if he ever would.

It had caused rows. Their marriage wasn't going well. He loved Glenda, but sometimes she acted as though he meant nothing to her at all, and he was sure she was playing fast and loose with someone, maybe even the producer. Sometimes he felt like bloody well going after him, having it out and half throttling him, but what good would that do? And he couldn't be sure if it was him.

A good idea would have been to hire a private dick but he didn't have the money. The small parts he was getting didn't allow for such luxuries, what with giving Glenda little presents so as to keep her interested in him. That was why he gambled, always hoping to hit the jackpot. So he drank a bit more than he should. So it upset his concentration and he did forget his lines, occasionally. But he was a worried man. He could see himself losing Glenda. If he had money, it would make all the difference.

Edwin had money. Edwin owed it to him to bail him out, if only temporarily. It was Edwin who'd bought his shares, leaving him with just enough to remain a member in the family business but not enough to give him much out of any profits it made, and lately it was making a bloody good profit. He'd been a fool to let his shares go. Edwin had known he'd been on to a good thing when he'd bought them, the crafty bugger. Well, now Edwin owed him. And this was why he was here. This was the only way he could see of keeping Glenda. Money.

"So where's Edwin, then?" he asked jovially, seating himself on one of the two sofas that faced each other in front of the plain but expensive-looking marble fireplace with its huge display of cherry blossom screening the empty hearth.

He thought he saw Helen frown, but it was only a moment before she smiled back at him.

"Oh, he's not usually here on Saturdays. He has to stay up in town. He comes home on Sunday just after breakfast."

Damn! thought Hugh. If he'd gone straight to the restaurant it would have been so much simpler. He'd leave here as soon as socially possible.

"Tea?" asked Helen.

He pursed his lips. "That'd be very nice. But you wouldn't have a drop of brandy around, would you?"

"Brandy? Yes, there is some. But you wouldn't fancy tea?"

"A coffee, if that's OK? And I wouldn't mind a glass of brandy to go with it."

Helen glanced at the push bell, hesitated, then got up and went to the door where he heard her call out softly, "Muriel, can you ask your mother to make us some coffee, please?"

Hugh smiled and thought of the days he'd spent as a boy at Swift House before the war, servants hurrying to orders issued in confident tones. Times changed. Edwin was trying to ape his ancestors, but it no longer worked. Poor Helen, thrust into that kind of life just so her husband could show off.

Hugh felt sudden admiration for her that instantly burgeoned into desire. Pregnant though she was, she still had that certain something that had once turned him on.

Eleven

It was midday. Letts was buzzing. People were coming to London to see the sights now the weather was getting warmer. He'd forgotten that. If he hadn't stayed with Helen so long he might have got here before lunchtime and found the place quieter.

He had made the mistake of asking after Helen's little girl, mainly to control the sensation Helen's nearness had produced between his legs in spite of her present condition. His mind had conjured up images of lying with her in her bed, making love to her, hearing her excited sighs. He saw her as lonely with Edwin hardly here, and as a consequence he imagined with relish her hunger for love as he took her.

Pulling himself together, he'd asked after the child, the only thing he could think of to calm down the feelings he was having.

Her reaction had been immediate, her whole face lighting up. "She's in the kitchen with Mrs Cotterell. Mrs Cotterell shows her how to make dough and she loves messing about there. I'll go and call her so you can see her. You haven't yet, have you? You'll like her. She's a real beauty." Helen had given a self-conscious laugh. "At least I think so."

He had been faced with the child, he who had never been at ease with children, trying to make small talk, mostly to please her mother. The kid had stared back at him as though he was some sort of unfunny clown. He was aware of consternation on her mother's face and the way she raised her voice to talk to her daughter. It was then that he recalled being told that the child had been born partially deaf. She didn't look idiotic, but her face was blank. A pretty face, rather elfin but she would grow up to be a beauty, he could see that, like her mother. Helen, for all her pregnant state, was still exquisite.

He had excused himself as soon as he could, mostly to get away from the woman who was disturbing him so. Now he stood in Letts' entrance, a young receptionist indicating for him to make his way down the marble steps to the restaurant below that echoed to the clash of plates, the clink of cutlery on good china and the babble of almost a hundred voices.

"Mr Edwin Lett around?" he asked her.

She looked puzzled. "Shall I say who's calling?"

"I'm his cousin," he supplied a little tersely. "Hugh Lett. Where is he?"

"Oh, he's in his office, sir. He won't be down here until this evening."

"Right!" Taking no further notice of her, Hugh hurried down the steps, across the lower restaurant and up the carpeted staircase to the mezzanine level. The dance floor at this time of day was empty apart from waiters traversing it. The bar, however, was busy, people sitting at the small tables, chatting, having sandwiches, coffees, lunchtime drinks. Ignoring them, Hugh made toward a door near the bar and went to open it.

"Excuse me, sir! You can't go up there. It's private."

Hugh turned irritably towards the young barman who had attempted to stop this trespasser.

"I'm Mr Lett's cousin. I understand he's in his office."

The young man was looking uncertain. "D'you want proof?" Hugh snapped.

The young man wilted and stood back, leaving Hugh to continue on his way without giving him a further glance, shutting the door behind him with an ill-humoured click.

The passage was dimly lit. It led to a single flight of stairs, at the top of which was the glass-panelled door to the office. It would be empty of staff this Saturday lunchtime, they having gone home after their morning's work.

He tried the door anyway. It was locked. Turning away, he carried on up a second staircase to another door. This one, far more elaborate, led to Edwin's penthouse. Hugh rapped on it.

"Hugh," he called to the voice that challenged him after quite a long pause. Seconds later the door was yanked open and Edwin's surprised face confronted him, the man in shirtsleeves, the collar undone.

"What're you doing here?" It was almost a challenge and he could see from Edwin's eyes that he'd been dozing, no doubt after a late night.

"I need to have a word with you, Edwin," he began. "Didn't mean to disturb you. I've been at your house and had a coffee with Helen. She told me you'd be here. Said you usually stay in town on Saturdays – sometimes Friday nights too. You must be damned busy."

Edwin had recovered his composure. "Well, come on in. This is a rare treat. Don't see much of you."

"I've been rehearsing for a new play," said Hugh as he followed Edwin into the cosy lounge. From the window, with its drapes pulled right back, he caught a glimpse across London. A fine view, but no longer across the rooftops of London, high-rise buildings going up everywhere.

"Managed to get a few hours off," he excused, taking the armchair Edwin offered him.

Edwin came and sat opposite him. "So you're doing OK, then. And how's married life treating you? Haven't seen you since you got married, except to see you in that play – can't think what it was called now."

When Hugh failed to enlighten him, he repeated ineffectually, "So, you're doing OK, then? Getting some good work, good parts?"

Hugh found himself pulling a face. No sense putting on an act. That would ruin his initial purpose in being here. He took a deep breath and leaned forward in his chair.

"Truth is, old man, I'm not doing so well."

Edwin's expression was one of surprise and commiseration. "Why not? What's eating you, Hugh? You look thoroughly downhearted."

Again Hugh allowed himself a deep sigh, leaned even further forward. "I need to come clean, Edwin. I'm at rock bottom at the moment. And my marriage looks like it'll come to an end before the year's out. Truth is, I think Glenda's carrying on with someone."

"Oh, no…"

"I can't give her what she's looking for," he hurried on, brushing aside Edwin's token sympathy. "I don't mean a family. She's not interested in that – says it'll interfere with her career. She's going to go far, that I know. She's a wonderful actress and she's had some really good offers. Me, I'm just her shadow, dragging my feet, in her way, holding her back. So far she's kept me afloat, put up with

139

me, but I can't see that lasting. She's beginning to make it plain that she's getting tired of me – wants out, though she's not said as much yet. Thing is, it's getting to me. I don't know what to do and the only thing that gets me going is having a drink or two and… By the way, you don't happen to have a whisky, do you? I know it's early in the day, but this is taking a lot out of me, coming here telling you my troubles."

Edwin got up and, going to a decanter on a small side table, poured a shot, bringing it back to hand it to him. Hugh sat for a while rolling the tumbler between his palms. He must not show himself up by tossing the drink back. Let Edwin see he wasn't that desperate.

"I'm not a drunkard, Edwin. I can take my liquor all right, but it does tend to make me irritable I suppose, more perhaps than normal. But I have cause. I watch her getting on, using her looks, making up to that bloody director fellow. They don't call them producers any more. It's the American way – they're directors now. He can get her places and she knows it. I know there's something going on between them, the way he looks at her and she at him – sometimes right in front of me. She goes out without me, says it's to see friends. When I put my foot down it starts up a blazing row and she flounces off anyway. What can I do? I know she's seeing him – it'll have started as the old casting couch lark, though I think it's more than that now. But of course I've no proof. She's tired of me, that I do know, and I don't know what to do."

"I don't know how I can help you," Edwin was saying, but again Hugh brushed the sympathy aside.

"If I had a bit more money, I could take her places, show her a good time, like he's no doubt doing. I'm desperate to raise a bit of cash. I have a flutter on the horses. Well, it's more than that. Your father used to do well, casinos and things, and I know of a few places. But I don't have his luck. Sometimes I win, but most of the time…"

He broke off to take a long swig of the whisky, then sat staring into it. Finally he looked up at Edwin, his expression abject.

"I've got to find a bit of cash from somewhere, Edwin. And because I can't concentrate for the worry of everything, my career's going downhill. I need to come clean with you, Edwin. I've not managed to get a few hours off from rehearsals, I've walked out. Couldn't stand the way I was being spoken to. You can't tell me it wasn't designed to make me feel small in front of the whole cast – everyone smirking at me, knowing what's going on. I told him I'd had enough and he could stick his part. He leered at me and said if I walked out I needn't come back. And her, she just stood there and watched me go. She looked a bit taken aback, but she didn't bother to stand up for me. So I'm out, and I don't even know if she's coming back. Without her I'm all washed up. I'm lost without her. All I can think of doing is topping myself."

Edwin was looking horrified. "Don't be silly, Hugh! She'll come back, I'm sure. Don't give up. And you'll get another part. Things are never as bad as they seem at first."

"Oh, yeah!" Hugh turned on his cousin, his heart full of wrath. All full of trite cliches and bloody empty air, this man wasn't going to help him.

"Easy for you to say – someone like you, with everything. When did you ever have it hard? Everything has dropped into your bloody lap, hasn't it? You got the girl, you got the restaurant, you've money coming out of your fucking ears! And all you can say in that damned patronising tone is that it's never as bad as it seems. What do you know about bad? What d'you know about rock bottom? I've not got a bean right now and I don't know where to turn, so what's the point of it all?"

He was beginning to break down. He hadn't intended to make a spectacle of himself, his voice cracking, the muscles of his face contorting, his vision blurring with tears. But he was at his wits' end and all he was getting out of this man was that nothing was ever as bad as it seemed. Giving up to his misery, he slumped forward, his head in his hands, while Edwin looked on, at a loss what to do.

Edwin's mind was in turmoil. Was his cousin asking for money or help? He could give no advice, and if he offered cash, would Hugh take it as an insult?

"Something'll turn up," was all he could think to say, then, on a surer note, "Can I do anything?"

Hugh lifted his head, his expression filling with new hope.

"If I had something to tide me over," he said unevenly. "Until I get another part somewhere."

So it was money he was after. Dim recollections of what he'd been told about his father's incessant borrowing from his brother assailed Edwin. But that had usually been to settle gambling debts. This was different. This was Hugh's career on the line. Even so, some instinct made him stall. He wanted to say that drinking and gambling wasn't the answer, but thought better of it.

Instead he said, "You've got shares in Letts still. You get a regular income from them."

It couldn't be much, he knew. Hugh had been ready to sell every last share he had in the business, just as his stepmother had, their heads turned by all that cash. It was only because Edwin had persuaded him to hang on at least to a few that he still had some.

"The way the restaurant's going," he said, "profits up, you're getting good returns. You must have saved something. Can't it tide you over for the time being, that and what you make with acting?"

Hugh's answer was to glare at him. "What do you think acting brings in, for Christ's sake? I'm not one of your famous celebrities earning a fortune." In his anger, he got up and began pacing, waving his hands as theatrically as though he were indeed acting. "I play bit parts, supporting, I get peanuts. One day I might make it, make thousands. But that's not now, at this moment. At this moment I'm bloody stony broke. And what shares you didn't take hardly keeps up with paying for food."

"If it wasn't for my insisting you didn't sell them all to me," Edwin reminded, watching him and trying to keep his own feelings under control, "you'd have got rid of them too. You are at least still part of this business."

"What bloody good that ever does me."

He looked so woebegone that Edwin knew he had to do something. "Look, if I give you something to tide you over, how would that be?" He could see immediately from the other's expression that this was what Hugh had been waiting for. "How much do you need? To tide you over until you get settled again."

Already he could see shades of his father and uncle. This must not become the thin end of the wedge. But before he knew it he was writing a cheque for five hundred pounds with the uncomfortable feeling that this was indeed setting a precedent. A year, perhaps only a few months from now, Hugh would be at his door again, shamefaced and imploring, saying he was in dire straits yet again.

As Hugh took the cheque from him, his face shining with gratitude, Edwin was almost urged to say, "And don't use it to gamble with," but once again thought better of it and kept quiet.

–

Helen's second baby was another girl. Helen had to admit to being very happy about it and though she knew Edwin would have loved this one to have been a boy, he was pleased that the birth was much easier this time.

"The second one usually is quicker," said one of the nurses who had attended her in the hospital. "And she is bonny, isn't she?"

Yes, she was. What the nurse didn't see as the fond parents nodded agreement, gazing down at their daughter in adoration, was that behind the proud father's smile was an aching fear that there could be some hidden affliction similar to that of his first daughter.

Angel – even Helen had come to call her that – no longer had the difficulties with speech she'd encountered at first. A quick child, she had soon picked up the way she had of watching people's lips, grey eyes bright and attentive, pretty head slightly to one side, giving her an appealing look that endeared her to everyone. No one would have thought for one minute that she had trouble hearing.

Even so, it hung heavily on Edwin that, having had one child slightly defective, the problem might be repeated in the second one. It was to trouble him for months, as it did William Goodridge, suffering appalling guilt and self-condemnation that even now he did not have the gumption to reveal that secret he held. Hating himself, he could only smile as his second granddaughter was handed to him, Helen proudly but innocently announcing, "We're calling her Georgina Mary. I thought you'd like that, Dad."

Mary after Helen's mother. Georgina – Edwin's choice – after his father Geoffrey. Angela's second name, Pamela, had also been requested by him for his mother and although William hadn't been too pleased about that, he kept his dislike of the woman to himself. Though Georgina, he had to admit, was a pretty enough name.

After all, Edwin would have loved his mother. William wasn't sure if he had spoken of Geoffrey Lett's callous divorcing of Mary when Pamela had come along. He'd been so carried away in that pub all that time ago, when persuading Edwin to take over the family business, that these days he wasn't sure what he'd said aloud and what had only been recalled in his head. Of course Edwin would want to honour his dead mother. No doubt if one of his children had been a boy he would have wanted the name Geoffrey added. It was only natural.

–

Glenda was divorcing him. For cruelty! God, he'd only hit her the once. Blacked her eye, that was the trouble.

Well, he had lashed out at her before, he had to admit, but then who wouldn't? The way she cocked a snook at him all the time, taking him for a dummy. For the last six months they'd done nothing but argue. Always over the same thing – what she was getting up to behind his back.

He remembered that first time he'd hit her. He hadn't meant to. It was the first real row they'd ever had, the day she came in after the show six months ago.

She was doing well for herself – with the help of Simon Jenson, that bloody director also going places, promising her the lead role in his next show. And he would have a next show, perhaps in the West End. Give him his due, he was bloody good at it and he had money. Glenda liked money.

He knew she was seeing him, knew which side her bread was buttered. That she still clung on to her marriage was a wonder to Hugh, but he knew why. Jenson was already married. He'd heard the gossip, Jenson a one for the ladies, but it seemed his wife was devoted, didn't want to let go, always hoping for that miracle – her husband to become suddenly loyal.

As for himself, Hugh still toyed with the idea of hiring someone to follow them, catch the pair of them at it, giving him grounds for divorce. Trouble was he didn't want to divorce her. He still wanted her. The only time he forgot to want her was when Helen was around and then everything would go out of the window as the sight of her got to him. Once she was out of sight, however, his thoughts would whisk back to Glenda and how she turned him on. But Glenda was turning someone else on now, the bitch, and enjoying every second of it.

He decided he wasn't going to put up with it any more when she came home looking stunning in a pale gold New Look evening dress, all long flared skirt and hardly any top, tits almost falling out. She'd put on a bit of flesh up there and the sight of it turned his blood both to fire with desire for her and curdled it at the thought of someone else already having been fondling them.

Whore! he thought as his gaze followed her self-satisfied entrance into the lounge. And him, the bloody lecher! Where had they been, those two? He could see it all: some hotel room, the bed, the mirrors, the rumpled sheets, those two luxuriating over each other, and him here alone, stewing, just a couple of copies of *Esquire* and a bottle of scotch to keep him company.

"Had a good time?" He couldn't keep the sneer out of his tone as she passed him, dropping a nonchalant kiss on top of his fair hair, as if nothing at all was wrong. She wrinkled her nose.

"You've been at the bottle." She didn't care, did she? Well, one day he would make her care.

"Where've y'been?" His words were slurred.

"Going over the script for another show," she said as she went to pour herself a drink. "This one's likely to be in a West End theatre. I might even play the lead."

Yes, of course she would! They'd not worked together for ages; she'd gone on without him. While she was forging ahead he was still doing bit parts, still dreaming of acclaim, Shakespeare gone out of the window with him having trouble these days remembering his lines for quite mundane parts let alone those of the Bard. But with his mind always on Glenda and what she was up to with that sod Jenson, how could he concentrate? Reduced to less and less significant roles, no recommendation at auditions, he wasn't even being given supporting roles any more.

He'd had to go back to Edwin twice since that first time, Edwin each time writing out a paltry five hundred quid cheque and expecting him to be grateful for it. It was his own money he was getting, for God's sake, Edwin taking his shares like he had. Worth twice as much now as Edwin had paid him. Yet he handed out the odd five hundred as though it was part of his own flesh. True, the racetrack had reaped that much again at one time which had kept him going for a while – but that too gradually dwindled.

"Took a time going over one script," he said pointedly as Glenda sat down with her drink, letting her musquash fur stole slip leisurely from around her shoulders, making him squirm to touch her as he continued to sit tight.

"It took ages to get through. It's a big part."

"I bet that wasn't all that took ages," he remarked sardonically.

That had got her going, asking him exactly what he was implying. He'd told her he was sick of playing second fiddle to her, and she had started up in anger.

"And I'm sick of you suspecting me of doing things behind your back." Her voice had risen in a wave of injured pride. (These days she was more blatant about it, flaunting her lover, but at that time her indignation almost had him believing for a moment that he must have got it wrong.)

"I work hard," she went on. "It's a pity you don't. I mean to go places, Hugh, even if you're no longer up to it."

That did it. He'd leapt up, confronting her as she too sprang up from the armchair. "And who is it helping you go places? Don't lie to me, Glenda, I know all about you and Jenson. It's true, ain't it?"

For a moment she had stared back at him, then her lips curled. "So what if it is?" she had taunted.

Pointing a wavering finger in her general direction, he'd roared, "I knew it! You've been with him, with that... that..."

Lost for a suitably foul enough epithet, he aimed a swipe at her instead, managing only to catch her bare upper arm in a badly aimed blow meant for her face. Clutching the already reddening place, she'd staggered back from him as though she had been punched.

"You struck me! I'll never forgive you! You hit me!"

He'd not hit her again. They'd had blazing rows time and time again, but he'd never struck out at her again. Until last week when she had openly flaunted her love affair in his face, telling him he was nothing to her. Now he had blacked her eye and with this glaring evidence of cruelty she'd sought a solicitor and had immediately instituted divorce proceedings. From now on, to add to his burden of debt, he was going to have to support an ex-wife.

More and more he was going to have to see Edwin, who in a way owed him, as he saw it – climbing on his back to get Letts for himself.

Part Two

1959–1968

Twelve

It was Angel's fourth birthday. There would be a party for all the children in the neighbourhood, and afterwards an evening for the adults. Caterers had taken care of everything but still Helen was rushing around making sure all was in order and nothing overlooked; like most people with time on their hands, she felt it had to be spent worrying over unnecessary little things, keeping the mind occupied, the hands busy.

"Are you sure you've covered everything?" She'd phoned the caterers, to receive a patient assurance that their reputation never allowed them to leave anything undone.

"You have nothing to worry about whatsoever, Mrs Lett. Just leave it all to us."

But if she didn't worry, what else was there to fill her time? This last week it had been well filled buying invitation cards, writing them out, sending them off, having a firm of cleaners in to be doubly sure the house looked its best, carpets and drapes cleaned, small repairs done, a little interior decorating here, a little exterior painting there, the grounds just so, being that November could play havoc with gardens. Now there was nothing left to do but worry herself.

"I don't know why you're making so much of this party," Edwin said when he did manage to get home.

"Don't you care about Angel enjoying it?" she had snapped at him.

"Of course I care," he'd snapped back. "But you never made so much fuss about Georgina's party in September. That went smoothly enough."

"It was only her second birthday – much easier to organise. She's too young to appreciate anything too involved. But Angel's going to be four. She's begun to look at things a different way."

Edwin had looked peeved.

"I don't like the way you pay so much more attention to her than Gina." He often called her that, copying the way she pronounced her name.

"I don't," Helen had protested, but it was true. Angel would always have a special place in her heart, and she would always have a natural instinct to protect her elder daughter from the world, while Georgina, even at two years of age, already stood on her own two feet, metaphorically speaking, and always would. She already promised to be a positive child – wilful might be a better word – who even at two appeared to know where she was going, leading the way and ready to run rings around everybody – and if they wouldn't have it, she would throw a tantrum until they gave in.

Angel, on the other hand, was sweet-natured and understanding. No matter how badly Georgina behaved, it was Angel who could calm her, putting an arm about her younger sister, gazing into her face and talking gently to her. She'd even let her have whichever of her toys she wanted, placidly giving them up. The two were like peas in a pod; Angel tending to be small and petite, her sister was already catching her up in height so that they were more like twins to look at. But there the resemblance ended as Angel moved contented and smiling through her little life while Gina tended to romp and demand and scowl.

Of course Helen would feel protective towards the sweeter, more vulnerable of the two. Edwin had no right to accuse her of favouritism. She loved them both equally in her way. And he was here so rarely, what did he know?

-

The party and evening went off as smoothly as Edwin had said it would. All his acquaintances and friends had come in the evening, their large cars gliding up the tarmac drive to a stop in front of the new portico entrance to empty out and be taken off by someone hired for the purpose.

In a way this incorporated a second house-warming, the first a few months after he'd bought the place, it not being shown to its full advantage at that time with all the things yet to be done to it to make it the mansion it was today.

Of course the family was there, and Helen's father. Hugh had been asked, and invited to bring whomever he wanted with him. But Hugh had come alone.

"Can't look at females with this damned divorce going through, old boy," he'd lamented, while making it sound like a defiant quip. "Still into adjusting to her not being around, but I'm not prepared to stand by and watch myself being cuckolded. And I'm certainly not going to be humiliated by having her claim against me for adultery. No sir!"

He'd let out another short chuckle. "So I'm completely celibate at the moment." Then, the bravado melting away, he'd added, "And it's killing me!"

Edwin eyed his cousin with sympathy and some contempt. Hugh should never have sold so many of his shares so impulsively but, influenced by his stepmother, he'd only seen ready money in his hand, just as she had. What he'd overlooked was that she had not truly been family, wanted out, but he was related and should have taken that into consideration. Edwin felt remiss at not having drummed that into him more effectively. Hugh would have been reaping a decent profit by now, though Edwin imagined he would have blown it all just the same in gambling and generally having a good time.

He looked away from Hugh's bleak expression and hardened himself against too much sympathy lest Hugh once more came the old soldier in need of money.

"I'm really sorry about your marriage," he said inadequately and Hugh gave a miserable nod.

Divorce proceedings hadn't even begun until this year. Under the law a couple had to be married for three years before any divorce could be initiated unless in special circumstances and all Glenda had was that he'd hit her on occasion, not beaten her up. Yes, he could have had her for adultery, but deep inside still lived the hope that she'd tire of Jenson and come back to him. He'd tried to entice her back but she would have none of it. Jenson's marriage was finally on the rocks, and he gave all his time to Glenda. He was going places, and was happy to take her along with him. Hugh would grind his teeth every time he thought about it.

The three years had been up in September. Now would come the lengthy process of divorce itself. Last year had been the longest of his life, and there was still a long way to go. Proceedings would take at least another year, and all that time he was expected to suffer, knowing that she was with her lover.

"I'll be glad when it's over," he said, following Edwin into the large reception room, brightly lit, already decorated for Christmas and crowded with people holding glasses while a couple of waitresses moved among them with trays of dainty refreshments.

Seeing Helen talking to someone, Hugh's heart leapt. But as he made towards her, did she turn her back on him deliberately or had she genuinely not noticed him come in?

–

The party had gone well and she had enjoyed it, but Hugh's arrival had unnerved her for a moment. He hadn't replied to the invitation, and she'd rather hoped he wouldn't come. She was going along OK with her marriage, even if Edwin was forever in town with his beloved restaurant. She didn't need Hugh coming here to upset it. Because that's what he did, whether he knew it or not, awakening feelings inside her she'd rather not have.

That eager look of anticipation on his face had been evident before he'd got anywhere near to her but thankfully he'd taken the hint of her turning away from him and had kept his distance, only coming over to talk to her when she'd been with Edwin. Trouble was, that in itself spoke volumes. But now the party was a fading memory, they were three months into 1960 and Hugh hadn't come nigh or by since.

What bothered her was that thoughts about him still popped up to unsettle her when she least expected it. She had asked Edwin casually if he'd heard from him but he'd shaken his head.

"You know Hugh," he said. "All over us one minute, not a peep from him the next. I expect he'll come by when he needs something. He usually does."

That last remark sounded bitter, but Helen was only too glad not to hear from Hugh as she tried to put him aside and concentrate on her children instead, as a mother should. They in fact had become her whole life, living away from London as she did.

–

Her daughters were becoming inseparable. Angel tended to take her younger sister under her wing, including her in all she did. Helen would watch them playing together, grey eyes intent, golden heads close together, and feel the pride run through her veins. When something displeased Gina, when there was a toy or game she wanted to take over, Helen would see a brief frown on the other sister's brow before it cleared in a sort of understanding and the toy was offered or the game conceded to the other. At times it irritated her that Angel should give in so easily, at other times it brought such a surge of love that she could hardly bear it as she fought an impulse to pick her up and hold her close. To do that would make Gina jealous and that she did not want. Gina was hard going enough as it was, even at two and a half, without provoking her jealousy as well.

One other thing endeared her to Angel: the child was beginning to develop a fondness for dancing and already possessed an instinct for rhythm. When the beat was strong and loud enough on the radio, she would dance in time to it, her movements dainty and precise. She'd watch anything on television that had to do with pop music, taking it all in as though her little world depended on it. Cliff Richard fascinated her and she would emulate the movements of all the pop groups, with Gina in her infant way trying to copy her, and often Angel would show her how to do it better. For Helen, watching them, the sight was as fulfilling as anything could be.

If only Edwin were here more often to see it all. But by the time he came home both were in bed. When she tried to tell him what they had been up to, she often found herself talked into silence by his own relating of incidents concerning the restaurant. This had happened, and that had happened, and so-and-so had come in, and a waiter had been rude and had to be dismissed, and there had been a problem with the staff or the ordering or the hiring of a band for the evening entertainment or extra waiters for some special occasion. There had been an argument with Chef or problems with a drunk customer or they had had trouble keeping out the Teddy boys who would inevitably cause disruption so that nowadays they had to have a doorkeeper on during the evenings who was built more like a bouncer to dissuade possibly unsavoury customers.

On and on it would go, she giving up and listening to him, nodding her head in understanding on those odd occasions when he wasn't too weary to sit in the lounge with her to enjoy a drink after sharing a rare dinner with her. But finally something had to snap.

"Why can't you stop and listen to me for once in a while?" she burst out one Sunday evening with the July sunshine still streaming directly into the room at eight o'clock. "I'm trying to tell you about the children, but you don't seem to have any interest in them. You hardly see them."

He looked at her in amazement. "I've seen them nearly all day."

"Yes, today. Fortunately you've been home today. What about the rest of the week? You're never home to see them."

"I always see them on Sunday. I'm always home on Sunday."

She got up from where she had been sitting beside him and began to move about the room, her gin and tonic still in her hand. "Oh, thank you very much, Edwin. How could I have overlooked that you're always home on Sunday. How big of you!"

He followed her with his eyes. "What's got into you?" he asked calmly, and had her turn on him.

"*You've* got into me! You live, eat and sleep that damned restaurant of yours. Up in your flat. We were happy when I lived there with you. But here…"

"It's too small for us all. You agreed it was."

"I didn't."

"You came here," he pointed out, still infuriatingly calm. "That was agreeing, wasn't it? And the children wouldn't have got on so well where we were – cramped, no garden, London full of fumes. You agreed it wasn't the best of environments for them to grow up in."

Yes, she had to admit to having agreed to that. "But I thought you'd be here more often," she fought on, feeling that she was now losing the battle against his logic. "What I'm saying is that since we came here you've not seen the children growing up, nor appeared to want to."

"I can't help it if work keeps me away from here," he defended, finally losing his calm. "Do you want me to give it all up, then? If I do, we couldn't afford this place. You wouldn't have all the things you have now."

"What things?" she railed back at him. "What have I got? I don't go anywhere. I'm stuck out here in the sticks. You never take me up to a show, or out to dinner. So I can have all the clothes I want, but what's the point if I don't go anywhere to wear them?"

They were getting off the point. But he brought it back for her by saying angrily, "You'll hardly ever leave the children to go out." And that was true. "I've suggested they have a nurse or a nanny, but you won't have that. You say Angel wouldn't be comfortable with a nanny with her trouble. Oh, you let Mrs Cotterell look after the girls occasionally. But you insist Angel can't be left very often, almost never. You don't even try, so how do you know?"

"I *know*!" she flared, putting down her drink to come and stand in front of him. "Don't you think I know how my daughter feels?"

He was looking up at her, intensely. "You've two daughters, Helen. Remember that. Do you know how your younger daughter feels? Or don't you care, so long as you have Angel?"

Helen felt tears spring to her eyes. "That's not fair, Edwin. I treat them both the same. I feel the same for both of them."

He said nothing, but remained looking up at her and, disconcerted by the implication of that stare, she swung away from him.

"Sometimes I…"

She was going to say, hate you, but that was too strong. He angered her. She felt neglected. She felt he didn't care. There were times when she felt their marriage was in name only. Only rarely did they have sex these days. Did he imagine she was fulfilled in other ways, by the children, by her life here in this mansion of a house where he would throw parties and think that sustained her need to get out of herself? Where was the romance, the excitement of being taken places? She'd imagined once that that was how it would be, but it hadn't gone that way, Edwin was so full of his restaurant.

She felt herself caving in. "Oh, what's the point," she sighed. He would never understand. "It's just that I wish the children could see more of you."

He got up and came over to her. Her back still turned, he put his arms about her waist and buried his face in her fair shoulder-length hair. "Don't let's fight," he said, and so ended the argument for the time being.

Even so, his ways did not change. In another argument he pointed out that they'd sometimes go up to London to see a film. Yes, she thought, and when had that been – last year, to see *Ben Hur* with Charlton Heston. Persuading their cook, Mrs Cotterell, to give an eye to the children, they'd stayed in London to have dinner afterwards – at Letts itself, the first time she'd been in for months.

They had gone to London again in January, taking the girls to see a pantomime, and it had been good fun. But since then she'd been nowhere.

"I don't know why," said Edwin when she'd pointed this out. "You've got a car. And you have no qualms about driving into London."

Having passed her test last year he'd bought her a car in which she quite competently took them to visit their grandfather. But it wasn't the same as having Edwin beside her. And so the old dissension would rise up again and again, though she didn't quite go to the lengths of that argument in July. The only release she had was to let it all out to her father, though there was nothing he could do and sometimes she felt she was burdening him unnecessarily.

–

William, celebrating his sixty-fourth birthday with just Helen and Edwin and the children round to tea, had insisted on not making too much of it. "Bad enough knowing I'll be retiring next year. It'll be 1961 by then. The 1950s behind us, now into a new era, I don't know where the time goes. I tell you, the older you get the faster it goes."

She had given him an encouraging smile as she ate her slice of the birthday cake made especially for him – part of a nice spread that had been arranged – and had noted at the time how quickly he was getting older.

Visiting him with the children today, it seemed to her that his ageing was speeding up, despite the warm weather.

"I think you work far too long hours," she scolded him, and had him smile tolerantly at her, as though he knew she had been going to say "for someone your age", even though she hadn't voiced the thought. He had an uncanny knack of getting there before her.

"Well, I'm worried for you," she blustered as he raised little Georgina on to his lap.

The winter before this last one he had developed bronchitis and been unable to go into Letts, though that was more because it just wouldn't do to have the maître d' coughing and spluttering over customers, as he put it, than because of the illness itself.

This winter he'd been well, got away with just a brief cold, but that bout of bronchitis as she saw it had been a sign of advancing years starting to take their toll on him.

With little Georgina on his knee, William was well aware of his daughter's scrutiny. While he was always pleased to see his grandchildren, he wished Helen wouldn't fuss over him so.

Ignoring her, he busied himself cuddling the child to him while he played little teasing games with her older sister, which she enjoyed.

"Can you read yet? Can you spell?"

The large grey eyes anticipated this one, her head cocked to one side in that characteristic and charming way of hers. "Of course I can. Silly."

He smiled, knowing she was ready for him. "How do you spell cat?"

"C – A – T." She knew exactly what was coming but played into his hands. He grinned.

"Wrong. It's K – A – T."

"No it isn't! It's C – A – T. It's you can't spell, Granddad."

"Well, I always thought it was K – A – T," he capitulated after the game had been repeated several times and was growing stale, with Angel getting impatient. "So you must be right."

"Of course I am."

For all her amiable manner, she could be persistent when she wanted. She took after her grandmother in that. She certainly didn't take after him.

The thought, even as he smiled at it, brought him up sharp. Of course she wouldn't take after him anyway. How easy it was to forget that these two children were not of his blood. He shrugged the thought away. Did it matter any more? They were lovely girls and Angel's slight hearing difficulty appeared to be receding, or she was adjusting to it better. A bit of heartening news during her frequent check-ups had been that when she was older the chances were that the problem could be rectified and she'd hear as perfectly as anyone.

Even so, it was a relief to hear Helen say earlier this year that she'd decided two children were enough.

Thirteen

Edwin's heart sank down to his boots as he saw Hugh descending the marble steps leading from Letts' foyer.

Edwin hadn't set eyes on him since last November, Angel's birthday – ten months ago. There came a flash of memory, a remark he had made to Helen afterwards: "We'll see him when he wants something," or words to that effect. How true those words were as Hugh, having spotted him, quickened his step, his expression thoroughly woebegone. Yes, he was after something all right – a handout, of course. He knew that expression by now.

Sighing, Edwin went to meet him. If it *was* money Hugh had come for, he didn't have to give him a bean, yet he knew he would end up writing out a cheque. So long as it wasn't a vast sum, that was all.

"Hugh!" He offered his hand as he came forward. "Long time no see. What brings you here after all this while?"

"Just thought I'd look in, old man." The woeful expression hadn't altered.

"So where've you been?" asked Edwin as his hand was taken briefly, no life at all in the grip – part of the act, thought Edwin a little uncharitably.

"Been out of the country," explained Hugh. "At least for a few months. Rome mostly, the Olympics."

So he couldn't have been so badly off. Edwin wondered where he had got the money to go there. He'd probably begged off some other idiot. He'd obviously gone through it all or he wouldn't be here with that look on his face. Well, he wouldn't get much out of him – a few quid, maybe. Edwin could afford it. What annoyed him was feeling he should be helping him, feeling guilty if he didn't, and the fact that he was expected to help, of it all being taken for granted. He should say, "No, go and earn it!" But he did have money and he couldn't turn away his own cousin if he was penniless.

"So you've had a good time then?" he asked. "Fancy a drink?"

"Thanks, I would," said Hugh, and as he was led towards the bar, answered the first question. "I suppose I had a decent enough time, old man. But I'm in a bit of a dilemma."

I knew it, thought Edwin, aloud asking what he wanted as they reached the bar, Hugh promptly requesting a large whisky and soda.

"So what's the problem?" asked Edwin as he sipped his own whisky and soda, this time a small one.

Hugh gave a theatrical sigh. "It's a girl." After a pause, he continued. "I met her there and we were together the whole time. Had a good run of luck while I was there. Made a good bit of dough and it kept us going. I know I spent a lot of it on her, but she was worth it. Every penny." He became confidential, leaning close to Edwin. "You know with the divorce still going through, I shouldn't be seen with another woman or Glenda would claim against me for adultery."

"Would that be so bad?" asked Edwin. "You could divorce her yourself for adultery, come to that."

He watched Hugh grimace.

"Bad enough her claiming cruelty. I don't want to lose her. I still don't. I can't bear knowing she's going on from one success to another without me. While the divorce is taking its time I can still have some hope that this bloke she's got will get fed up with her and she'll come back. But if I'm found with another woman and she hears about it, it'll speed things up, and I don't want that."

"So what about this woman you met in Rome?"

"We had a good time and no one got hurt. Glenda was none the wiser. But this Delia, she wants to keep seeing me. I don't feel anything for her. We just had a good time. Now she doesn't want to let go, and if Glenda gets to hear…"

Edwin slammed his glass down on the bar. "You're a prize, Hugh, you really are. I bet you've spent your last penny on her, haven't you? And now she thinks you're the one for her, thinking you're rolling in dough. What did you expect? And why tell me?"

"Because I need to pay her off. Oh, it's not blackmail. She knows nothing about Glenda. I wasn't that silly. But apparently she thinks she'd clicked with me, and she's not that well off herself. Giving her a decent bit of cash I can get her off my back – lessen the blow of telling her I don't want to continue. I did hint about it on the way home when she started hearing wedding bells. She was upset but said I'd see things differently once we were home again. All I could think of was giving her a decent bit of money, enough to satisfy her, and then she can go her own way feeling a bit compensated for her disappointment. At the moment I can't get into any relationship."

The way he was rambling on, it was obvious that he'd already been drinking. With another despondent sigh, he tossed back his drink and placed the empty tumbler reluctantly on the bar, staring at it with such regret that Edwin felt compelled to get him another.

"Trouble is, I haven't any money to give her. But there's worse. I've had to get out of my flat so as to pay off a couple of hefty debts I ran up while I was away, what with the bank on my back as well. That run of good luck I had in Italy didn't last. I'm living in a hotel at the moment and they'll be wanting their bill settled before long."

"And you can't pay that either," finished Edwin.

Hugh stared into his drink. "'Fraid not, old man. Rather in Queer Street at the moment. I'll have to start thinking about getting back into the theatre again. Rather let it slide this year. It gets you down, old man, feeling you're not getting anywhere while the woman you married is going from strength to strength. She doesn't have to go auditioning for parts any more. Him, that scum she's with, he's finding scripts instead to suit her. She can't lose. I've heard through the grapevine that they're playing the provinces at the moment with a new play that's getting great notices, so much so that it'll be coming into London in the near future – the Theatre Royal, Haymarket, no less. And she's been given the lead role! I can't beat that. But I've got to do something. I've got to get money from somewhere. I have to land a decent part to bring in a bit of money at least. Otherwise…"

The second whisky and soda going straight down his throat, he held the empty glass to his chest as though it were his baby and looked intently at Edwin. "Couldn't have just one more, could I, old man?"

Edwin steeled himself. "You've had enough, Hugh." But he knew he wouldn't be able to steel himself for long –

with drink maybe, but not where money was concerned. He couldn't throw his cousin out on the street.

"We'll go up to my office," he said and saw Hugh's face grow hopeful.

–

"You did what, Edwin?"

"I told him he could move in here – for the time being – until he gets himself straight again."

Helen paced the gleaming block-wood floor of the small library. "No. I don't want him here. Not to live."

"It'll only be for a short while."

"Not here."

"Why."

"I don't like him."

Edwin looked bemused. "I thought you did. What's he done that you don't like him now?"

She stopped pacing, gazing out of the library window at the garden beyond, to trees heavy in leaves waiting to take on autumn colours in a month's time. "He's all right in small doses, Edwin. But to have him here all the time…"

"He won't be any trouble. He can have the top floor, the two rooms we never use."

At one time Edwin had planned to use those two rooms as an office, to work from home, but his penthouse on the premises had proved too much of a draw. The rooms still lay empty under the extensive roof of the house, large and roomy and bright with dormer windows overlooking the beech woods around Ongar.

Now she turned on Edwin, her face imploring, confusing him. "If you feel you need to help him out

170

– I know you've given him the odd cheque now and again, which I think is an imposition, and him stooping to scrounge off you is in itself enough to turn me against him – can't you perhaps sort him out with rent for a flat in London for a while until he's on his feet? You said he's been going on about going back into acting again. He won't get back into it stuck out here in the sticks. He needs to be in London."

Edwin sucked at his lower lip. "I doubt he'll ever make a go of acting. Too easily sidetracked – too much dreaming of fame, not enough dedication, that's Hugh. And he drinks too much."

"That's another thing I don't hold with," she cut in, but Edwin ignored her.

"I've put a proposition to him. He hasn't said yes or no to it yet, and I wanted to ask how you felt about it anyway. I know he'll never apply himself enough to reap what he'd always dreamed about so I suggested it was time he began knuckling down to something more substantial. What I suggested – and I need you to have your agreement in this – is that I take him into the business as a partner. After all, we are cousins. I've not spoken to the family yet but they'll be right behind me on this. But I've told him that he'll have to work and dedicate himself to it. He'd be silly to pass it up, a guaranteed regular income rather than this hit-and-miss lark of acting."

"Hold on, Edwin!" Helen stormed towards him. "You've promised him all this before—"

"I've not promised anything yet."

"Not before consulting me?" she finished. "And I'm expected to fall over myself to agree. I hardly see you from weekend to weekend. I'm all on my own here most of the time, but he can come here and live!"

"He'll be company for you, Helen."

"It's your company I want, not your damned cousin! I'm expected to be happy at being fobbed off with some substitute. I don't want Hugh's company. I want you."

Edwin lifted his arms in despair then reached into a nearby wooden box for a cigarette. He'd taken to smoking these days at home, mostly because it was always so fraught with Helen's complaints about him not being there. At work he hardly even thought of cigarettes.

"Don't start all that again, Helen," he said, searching for the table lighter, which didn't happen to be there. Lamely he put the cigarette back in its box. "I can't be in two places at once."

"I know that," she railed. "But once in a while couldn't we go out somewhere, just the two of us together – dinner or the theatre or even just to the local pictures?"

Now he was out of patience. "Look, Helen, I've virtually invited Hugh to stay here, just for a short while, and I can't go back on that. I'll make sure he keeps out of your way if that's how you feel about him, and get rid of him as soon as I can."

"As soon as you can!" she burst out. "Why not sooner? Why not now?"

The library door was opened tentatively, interrupting them, admitting a cautious Angela, looking worried, followed close behind by her sister. Having started school last week for the first time, she had become a little awed and Sunday, as today was, had done nothing to ease her mind about Monday morning. She had evidently been looking for comfort. Now she faced the two adults with wide-eyed concern.

"Why are you and Daddy shouting at each other, Mummy?"

With a final glare at Edwin, Helen hurried over to her and swept her up in her arms. "We weren't shouting, darling. We were just talking a bit too loudly."

Odd that Angela, who needed to concentrate on what was being said to her, could complain that something was too loud, for surely a raised voice would not be deemed as such.

"You was shouting, Mummy!" came Georgina's truculent voice. Just eight days off being three years old, she was finding her feet with a vengeance. "We could hear you right down in the kitchen."

She, like Angela, enjoyed being downstairs while meals were prepared. ("So long as they sit on a chair each up to the table to play and keep out of the way when there's any hot stuff about, they're fine with me," Mrs Cotterell would say.)

"Mrs Cott'rell said, 'Whatever's them two rowing about?' so we came to see. Mummy, pick me up too. I want to be picked up."

"Daddy will pick you up, darling."

"I don't want Daddy, I want you," Gina began to rage. Her small fists were clenched, and one foot stamped rapidly on the wood block flooring. It was left to Helen to hand the compliant Angela to her father so as to hoist her other daughter into her arms, Gina immediately quieting with a satisfied smile.

So dwindled out the argument and Hugh, attending Gina's birthday party, stayed on after the other guests had left.

-

It was unnerving having Hugh around the house. Not that he was around all that often. Mostly he'd head for

London beside Edwin in the car, or in the Jag he'd bought himself in the spring, only eight months after having been taken into the partnership, and often he'd stay on in town, sometimes until the next evening, sometimes for a couple of days or more. Helen guessed the reason for that. Hugh enjoyed his women – for the odd night or two, that was.

Hugh's womanising should have left her cold, but she constantly caught herself dwelling on it. She wasn't jealous, she sternly told herself - but if she was really honest, that was what it boiled down to.

When he was here, she could feel those vivid blue eyes following her every movement, and was acutely aware of being under what could only be described as suggestive scrutiny.

"Haven't you got something to do?" she'd snap at him, or hiss if Edwin was home. He was here far more than her husband. If Edwin was home more often she'd have felt less disconcerted having Hugh around.

Hugh's decree absolute had come through in June this year and for nearly three months he had moped about the house, staying out of everyone's way. He'd hardly gone to the restaurant, though Edwin appeared content to let him hang fire for a while.

"I can guess what he's going through," he told Helen. "It must be a rotten time for him, and I can manage. Though I wish your father was still in charge. I miss him, you know."

Her father had planned to carry on at Letts beyond his retirement, but January 1961 had done for his bronchitis. Confined to bed, his energy drained by a constant racking cough that made it a terrible job to breathe, Helen had feared for him. With the arrival of spring he had recovered slowly but by then he knew that his working days were numbered. Another bout in late April had convinced him that working beyond retirement was stupid. He did threaten to go in from time to time, missing the place dreadfully. But Edwin had been adamant. He had no wish to see his uncle's oldest friend fall foul of an ageing body and be killed by overwork.

Now her father sat at home, went along to the Pensioners' Club and the Dinner Club, comfortable on his state pension and a substantial one from Letts, plus interest from his savings and his shares. But he was lonely and isolated from all he'd known over the past forty years.

Helen visited him frequently and often brought him back to the house, not only because she wanted his life to be made as full as possible but also to keep at bay what was happening between her and Hugh. Perhaps Hugh wasn't aware of what he was doing to her – or was he? She wouldn't have put it past him. But the thoughts inside her were not healthy.

For a while after his divorce, it hadn't been so bad, with him moping around the house – though he was probably affected more by his ex-wife going on in the world of theatre without him than by his unrequited for love for her, or so it seemed to Helen. She had felt sorry for him; felt it safe to offer her sympathy and understanding without feeling threatened.

But now that had all changed. Snapping out of the doldrums in a remarkably short time, Hugh had become his old self again.

He'd been here over a year now. Today was Gina's fourth birthday, and Helen was giving a small party for hers and Angel's little friends, with no evening do to follow. Hugh had offered to help in the kitchen and she had let him, for why behave churlishly when he'd been so down these previous three months?

"What do you want me to do?" he asked.

She pointed to the bread she'd cut. "You can butter those."

He made a good job of it. Outside, Mrs Cotterell, her daughter and the gardener, Arthur Brain, had taken over organising the fun and games, and the squeals of children seeped into the kitchen. There was only her and Hugh in the house. Edwin, as usual, had made his excuses not to be there though he had promised to be home early.

"Maybe you should have gone to help him today," she said idly as she took some buttered slices from the pile Hugh had made. "Then the two of you could have left earlier and got here in time. Gina's so disappointed."

"I don't think she is." Hugh's voice was husky. "I know I'm not."

His tone made her look up sharply at him. But before she could reply, he laid down the butter knife, reaching out to take hold of her wrist as she made to pick up another slice from the pile.

"It wouldn't have given me this opportunity to say how I feel about you, Helen."

"Don't be silly, Hugh!" she burst out, jerking her hand from his hold. But he reached for her again.

"I know how you feel about me. I see it whenever you look at me."

"That's not true!"

Her words were cut off as she was pulled against him, his fingers, expertly entwined in her fair hair, gently easing her head back while he planted a kiss on her lips. In anger and surprise she fought against him, finally breaking from the hold to leap away from him.

"That was uncalled for!" she hissed, afraid to raise her voice in case those in the garden heard her. "I don't know what you're playing at, but if you think I feel like that for you…"

He was smiling at her. "I know you feel like that for me, Helen. There's a hunger inside you. You get nothing from Edwin. I know that by the way you look so unloved these days. Your eyes are empty. Until they look at me and then I see them fill with longing – a longing to be loved."

Now she was thoroughly angry. "You think too highly of yourself! As if I—" She broke off, at a loss, unable to express herself with her senses contradicting every word hardly had it reached her brain.

She should have laughed it all off. A laugh would have deterred any further nonsense from him. Her mistake had been not to, and now he took her back into his arms and she returned his kiss as the need for the love that Edwin was failing to give her welled up inside her.

A loud, overwrought weeping tore her from his hold. By the time Gina stumbled into the kitchen in floods of tears, closely followed by a concerned Muriel Cotterell, Helen was back to making ham sandwiches and Hugh was buttering away like fury.

"Mummy!" An indignant Gina flung herself at her mother. "Make Katie give my trike back! Come outside and make her!"

Apparently to Gina's mind the birthday tricycle was sacrosanct, not to be purloined by anyone, not even her sister. That a friend should lay claim to it even for a moment or two was to her the worst thing in the world.

"Mummy, she'll break it! Come and get it back!"

"All right, darling, I'm coming." Taking the small hand, Helen let herself be practically dragged out to the garden to do her duty, at the same time throwing Hugh a warning glance.

It took quite a while to sort out the problem, gentle words finally persuading the little friend to relinquish the trike, only for Gina to explode again as another little friend felt she could borrow her birthday doll.

"You can't play with both at the same time," Helen admonished her daughter, aware that the second friend was about to burst into tears. In frustration she prevented Mrs Cotterell plucking the doll away from the pouting friend and starting off a new set of tantrums, at the same time appealing to six-year-old Angela, "Darling, tell Gina she has to learn to share."

"But she's going to break it!" squealed Gina in panic, glaring through her tears at the second little friend.

Angel came to the rescue. Picking up one of her old toys, a brightly coloured, soft-bodied stuffed clown, she thrust it into the child's arms. The clown's many colours immediately attracted the three-year-old, and the doll was easily retrieved. Going to her sister, now on the trike but still tight-lipped and tearful, Angel sat the doll on the handlebars while Gina reached to steady it, tears quickly drying, leaving Helen to fondly gaze at her older daughter.

Harmony restored, she returned to the house but there was no sign of Hugh.

--

Helen glanced up to see Hugh standing just inside the doorway of the lounge, where she'd been engrossed in a novel by Daphne du Maurier, one of her favourite authors. Edwin in London, the children in bed, the radio playing quietly to itself with nothing on the television to interest her, she'd been immersed in the world of du Maurier's *Mary Anne*, the Cockney courtesan who had shocked a nation.

The lounge door being open, she hadn't heard him come in but had sensed movement from the corner of her eye. He had a disconcerting habit of creeping up on people and, remembering the episode in the kitchen during Gina's birthday party the previous Friday, her muscles instantly tensed.

He had kept out of her way since then but with Edwin around over the weekend that was no surprise. On Monday Hugh had gone in with him and they had come home together each evening for the next four days. "God knows what's got into him, being so eager to be there," Edwin had remarked.

Now, on this Friday evening, he had come back alone, leaving Edwin to carry on at Letts – perhaps even glad to see the back of his cousin, as he had so often remarked. Helen hadn't even heard him come into the house and she wondered if he had used the back door. Still in his outdoor coat, he'd been regarding her. Anger flew up inside her.

"Hugh! You gave me a start! What do you want?"

"I've come to apologise," he began, "for that business last Friday. It was unpardonable."

"Yes, it was."

It was all she could find to say. Keeping a tight hold on her book as a shield against his coming any nearer, she glared at him over the top of it.

He was smiling affably. "Can you forgive me?"

Somehow she nodded, accompanying the head movement with a shrug, hoping he wouldn't come any nearer. She just wished he'd go; his presence was already causing that familiar discomfiting sensation pulsating inside her.

But, having moved two or three steps further into the room, Hugh came to a standstill.

"I've come to a decision," he said. "I've decided it's time I left. Truth is I seem to have overstayed my welcome, at least where you're concerned. It's time I moved on."

She remained staring at him, aware of a sudden and disturbing empty feeling.

"I'm going to spend a few weeks in Cambridge." His statement brought Helen back to earth.

"What about the restaurant?" she asked sharply. "And Edwin?"

"I've squared it with him. He's willing to let me go, seeing it as a short holiday. I think he owes me that."

Short holiday! A few weeks! Edwin begrudged himself holidays, so why give his cousin time off? Hugh had skived off plenty of times as it was since coming into the business. Edwin was far too soft on him. But who was she to argue? She wished only to see the back of him and the temptation he brought with him. In fact, she told herself, she couldn't be more relieved.

–

What he had told Helen had not been true. Hugh smiled to himself as he drove to Cambridge in his Jag. A few weeks could stretch into a few months or even longer, maybe forever.

The real truth wasn't that he needed to get away from Helen, who could turn him on every time he saw her, but that the chance had come up of a plum part in a new play – one he could not refuse.

An old Oxford chum had written to him about it. In fact it was Rodney who was putting on the play.

I want you for the lead part. It's perfect for you. In fact I wrote it with you in mind, though I didn't realise that at the time. I think it was because I remembered how good you were when we were in OUDS and it kept plugging away at me. So there it is. Say you'll come up and we can have a chat about it. It's a great script. It'll be playing in Cambridge and there's every chance of it eventually being transferred to the West End.

Hugh had replied that he would be delighted to come up to Cambridge. Rodney, in the days of Oxford a promising playwright, now actually putting on a play and asking him to play the lead – it was like manna from heaven. Hugh saw his future stretching bright and golden before him as he drove. He saw the play running for weeks, perhaps months, a total success, brought into some prominent West End theatre to reap great acclaim, brilliant reviews, excited critics, and packed houses. He was on his way at last.

Fourteen

"I want him out of here!"

Helen hissed the words over the breakfast table, fearing that Hugh, still upstairs in his rooms, might hear her. But their vehemence had Edwin looking up sharply from the piece of toast he had just reached for, his expression one of injured surprise. "What's he done to upset you, then?"

"He hasn't upset me." She forced herself not to sound agitated, though after this weekend it was hard not to be.

Hugh was living with them again, had been here six weeks since his return in late July after an absence of ten months. In that time there had been one letter from him, received after two months away and full of apologies to Edwin. He'd explained that he hadn't intended his time away to be so long but that he'd unexpectedly landed an absolutely marvellous part in a play:

"I was as surprised as you are," he'd written quite unashamedly.

> *But it was something I couldn't pass up. I know you'll understand. I hope this doesn't affect our relationship, business-wise or cordial, and I'm certain you can carry on without me for a while.*

There had been a full page of drivel. Edwin had been furious and so had Helen. "He treats you like shit!" she'd said, feeling the need for crudeness, so beside herself was she at Hugh's cavalier behaviour.

For once Edwin had agreed though as the months passed and he acquired a good restaurant manager, Michel Marat, a young and energetic man – Helen's father had retired permanently now owing to ill health – he often remarked on being better off without Hugh around.

Now Hugh had come back and in that short while had begun to cause her more trouble than before.

At first he had behaved himself, but soon it had all started up again. She sensed him hovering, never far away, found him there beside her when she least expected it. When he wasn't in London with Edwin, which seemed too often for comfort, he constantly watched her. This weekend had been the last straw.

"Don't you think he's been here long enough?" she asked now. "It's about time he found a place of his own. He lives off us, don't you see? And you let him. All that time he was absent, we heard hardly a word from him. Now he's back why can't he start putting in the same hours as you? He's always loafing around this place while you work your socks off."

Edwin began buttering his slice of toast. "To tell the truth, darling, I'm rather glad he's not there. He gets under my feet too. I'm glad to see the back of him sometimes. He has no idea of what's involved in running a restaurant, even after all this time. He had a hard knock earlier this year but it hasn't cured his love of acting. Given half the chance he'll be off again. I haven't entirely forgiven him for going off like that."

"You should never have allowed him back," Helen fumed.

She saw Edwin give an apathetic shrug.

"He is family. Getting rid of him would mean going through all that performance with the rest of them again. It's simpler to let him stay on."

"But you're paying him good money for nothing."

Again Edwin shrugged, this time with a more positive negation. "I can't be dealing with this just now, Helen. Sometimes I wish your father were still with me. I miss his help and advice. Michel is very good, but he's not William Goodridge. There'll never be another to match your father in all he's done for Letts."

"He was so ill last winter." Her initial point was slipping away from her. "He had to retire in the end."

She remembered how bad her father had been earlier this year. She had gone to stay with him whenever she could, leaving the girls in the care of Muriel Cotterell who was proving to be an apt and trustworthy nanny with whom they both got on very well.

"I know, but I still miss him." Edwin bit into the toast he had now spread with marmalade. "Hugh is worse than useless."

"You should have guessed that much before you invited him into the business in the first place." She was dying to get back to her original point.

She saw Edwin give her a wry smile.

"I couldn't see him out on a limb without a penny."

"After walking out like he did, he came crawling back with his tail between his legs."

It seemed the play in Cambridge hadn't lasted that long; had proved a flop. What money Hugh had made had apparently gone on gambling: cards and the horses. He'd even had to sell his car to honour his debts, had turned up at the restaurant in July with a handful of IOUs which, taking pity on him, Edwin had settled. Now he had a new car, so God knew what he was getting out of Edwin at the moment. Edwin refused to say. No doubt he felt guilty in front of her while Hugh paraded around the place as though he owned it, making eyes at her, and then making that preposterous invitation on Saturday evening.

"And already he's been able to buy another Jag," she continued. "Not any old car, but a *Jag*! How on earth can he afford that in that short while?"

She needed to get back to her original idea of getting rid of Hugh. At first he'd been the soul of good behaviour but it hadn't lasted. She wasn't sure whether to be angry with herself or him at the way things had begun to take a turn. She was annoyed with herself mainly, aware of the old attraction stirring inside her. She'd tried to ignore it but he must have sensed something.

This time she hadn't had the children as an excuse to keep him at bay. Angel, seven in the autumn, was in her second year at infant school and Gina had been allowed into the infants this month. She was the youngest in her class but bright enough for them to have stretched a point since there were only two weeks or so to go to her fifth birthday.

Her only escape from that probing gaze Hugh had again begun giving her was to visit her father. Since the most recent attack of his bronchitis last winter he was no longer his old self, but he welcomed her visits though she never let on why she came so often.

Today had been spent stewing over Hugh's proposal, his presumption as ridiculous as the tingle of temptation she'd felt had been abominable. How dare he imagine she would go to bed with him? Yet, with the children staying the weekend with Aunt Victoria – she would not be present at Gina's birthday party and had asked for them to spend the weekend with her – with Edwin having broken his promise to come home Saturday evening, though he'd be home on Sunday, and with Mrs Cotterell and Muriel gone home for the weekend – she and Hugh needed little looking after – they were entirely alone. Indeed, he'd begun by mentioning the fact.

Having come home around ten and gone up to his rooms, he had come down again to stand in the doorway to the sitting-room looking at her and grinning. When she had asked where he'd been, he had said, "Down at the pub." Judging by his silly grin he'd knocked back more than a few whiskies.

When she'd asked what he was grinning at, made uneasy by it, he had said, "Seems there's only you and me here this evening. I thought I might keep you company. Cheer you up a bit?"

She'd told him coldly, "I don't need company and I don't need cheering up. I've plenty of things to do before going to bed."

"Such as what?"

She'd stared hard at him. "Such as – well…"

There *was* nothing to do. She missed not having the children here – no creeping into their bedrooms to kiss each of them goodnight before going to bed herself. Most of the evening she had been lounging full-length on the sofa watching television, which was what she usually did until bedtime. She'd been contemplating having a leisurely soak in the tub before retiring to read for a while, but ten o'clock was rather too soon to go to bed. Thinking back it was what she should have done.

Her hesitation encouraged him. "I can keep you company, Helen." His voice was low and seductive. "We can have a drink or two and a chat."

"We've nothing to talk about," she said coldly, but he wasn't to be deterred.

"Oh, I don't know." He shrugged. "You can always find something."

"I don't feel like chatting," she said. "I'm thinking of going to bed."

He sauntered into the room and came to sit next to her, first gently easing her legs off the sofa to do so. "No Edwin then?"

"You know there's no Edwin!" She felt cross that without protesting she had allowed him to alter her position like that, as if it was his right to do so. "He's at work – where you should be instead of boozing in a pub."

Telling him off made her feel better about having him touch her without permission. But he merely smiled, gazing down at his hands.

"He did say he wouldn't need me tonight. Nothing much doing in September. Better to be there as it gets busier towards Christmas." He looked up at her, his face brightening. "So here I am, helping him out in other ways by keeping you company for him."

"I don't want your—"

She broke off as his hand stole over hers, the other arm moving around her shoulders. "Come on, Helen! Don't try telling me you enjoy being all on your own. Don't you miss his company?"

"Of course I do, but…"

"Don't you miss… this?"

He leaned over her and before she could resist the arm that had eased her body towards him, he kissed her, a lingering kiss that nothing would interrupt this time.

Had it been loneliness that had made her not pull away – a hunger for some comfort that Edwin, so full of his

187

restaurant, failed to give and that she had lost the will to ask of him? Was their marriage going slightly stale without either of them realising it? Whatever it was, she hadn't drawn back from the heat of his lips against hers, his hand on her breast, warm through her blouse then slipping through the opening that had somehow appeared between the buttons, and the oh-so-lovely manipulation of her bare flesh, all of it sending a need through her body that had been so long lain aside.

No words were said. She felt Hugh's hand leave her breast to slip down to the securing button of her slacks, the hand travelling firmly down over her abdomen and on between her thighs, fingers probing. It was the sudden shock of her natural response to the sensation it produced that brought her to her senses. She struggled a little. "Hugh, don't!"

When he failed to stop, her voice grew louder. "Hugh, I said stop!" She'd struggled more fiercely, grabbing his wrist to try and jerk it away. "You can't do that here!"

She hadn't realised how those last words could be misconstrued. He had let her pull his hand away – or rather his fingers had withdrawn to leave her quivering – and he leaned back to gaze at her.

"You'd like it more in bed, then?"

"What?"

"You want us to go to bed? I'll guarantee to make you happier than you've ever been, Helen." He got up and as he pulled her up with him the last of the reeling sensations fled, leaving her astonished at what she had let happen, and filled with fury that he could dare to assume her compliance to such a suggestion.

Seconds later she had given him a resounding smack across the cheek. She thought he was going to hit her back as his hand went up to be clapped to the already rising redness, his eyes blazing.

"You fickle bitch!" he exploded. "You lead me on and then back out. Is that your style?"

"I never led you on," she yelled at him. "You thought you'd play on my feelings about Edwin always being away working – take advantage of it. Well, I am lonely and I want Edwin here. And maybe things aren't as rosy as I would like. But I'm not that frustrated!"

He looked at her with a crooked, knowing grin. "Oh, I think you are, my dear. I think you'd take anyone who happened to be handy if it wasn't for your blasted high morals. Don't you think I knew that by the way you rose to what I did? You were ready for it. I just jumped the gun too soon. If I hadn't, you'd have let me take you, I could feel it. I could feel you pumping—"

She had screamed at him then. With no one else in the house to hear, and the house isolated from others around, she had shrieked at the top of her voice, had run past him to her bedroom and, locking the door, had flung herself on her bed to weep with fury at him, at herself, at the circumstances which had almost caused her to succumb to temptation, and made her still want to, even as she wept.

Edwin had put in an appearance, that was virtually all it was, yesterday mid-morning, full of contrition at having left her on her own on Saturday night and trusting she hadn't been too lonely with the children away as well. Mutely she'd waved away his excuses, the replicas of those he'd given on the phone on Saturday afternoon, ones that she had got used to hearing over the years.

Now at the breakfast table this morning, with him saying he would be leaving for London in a couple of hours or so, she had begged him to stay home.

"There can't be that much doing at this time of year," she had cajoled. "Why not give yourself some time off? You work so hard."

"I don't have your father there now to help out."

"But you have other staff. Surely you can rely on them."

"I'd sooner be on the premises making sure all goes well."

"It will."

"No, Helen, I'd rather be there."

Yes; he would rather be there than here with her. And see what had nearly happened because he wasn't giving his time to her! It was a good job she had had the presence of mind to stop it before it had gone too far. But would the will power be there next time? The sensation of Hugh's probing fingers still lingered in her mind.

"If you must leave," she had demanded, "then take Hugh with you."

Totally innocent, he'd pulled a wry face at her over his breakfast cup and said, "Between you and me, I'd rather he stayed away. More trouble than he's worth."

It was then that she had burst out, "I want him out of here!"

Edwin had shaken his head, annoyingly playful. "Don't foist him on me!"

When she had repeated it even more vehemently, prompting him to ask, "What's he done to upset you, then?" there had been no way to explain.

The idea of being alone with Hugh for another day appalled her. She made a great pretence of thoughtfully stirring her coffee.

"I was thinking, I might pop up to London myself and spend the day with my father. It'll be nice for him. I could stay overnight if you're not coming home. I'll ask young Muriel to get the children from school and perhaps Mrs Cotterell can stay the night." For extra payment Mrs Cotterell was always willing, saying they were never any trouble. "They'll have their eyes glued to the TV until bedtime anyway," Helen ended.

On Tuesday she would browse through the shops in nearby Chelmsford, have lunch out, then pick up the children from their school and take them to the pictures in Chelmsford – a Walt Disney film was showing there – and they could have a nice meal before coming home. Anything to keep out of Hugh's way. On Wednesdays she attended a local women's guild – she could remain behind helping out until the children were ready to be picked up from school, and maybe on Thursday…

Helen brought her mind back with a stem jerk. She couldn't go running off here, there and everywhere forever. Something would have to be done about her and Hugh. But what?

It was Hugh himself who solved her problem. Whether he had got the message that Saturday evening or not, he kept out of her way for the rest of the week, announcing on the Tuesday that he would be spending some time in London. No doubt looking for someone else to seduce, she told herself, not without a disconcerting stab of regret which she fought to ignore. At least she could relax – if that was the word.

To Helen's immense joy Edwin decided not to stay in London the next Saturday evening. "About time I had a weekend off," he told her. "I can go back on Monday."

Michel Marat had now been there several months and Edwin, for all his capacity for imagining that no one could run the place as efficiently as he himself did, apparently now felt he could leave the man in charge.

It was wonderful having him home for a whole weekend. And no Hugh, though it wouldn't have mattered if he had been around with Edwin here.

–

He was in his study on the Sunday evening when Hugh turned up.

Tapping on the study door, Hugh entered to his cousin's invite. The first words out of his mouth were, "Can I have a word with you, Edwin?"

Frowning at the now familiar hangdog expression, Edwin prepared himself for the worst. Hugh was short of money again, no doubt, yet he reaped a decent enough salary.

He tried not to sound too terse. "What is it?"

"I know you're not going to be too pleased about this," began Hugh, seating himself in the nearby armchair. "The thing is, I just happened to be reading the *Theatre News* and noticed there was a company doing auditions for a new play. I thought I'd pop along to see what it was all about. Just to keep my hand in, you know. The thing is, I've been offered a part."

Hugh's eyes grew full of entreaty. "Edwin, I can't turn it down. It's a great chance. Trouble is, I won't be able to be in the restaurant and the theatre at the same time. I wanted to know what you thought."

"You're seldom in the restaurant as it is," remarked Edwin.

It was obvious that Hugh was taking his comment as hopeful rather than caustic. His handsome face began to beam. "So you don't mind, then?"

Edwin wanted to kick himself for his mistake. He did not return the smile. "As a matter of fact, Hugh, I do mind. I took you into the business in good faith, but what help you've been is minimal."

He could see his cousin's face begin to drop, but he ploughed on. Something needed to come out, something that had been stewing in him ever since taking Hugh in.

"I did it for you, not for myself," he continued. "Aunt Victoria and the others were well pleased. But I think I'd have done better to have persuaded Sheila's Paul into the business rather than you."

Eighteen months back his cousin Sheila had married a promising young junior executive in her father's own company. With William Goodridge now retired for good, Edwin had mentioned the young man coming into the restaurant business, feeling he owed Sheila something as one of the family, but the offer had been turned down flat. Sheila's husband had thanked him but said that he wanted to get to the top of his own tree. It had felt akin to a snub and Edwin had smouldered under it for some time until Hugh had taken up his offer.

"But you're my cousin," he went on. "My nearest relative. I had the temerity to imagine it would make a good future for you. It seems I've been barking up the wrong tree."

"Edwin," appealed Hugh. "You can't begin to under- stand how people like me feel. The theatre is in my blood. I can't help it."

"That may be," said Edwin, "but it doesn't mean you're any good at it. You've said you've never made much headway – bad luck, I think you term it. Well, when you hit bad luck yet again don't come to me asking for a hand-out or to be taken back into the business. I won't be so stupid next time."

For a moment Hugh glared at him, then the comers of his lips moved down into a sneer. "You can't brush me off like that, old man – take me into the business then take me out again as you please. I'm in for good unless you want a legal wrangle over it."

Edwin fought not to show his anger. "That's true. But whatever bed you make for yourself you've got to learn to lie in it. You can't just keep swapping beds as and when you please."

"I can't see Aunt Victoria and the rest of them being too happy if you do brash me off," said Hugh.

Edwin shrugged. "It seems I can't prevent you doing what you want. All I'm doing is putting things on the line so you know my feelings about it."

"So it's OK for me to take this offer?"

"If you feel you need to. You might as well. I don't think I'm going to miss you, Hugh, what little asset you've proved to be to Letts."

"But I'm still in, aren't I?" Hugh had cheered up considerably. "The thing is, old man, it may all come to nothing. This play might not have a long ran. No one can tell. And if I can't get another part... But I have to try. I can't miss this opportunity. And I am still welcome in your home? I can still pop in to see you and Helen?"

Edwin gave a sigh. "Yes, I suppose so," he said.

Fifteen

It was this virtually starting from scratch that was humili-
ating.

This time he didn't have Rodney to prop him up with
a lead role. This time he was on his own. Taking his turn
among all the others auditioning for this new play that
was being put on in Oxford, he finally stood alone in
die large, bare, echoing room while the director, seated
with a script on his lap, fired questions at him: "What do
you do?" and, "What have you been in?" and the worst
of all, "When did you last work?" He'd had to admit to
some quite lengthy intervals between parts, adding that
he'd been in business with his cousin managing a famous
high-class London restaurant. His over-confident remark,
"You must have heard of Letts," reaped a blank stare and a
probably well-deserved sarcastic comment: "So you really
think you'd be in the running for this part, do you?"

Even so, he was tested, dragging up some talent from
somewhere as he went through the part given him to read.
He grew aware of the look of approval he received at the
timbre of his voice and the way he held himself. Later that
afternoon he was informed that the part was his – not the
lead, but a substantial one – and was told where they'd be
playing and when rehearsals would start.

Two weeks later he was back in the same echoing
room, seated on a chair in a circle with the rest of the

chosen cast, his script shaking slightly in his excited grip. He was determined now to get to the top this time. No looking back. No more would he toady to restaurant customers, having them look down their long noses as if they were better than him. He'd be a name and one day show Glenda that she wouldn't be the only one to succeed.

His one worry was that time was running on. At thirty-six he was pushing his luck a bit. Fifteen years ago, when he'd first started – good God, was it that long ago? Still an undergraduate but well in with the Oxford University Dramatic Society, he'd dreamed of a bright and promising acting career as a Shakespearean actor. He had a good sense of drama, loved of his chosen career and was blessed with a resonant voice that could carry clear across any quad. His very first big part with the society as King Lear had found instant acclaim and, dazzled, he had vowed to reach the pinnacle of his calling, seeing himself eventually as another Olivier or a future Gielgud.

But things had changed. Life had happened. Where had it gone wrong? Meeting Glenda, perhaps, being upstaged by her in everything, including her preference in men. She'd finally made a complete fool of him, laughing in his face. Why? He'd been good to her, treated her decently, wasn't half bad-looking – he'd seen other women look at him, though he'd had eyes only for her. Well, there was Helen, but he'd have forgotten her if Glenda hadn't turned out a two-timer. Glenda's excuse for wanting to be rid of him was that he drank too much, gambled too much, was more interested in himself than in her, and that her lover did more for her than he ever would. He reckoned sourly that had he enjoyed better luck gambling, had he been able to shower her with diamonds, she'd never have left him. No, he had crumpled too easily before adversity – should have been more determined, fought his corner better. But Glenda had undermined him so much that he'd lost the will to fight. Her fault, not his. She was still a thorn in his side. So was Helen, turning up her nose at him, yet she wanted it. She wanted it like mad. And once he'd made a name for himself, she'd be throwing herself at him. This time round, things would be different. He'd show them. He'd show them all.

"I've had a letter from Hugh."

Helen laid the sheet of scrawled writing in front of Edwin during one of his rare Sunday lunches at home. His weekends at home were growing increasingly infrequent with the Christmas period approaching and more and more bookings beginning to flood in. It was to be expected but it didn't mean she had to be pleased about it.

He hardly glanced at the letter as he babbled on about a party of diners they'd had in – name-dropping almost – revelling in the way Letts was being continually patronised by this and that American film star, this and that famous stage actor or actress until at times Helen felt she could have screamed at him that she would have liked to talk to him about herself now and again. He would talk on and on about the odd impromptu party to which he had been invited, never once realising that she was being left out.

"I would like to have been asked," she had said in the past, but his reply was always, "These things happen on the spur of the moment. I can't come rushing here to get you. By the time you'd got the children minded and got ready and we'd driven all the way into London, it'd be over. It's silly to talk like that." She didn't even bother to ask any more.

"Aren't you going to read Hugh's letter?" she pressed, halfway through Edwin regaling her with an enquiry regarding a booking from no less than someone to do with Frank Sinatra.

Frustrated, he sighed, picked up the sheet of notepaper, scanned it briefly then put it down. "It says he's doing very well, the play is doing well and set to run on well into 1963. Nice start to the new year for him."

The faintly sarcastic remark revealed that Edwin still hadn't got over the sting of his cousin's disloyalty to Letts. The letter was returned to her while Edwin fell to eating the ham salad before him. He was so used to the fine cuisine supplied by Letts that plain food came as a welcome change.

Slowly Helen reread Hugh's letter. None of it was personally addressed to her. There was no reference to how he felt about her. But of course, if there had been, she wouldn't have shown it to Edwin.

Hugh seemed to be doing fabulously; the whole thing was fall of how well he was doing. "This play could go on and on by the look of it. We're playing to packed houses and there's been talk of it going into London, into the West End later in the year. Then I'll be seeing more of you both."

It was the nearest the letter came to being personal but, reading more into it than, perhaps, he'd intended, she felt her insides shiver deliciously. He'd been gone over three months and yes, she missed him dreadfully.

"So, everyone, next month, August, we'll be playing the West End." The voice was excited but now fell a little. "Of course there'll be some changes. Some of you may be dropped; the new management always has the last word, as you probably know." The tone lifted again. "But for the rest of you this is a really great opportunity."

Hugh listened confidently. No one would drop him. He'd been playing the lead since the actor originally playing that part had fallen ill three weeks ago. It now seemed the role was his, the other man having had to drop out permanently. So far he had gone down well with the audiences and was certain in his mind that he'd be one of the company going on into the West End. His future was at last assured.

Over the past year, it had of course been a relief not having to deal with Hugh's foolish hanky-panky, but she still missed that sudden and infectious laugh of his, the jaunty way he had of talking, unless he was quoting Shakespeare when his voice would strengthen, become resonant, almost seductive to listen to. This was when he wasn't moping around offloading his bouts of despair on to her – but she chose not to dwell on those times. All she knew was that without him the house was silent.

Angela and Gina were at school all day; Edwin was hardly at home; life had become increasingly dull. Her only pleasures were ones she went out and found for herself. Last year, in frustration, she had joined the local WI and, although she found it restricting and a little boring, she had made a friend through it. Carolyn John-ston was some five years younger than she but her husband came home every evening from his office in London, which made Helen faintly envious. She and Edwin seeming to be growing further and further apart.

"We've nothing in common any more," she told her father on visiting him just after Angela's birthday. "He's never there. We never go anywhere together any more. He has his restaurant. I have my home and the girls. That's the sum total of my life these days."

Without them she would have been utterly lonely. There had been a letter from Hugh around the end of August, full of bitterness, saying that he had been dropped from the cast when it had gone into the West End – his role had been given to a well-known actor who could guarantee to pull in the crowds. "There's no fairness out there!" he'd written.

Since then they'd heard nothing more from him. None of the family had any idea where he could be. It was nearly eighteen months since she had seen him and, the way her marriage was going, Helen often wondered why she hadn't taken advantage of that offer to sleep with him. At least she'd have had something to remember him by.

"Just me and the girls," she went on bemoaning to her father as she sipped her tea and nibbled a biscuit from the tin he'd produced. "That's the sum total of my life these days – the girls, my friend Carolyn and the WI. I wish Hugh was still with us, nuisance though he was. At least he was some company for me."

She'd told him of Hugh's letter about having been dropped from the play. "We've heard nothing since. No word of where he is. Edwin just shrugs and says that at least it's a weight off his back and that Hugh's old enough to know what he's doing. Edwin can talk! He's thirty-five and should be able to see where our marriage is going but he's too wrapped up in his blessed restaurant. I don't think he even cares about me any more. We live separate lives these days. Hugh being home did help compensate for it, but now he's gone too and I miss him an awful lot, Dad."

Noting the glum way Helen was sipping her tea and nibbling at her biscuit, William had a sense of alarm bells ringing inside him. How close was she to the man she knew only as her husband's cousin? The way she had said so plaintively "I miss him an awful lot, Dad" had too many connotations for his peace of mind.

Both of them were totally unaware of their blood ties. Hugh would see Helen as fair game were her marriage to fall apart. Please God it wouldn't, for more reasons than just the pity of it. Perhaps it wouldn't get that far. Married people always had their ups and downs. But what if it did and Hugh saw his feet fitting under her table? God forbid!

Something had to be done. But perhaps he was being somewhat over-imaginative. Helen would never be unfaithful. She still loved Edwin, it could be seen at a glance. What Edwin needed was a good talking-to. Although Will still hadn't the courage to enlighten Helen on the unthinkable, he did have enough in him to alert his son-in-law to the risk any man ran by neglecting his wife, good and faithful though she was. He would put him straight this very week.

"So what do you do with yourself all day, then?" he asked, getting up to switch on the light.

Not yet lunchtime and the December day was as dingy as if it were already evening. Later they'd have lunch, then she would drive home in time to pick the girls up from school. Angela – he had never called her Angel as her parents did – was now eight years old, Gina six. Once they were in bed with school the next day, Helen would be alone. William felt for her and again vowed to sort Edwin out.

She had told him that two nights a week she took them to ballet and tap classes, so that helped he supposed. She had her friend Carolyn. She'd told him that she and Carolyn went to the local cinema once a week, went shopping on Tuesdays and had lunch out, and that she attended these WI meetings on Wednesday afternoons, or was it Thursday? She was filling her lonely weeks, but how deadly dull they seemed.

He thought of Mary, the life she'd had before Geoffrey Lett had left her for someone else. She'd enjoying her society life, meeting celebrities, sailing to New York, holidaying in the south of France – a dream come true for a girl who'd once been a waif and stray. He, William, had rescued her from that, as he'd rescued her from the shame of being an unmarried mother by marrying her, doing Henry Lett a favour. Henry had been grateful, but he could never know what mess would come out of it later. William could only hope that Helen's interest for the man who was in fact her half-brother was merely of the affectionate kind.

He came back to the present to hear Helen saying that she and Carolyn had been to the pictures to see Alfred Hitchcock's *The Birds* and that Carolyn had been scared stiff. But all he could find to say was, "I hope you enjoyed it," his mind still hovering around her and Hugh.

Helen came away with concern nagging at her. She hoped her father wasn't in the process of becoming ill again. He'd had a brief coughing fit just after lunch. He'd shrugged it off as something caught in his throat, but it had sounded a bit rumbly to her. She just hoped it wasn't the start of his bronchitis again. December was the month for it, the weather dull and wet and pretty chilly. She hoped to have him at home for Christmas but if he fell ill again, they'd have to come here – awkward, but necessary.

Nor had she been all that happy about the way he had gone off into a reverie when she'd told him about the Alfred Hitchcock film. She had meant it to be funny, but he hadn't laughed, his thoughts obviously elsewhere.

She'd felt it best not to go on to relate the tale of her and Carolyn's other jaunt to see *From Russia With Love*. Not because it was prattle and he'd have lost interest in that too, but because although Carolyn had said it was for her a boring film, she herself had seen something of a resemblance between Sean Connery and Hugh which practically glued her eyes to the screen, wondering with a sudden longing where Hugh was at that moment. To have related that sort of feeling to her father would make her seem far too interested in Edwin's cousin than in Edwin himself.

–

Falling midweek, Christmas saw Edwin at home for the two days. But the restaurant was too busy for him to be spared on Christmas Eve, and it fell to Helen to wrap up the girls' presents and put them at the foot of their beds for them to find when they awoke the next morning.

To Edwin's credit, he would drive through the early hours in order to be there in time for his daughters to open their parcels on Christmas morning. But often after entertaining into the night he was too tired to appreciate the joy on their faces as they tore open the coloured wrappings, or to laugh at their gasps of surprise and delight on discovering the contents. Still, Helen supposed she ought to be grateful for small mercies, and she tightened her lips against censure as she continued wrapping their gifts all on her own.

She was still up when Edwin got in at around four in the morning. He looked so worn out and so cold that any reproach melted as she took off his overcoat for him, hurried to pour him a brandy, got his slippers and made him comfortable in an armchair by the fire she had kept going against the fierce cold outside. Seeing him sitting there, supping his drink and gazing gratefully into the fire, the logs of which she had stirred up into cheery flames, love for him flowed out of her and she came to sit at his feet. At times like these how could she ever think of Hugh?

For a second she felt anger against herself that Hugh's name could come into this cosy setting even in that negative manner, but as Edwin laid his hand on the crown of her head, his fingers fondling her hair, she cast Hugh's name from her and smiled up at him.

Edwin was smiling back at her, tenderly, thoughtfully. "Do you want your present now, darling?"

Helen came to herself. "Shouldn't it wait until we open all of them together, ours and the girls'? Yours is a bit too big to drag out now."

"I'm not worried about mine," he said quietly. "Though I shall be eager to see what it is. But I'd like to give you yours now, while it's quiet and there's only us two here."

Not waiting for any further protest, he put his brandy glass down and reached into his coat pocket to bring out a square, black velvet box which he handed to her.

"And this as well," he added before she could open it, reaching again into his pocket to extract another box, this time much smaller. "Open the bigger one first," he told her.

Helen felt her breath explode from her in delight as the opened lid revealed the creamy lustre of a three-string pearl necklace with matching teardrop earrings.

"Oh, Edwin! Oh, they're wonderful – they're absolutely gorgeous!" She had a pearl necklace but nothing like this. These had to be natural rather than cultured, they looked so expensive.

"And now the other box," ordered Edwin.

As she opened this one, Helen forgot even to gasp. There, nestled at its centre, was a diamond eternity ring, sparkling and flashing its richness into her amazed eyes.

"I thought it was time I declared my love and gratitude to you," he was saying in a low voice, "for all the times I have to leave you alone. You never complain, do you? I wish sometimes it wasn't like this, but I want you to say you understand. I want—"

He was spoiling it. He was talking too much. She reached up a hand and laid it tenderly across his lips.

"Shush, darling," she warned. "Just say you love me, that's all."

He gazed down at her. "I love you," he said obediently.

"And I love you," she returned. All the past hurt born of loneliness and imagined neglect were poured out into those words. Hugh was far away now, gone, banished, she thought, yet again she felt angry that even to this small degree his name should enter her head.

–

Fortunately her father's bronchitis hadn't developed until after Christmas, so he had been able to spend it with them. Nor, thank God, had it amounted to too much this winter. Instead, Aunt Victoria's husband died of pneumonia two months into 1964, to be buried in bitter cold February weather with all the family around him except Hugh, no one knowing where to contact him.

Helen had come home from a day in London with her friend to a phone call from Uncle Harold's daughter, Sheila, telling her of his death. It hit her a little savagely after having had such a lovely day despite the cold.

She and Carolyn had seen *Cleopatra*, starring Elizabeth Taylor and Rex Harrison, after shopping at the sales, though the Mary Quant dresses they'd both treated themselves to had been impulsive and expensive and they'd needed to go to the pictures to calm themselves down. As Helen said to Carolyn, "I'm a bit too old at thirty-six to carry off this sort of thing. It makes me look like a mod!" But Carolyn, five years younger, had put her straight, saying that her slim figure could carry anything off – even sackcloth, she'd added laughingly and not a little enviously. Carolyn's was a much fuller figure but it hadn't stopped her going in for the bold designs and short skirts of Mary Quant. "If I fancy I can wear it," she'd said, "then I'm definitely sure you can. And I think we should have our hair cut in the new short style to go with it."

Very daring, they had gone on to the pictures, completely new women, Carolyn giggling that she hated to think what her husband would say when he saw her hair. Helen said nothing. After that romantic Christmas when she thought Edwin had altered, he had gone back to being consumed by the business. She was left alone day after day, night after night, and he was so preoccupied that she knew when he came home he wouldn't even notice her new hairstyle, nor would she point it out to him.

She had felt no compunction in thinking of Hugh again as she went with Edwin to buy black for them both for the funeral. It was of course a dismal affair, as are all funerals and, as she had expected, there was no sign of Hugh.

"It's quite disgusting of him," sighed Victoria to her daughter Sheila. She didn't sob or weep, merely dabbed her eyes and shrugged off anyone who came to offer a sympathetic arm. "I'm all right," she tersely told them all. The only one she would speak to was Sheila, ignoring even her daughter's husband as she sat with their two-year-old boy on her lap as coldly as if he were a cushion she had picked up.

"Hugh is exactly like his uncle, my brother Geoffrey, caring nothing for others, going off into the blue without a word. He thinks himself free of any responsibility – not to the family, not to the business, not to Edwin… How Edwin puts up with it I do not know. After all he has done for that ungrateful man, not to hear a blessed word…"

In fact it was two months later that Edwin heard from his cousin – pages of frustration and bitterness addressed to him from Las Vegas, USA. He told no one of it, not even Helen, he was so furious at what his cousin had to tell.

Sixteen

Hugh couldn't believe the run of luck he'd had this past year. And there he had been last September thinking his life had come to an end. He'd been thrown out of the cast to make way for a famous name – money, that's what it boiled down to, his name not good enough for a West End play that even before it opened was going to be great box office. Of course, with a name it would, and he was out. Along with much of the cast, it was true, but that hadn't made it any easier to digest. But now – now they could all take a fucking jump. He was in the money and doing all right.

Tonight he was wandering along the Strip in Las Vegas. It was one o'clock in the morning. The night breeze was warm even in April and his face was lit up not just by a million coloured electric bulbs but by utter self-confidence. He had money in his wallet and a girl on his arm – his girl, who had said yes when he'd proposed to her on arriving here one week ago. He would make a little more money in one of these casinos and on Saturday they'd visit one of those little chapels that dotted this city, specialising in instant marriages.

He'd met Amanda on stage, and when they'd both been dropped from the cast they had consoled each other in mutual misery with several gin and tonics and whisky and sodas. They'd gone on to the neat stuff, Amanda had produced a couple of small white pills to help them feel even better, and they'd formed an alliance.

The next day, feeling like shit, he had bet his last few quid on a horse. It coming up trumps he'd recklessly gambled his whole winnings on another. That too had won. Despite Amanda pleading for him to walk away while he could, he knew he was on a winning streak and it would be stupid to back out.

On a roll from all he'd made, he'd gambled the lot on an accumulator – a "Yankee" – four horses to place or win in different races, any winnings to go on to the next. It was a long shot, but he had felt reckless. Knowing he couldn't pull out once it started, his heart had been in his mouth as the first horse came in, the winnings automatically going on to another horse to win or place in the next race. That too came in, the growing winnings going straight on to his third choice. He remembered how he had felt sick, knowing it was too good to be true to expect the fourth to come in. Yet it had. He'd practically staggered away from the racecourse with a pot of around twenty-five grand, having had enough sense to heed Amanda's frantic advice to leave while he was winning. She'd been right. Half tempted to have just one more stab, he'd used great will power and backed off to see the nag he would have laid money on come in nowhere. He'd been elated. Lady Luck was looking after him.

He could still recall the build-up of excitement in his belly and remembered saying to himself that the theatre could stuff its allure and that Letts Restaurant was way, way behind him. There had come an overwhelming desire to tell Edwin what he'd won and that he too could get stuffed, but better senses prevailed. Don't tell people too much. Instead he'd get out and see the world. See Paris. See the USA.

He'd settled for the USA to start with, saw the bright lights of New York, took in a few shows, then jetted off to the west coast. He'd taken Amanda to San Francisco – too cold – then down to Los Angeles – warmer – driving his brand new American car down the Big Sur Highway. They bathed in the Pacific, took a suite in a high-class hotel, went sightseeing then, with the money dwindling, drove off to where it all went on – Las Vegas.

It seemed he couldn't lose. Playing the tables he might have lost some here, a little there, but more often he won. This evening his wallet was bulging; tomorrow he would bank some of it – it was too easy to have it stolen. There was money already in the bank. It was a good feeling to write cheques without fearing they'd bounce.

Yesterday he hadn't been able to resist it any longer – he had written to Edwin and Helen telling them all about his stupendous luck. Edwin would be green with envy – all this money being made without having to work for it, to put in all those hours bending to the whims of bloody customers. Edwin was a sucker if ever there was one.

He'd also told them about Amanda and mentioned that they were getting married here – next Saturday, just a week away. His head was reeling from all his success. What was the song? "The Man who Broke the Bank at Monte Carlo". But this was Las Vegas and it was he who was going to break the bank.

"Where do you fancy, darling?" Masterfully tightening his grip around Amanda's small waist, he glanced up at the myriad lights all around them before returning his gaze to her.

She smiled up at him. It was a sweet smile, capable of turning his innards to jelly – the bright red lips parting to show small, even, white teeth, her pert little nose lifting, her blue eyes made bluer and more startling by that dark eye make-up girls were wearing these days. She was full of enticement, the waft of her Christian Dior perfume, the warmth of her flesh through her summer dress turning him on right here in the street.

"Let's try the Oasis again, you've been so lucky there this past week," she purred, and suddenly he didn't want to try any of them but take her back to the hotel and make love again.

It was what he should have done. Instead he conquered his desire and they went on in under the huge glittering facade of the casino. But from the very first bet on his favourite game, roulette, something told him that he had made a wrong choice.

–

A pale dawn grew rosy but Hugh, with eyes trained on the expert fingers of the blackjack dealer, took no heed of it. Inside the casino, its vast cavern bereft of windows, the lights were never switched off entirely although, as morning came, some were. Another sign of a new day was a decrease in punters though, like him, some die-hards stayed on under the begrudging cold glow above any table still occupied. While the slot machines clattered on, fewer of them were in use, but hopefuls still lingered, many of them housewives who'd enthusiastically flown in to spend a few days' housekeeping money and would either fly out again or leave by less comfortable Greyhound coach depending on whether they had made money or lost it. An army of cleaners were sweeping up the debris of the night before, but Hugh noticed nothing, his whole attention riveted in mesmeric desperation on the dealing of the cards.

He had a good enough memory. He knew he was pretty good at counting cards. For God's sake, he was an actor, wasn't he? He could memorise lines, and if he could do that, he could count cards, at least to some extent. But with Amanda moaning about going back to the hotel, saying she was tired of waiting around for him to win, how could anyone concentrate?

Perhaps it was he who was at fault, out of his depth at blackjack with its fast dealing, hardly giving him time to divide his cards, lay bets on each, seeing them scooped up again and again as he made a wrong decision. The cards weren't being good to him. He was a fool to have left the roulette tables where he'd felt comfortable. He wasn't comfortable here, but now here he meant to stick at it. In time his luck would turn. Even roulette hadn't served him well these last few days. Things had to change. Damn Amanda, worrying him like this, just as he was beginning to feel his fortune turning. It would turn, so long as he stuck with it, so long as he didn't lose everything he had. Maybe he could borrow off Amanda, but somehow he didn't think so.

Amanda was sulking, her staccato complaints expressed at regular intervals. "I want to go back to the hotel, Hugh. I'm worn out. I've had it. You can't keep on losing. We'll have nothing left. Let's get some rest and you can try again later. Your luck's bound to come back. Come on, darling, let's call it a day." But he ignored her. The next hand would bring a return of that winning streak he'd been enjoying all week.

It didn't. Nor did the next, or the next. How could luck change so quickly? How could it go on so long? What had put the jinx on it all? Swearing to himself, he kept going. Things had to change. They would soon. They had to. He was almost out of cash. If things didn't change soon he'd have to get to the bank.

The sun came up. Amanda wandered out to feel its warmth on her weary, smoke-paled face. She came back in, went to the ladies' room to freshen up and to the restaurant to have breakfast, ludicrously inexpensively. With the casino bringing in enough cash from idiots like Hugh they could afford to practically throw the food at customers – it was a dollar for a breakfast enough to feed three. She returned to Hugh to glare up at his glum features.

"Not won anything then?" she accused.

Hugh shook his head testily.

"You'd have seen if I had," he snapped and Amanda's lips quivered from tiredness and disappointment and resentment, all the joy of Las Vegas, its casinos, flashing neon signs, sparkling entertainment, vast hotels, desert sunshine and relaxing landscaped swimming pools, vanished from her mind.

"You don't have to be nasty with me, darling. It's not my fault you've been losing. I only asked."

"Then don't!"

Amanda fell silent. Hugh watched the dealer's slim fingers. A girl had taken over, the man going for a well-deserved sleep. She was fresh and alert, supple fingers flicking the cards dexterously. Hugh put in his selected chips, picking up each card in turn – a two, a five, a three, great! He increased his bet, his heart in his mouth. Another three! Thirteen! His heart was racing.

Stupid to stick on thirteen. A dilemma, one he hated. So temptingly near a five card trick. What were the chances of her going over twenty-one? He might yet recoup his losses. If the next card were under a nine, it would suit him fine.

She couldn't beat it except with a pontoon, a picture and an ace. Should he take a chance on a really large bet? Nothing ventured nothing gained, or was he being foolhardy? But perhaps his luck was turning...

"I've had enough!" snapped Amanda, breaking his concentration. "I'm going back to our hotel. If you don't want to come, I'll go on my own."

Caught out by having her walk off, his ability to think distracted, Hugh picked up several chips of large denominations for that fifth card. He knew seconds before it slid towards him that he'd done the wrong thing. Picking up the card, Hugh gazed at it in a kind of numb disbelief. A bloody nine! Twenty-two! All he'd wanted was anything under that. An eight or under and he'd have cleaned up. Even in this fate denied him. Of all the fucking luck! In dismay he saw the hand scooped up, his chips with it.

"Now look what you've done," he hissed, but Amanda had turned on her high heels, already making for the exit.

A split second later he was hurrying out after her.

"I might have won if you hadn't been so bloody touchy," he snapped, catching her up. "I was about to make up my mind whether to stick or not and when you put your damned spoke in, I'd just decided to stick. She might have bust and I'd have got something back. Now I'll never know. My luck was just beginning to change, I know it was."

"So you've been saying all night," she said without turning.

She was striding ahead of him, addressing thin air although he was right behind her. "You're nearly out of money. So what are you going to do if you don't start winning soon? Rob a bank?"

"Don't be so damned stupid." He was angry too. "There's still money in my account. I can use that."

"And when that's gone?"

"I won't go on losing. No one goes on losing forever. It's against the law of averages. I'm not worried so why should you be?"

"I'm just tired. I need to get back to our hotel and rest. Then this afternoon I'll be down by the pool and I'll stay there the rest of the day, get a deeper suntan. What you do is up to you. I don't care!"

At a loss, he followed her around like a puppy, spending the morning in bed, making love to her as she slowly melted to him, lounging restlessly by the pool, finally going to the bank to draw some money.

There was less there than he had thought. Several large cheques had made a hole in it. Clenching his teeth, Hugh drew what was left and closed his account. Tomorrow with his winnings he would open another. Roulette tonight. He'd had enough of blackjack.

By the evening what he'd drawn had all disappeared. Amanda got a taxi back to the hotel, leaving him to it. By the time he followed her back, around two in the morning, his gold watch had gone to pay the debt he'd run up at the table.

A hole inside him as large as the one in his pocket was more than he could bear. Tonight, however, Amanda refused to let him make love to her.

"Don't you love me any more?" he asked plaintively. She didn't reply. "I'll make it up to you."

"How?" she asked.

"We'll get married. Tomorrow. You said you wanted us to get married."

"What on?"

"Sorry?" From lying beside her on the bed he sat up.

"I said, what on? How're you going to pay for it?"

"I can hock my cigarette case and my lighter. They're gold. They'll bring in a few bob, enough to get married on."

"I'm not getting married on borrowed cash." She too sat up. "And anyway, I know you'll go straight back and gamble it. Then where will we be? How would we ever get home to England? I don't want to stay here."

"I might win. I will win. We'll be in the black again and we can—"

Amanda shot out of bed, for once wearing a filmy black nightie rather than sleeping naked as she usually did. She'd refused to take it off, said she was worn out and needed to sleep. He had understood and forgiven her, but now he was rankled. She was having her own back on him for losing. Silly bitch!

"No, Hugh!" she burst out. "No, I'm not going to marry you. You're a loser. You always will be."

He stared at her. "But I've been winning like mad for nearly a year."

"And it's come to an end. I'm not prepared to stand by, living on the breadline while you try to get back your so-called winning streak. I want to be the wife of someone with a regular, well-paid job, someone respectable, not some – tuppenny-ha'penny gambler."

Hugh gave out with a burst of cynical laughter. "You? Marry someone respectable? A second-rate actress? You must be joking."

For a moment she stared at him, then she turned and rushed to the huge wardrobe and dragged down her suitcase. "That's it! I've had enough of this. I wouldn't marry you now if you were the last man on earth! I'm going home. I might be a second-rate actress to you but I'd sooner go back to acting than stay here and watch you gamble all your money away. The theatre's a dicey enough business but nowhere near as dicey as what you do."

She began throwing clothes into the case. "I've had it, Hugh!"

He watched helplessly, too stunned to stop her as she strode about the room dragging her things from drawers. He felt all in. "Amanda, don't go. Give me one more chance and I'll prove I can look after you, keep you happy. This is just a hiccup. It happens."

He held out an imploring hand. "Look, stop doing that. We'll go down to the Strip. Caesar's Palace... no, The Golden Nugget, where we began and I won like mad – remember, just over a week ago? That's where my luck was."

She paused in her packing, turning a hard stare upon him. "And where's the money coming from? Just now you were ready to hock your cigarette case and lighter to pay for our wedding. Now you want to use it to gamble some more. Well, no thank you."

"Just one more time," he pleaded as she returned to her packing. "Maybe if we save my lighter and cigarette case for the wedding, we can get something on that necklace I bought you, and probably your ring."

She swung round at him, painted blue eyes blazing. "You bought that as my engagement ring when I said I'd marry you."

"It'll only be temporary," he persisted. "We'll get it back by tonight."

"And my necklace, and I suppose that bracelet as well. Why don't you sell *me* while you're about it? I'm pretty enough – got a nice figure – I'll bring in some decent money for you to gamble."

He shot to his feet in fury. "Don't talk to me like that! I've bought you everything. I've clothed you. We've lived in the best hotels. You'd never have had any of that if I hadn't brought you here, spent out on you. What money did you have? Nothing. But for me you'd be scrabbling around looking for another part. And now, because I'm having a run of bad luck, you feel it's time to walk out on me. Well, I'm not having it, Amanda!"

He saw her lips curl. "Just watch me!" With that she banged the hard lid of the expensive case shut, flipped the catches, then straightened up to lug the now weighty object off the sofa where she had been packing.

Standing in the centre of the room, Hugh sneered. "And what money have you got to get home on? All you have is what I'm giving you. And that's nothing at the mo—" He broke off, realising his words were condemning him out of hand.

Amanda was regarding him as though he were dirt. "That's right, nothing. But I do have the jewellery you bought me. I know the stones are real and everything's real gold. You wouldn't have bought anything less, you were so eager to throw money around. That should get me home."

"But the ring – that's your engagement—"

"Engagement's off!" she snapped.

"In that case," he railed in fury, moving towards her, "you can give it back." But Amanda stood her ground.

"Not on your life! It's the woman's prerogative to keep the ring if the engagement's broken off."

"You're breaking it off," he shot at her, "not me."

"Too bad," she shot back. "I need it more than you do. You've still got your lighter and your cigarette case – hock those. If I give you my ring you'll be broke again by tonight and it'll be gone for good. No, Hugh, I'm going and you can't stop me."

After she'd gone Hugh felt bad about hitting her. One enraged swipe across the cheek, that's all it had been. But it was enough. She'd reeled back then, hoisting the case in both hands, partly as protection against another attack, partly as a means to bulldoze him out of her way, she'd barged past him, leaving him gazing after her.

Seventeen

Last month the TV had had little on it but the Tokyo Olympics, in which neither he nor Helen were interested, though the girls were. Mostly they liked the women's gymnastic floor exercises, the nearest thing to real dancing there was. Anything remotely touching on dance had two pairs of young grey eyes so close to the screen that Edwin had to warn that they would ruin their eyesight if they didn't back away.

When they weren't glued, immobile, to the set they were dancing to any music there was on it. The new *Ready, Steady, Go* pop programme had the both of them jiving away to a beat that sounded to him like the same old thump to every song.

They were growing up fast – Gina had been seven in September, and in two weeks' time Angel would be nine. Both were tall, as his parents had been, and as willowy as their mother, where he was slightly more thick-set. He took after his Uncle Henry in that, knew that as the years went on he would become just a little portly, similar to Henry Lett in his late forties.

Where the girls got their talents from, he had no idea. Both were light as fairies on their feet and dancing lessons had taught them a lot. In fact they were consumed by it – tap, ballet, pop – and badly dealt was the rare evening they couldn't attend lessons because of a cold or some other cause.

He watched them now, this dull November Sunday afternoon, slim bodies supple, young limbs lithe, keeping in time to the rhythm of a Beatles record, and his heart marvelled at them in love and pride.

They could sing too, joining in with all the pop songs from the pirate radio station Radio Caroline out in the North Sea. Their young voices, as yet untrained, were nevertheless in key and pleasant to hear, immature but promising to eventually mature into very listenable ones.

A whimsical notion crossed his mind – what if they grew up to become entertainers? – instantly to be dismissed. Good schooling would find them something far more worthwhile. He took his gaze from his daughters and settled back with his *Sunday Times*, trying to ignore the penetrating beat and high-pitched yowling of the Beatles' apparent need to "Hold Your Hand". He found himself looking forward to being back in London come Monday morning.

Edwin had been home for the whole weekend. He'd made sure of that. With Christmas approaching he'd soon be snowed under at the restaurant. The place continued to do well. He had a good team, a good staff. These past couple of weeks, however, had been quiet, and he'd been able to take Helen out more often than usual. They'd seen a show or two in London, he'd taken her and the children to the cinema to see the new film "Hard Day's Night" – more Beatles – and he and Helen had gone out to dinner while Muriel enjoyed having her boyfriend keep her company while she gave an eye to the girls. He'd been worried about that, but Helen, eager to get out of the house, said these were modem times and so long as

Muriel didn't let whatever they got up to interfere with her assigned task, what did it matter?

Edwin had capitulated, weary of Helen everlastingly complaining at his seldom taking her out. To argue would have made things worse. It had paid off. Since then Helen had been completely manageable, and he hoped his attention to her would help compensate for his enforced absences as the Christmas rash came upon the restaurant.

Monday morning saw her amiable enough as he finished breakfast and began preparing to drive to London. He'd be back tonight and Tuesday night. From Wednesday until Sunday morning he'd be in the penthouse, on hand as the festive season, as always starting early, began to get under way and Letts, like all the top restaurants, began to hot up with late-night supper parties flocking in after the shows to stay until the early hours.

The post fluttered through the main door and Helen went to retrieve it. She returned, sifting through the four letters, taking the one addressed to her and handing the rest to him.

At his ease – he had plenty of time – Edwin opened the first two. One was a letter informing him of the change of address of a supplier – why it had come here instead of the office he couldn't be bothered to question. The other was from a colleague in the restaurant business inviting him and Helen to his twenty-fifth wedding anniversary party at his London home in January.

He passed the invitation to Helen. "Do you fancy going?"

Helen studied the silver-rimmed card and nodded. "I suppose it will make a change," she murmured, and Edwin creased his brow in frustration. Still she was harping on his inattentiveness and how lonely it was here when he was in London. For God's sake, lots of women, if they didn't work, were left on their own. It had to be her friend Carolyn who constantly unsettled her, her own husband doing a nine-to-five job and home every evening. It was pointless suggesting Helen find herself a job to keep her occupied. With the sort of money they had rolling in, why indeed should she need to?

"I'll be driving the girls to school in a minute or two," she said, to his mind deliberately and huffily changing the subject. He could hear them upstairs, giggling as Muriel helped them get ready.

Frowning at Helen's attitude, he slit open the third envelope, hardly noting the foreign stamp on it, unfolded the sheet of lined notepaper, the pencilled scrawl not even keeping to the lines, and began to read. Seconds later he had let out a roar.

"God damn the man!"

On her way out to call the girls, Helen turned to stare at him. "What's the matter?"

"This!" he held the letter towards her. "It's from Hugh! And he's after bloody money again! Well, he's not getting any – not this time."

Coming back into the room Helen stood there as Edwin began reading aloud what the letter had to say, his tone hoarse with fury.

She hardly heard the first words, her mind casting back to the joyous letter Hugh had sent them earlier this year. Edwin had been annoyed then, reading aloud at that time also. Hugh had been in Las Vegas then, was about to get married to a girl named Amanda. The letter had been all about how he had met her, how they had come to Las Vegas and how he was making a fortune at the gambling tables there.

Helen remembered her heart dropping like a stone at the news of his marriage, her face hot that his news should affect her so. She'd spent the next months wondering if he was happy and if he had forgotten her entirely. He probably had, the way he'd enthused about Amanda. From then on Helen forced herself to put aside all thoughts of him. But it had been hard at times.

Now she felt a strange eagerness mingle with the horror of what Hugh had to tell them. Perhaps what he was going through might make him come home, and, though she was ashamed of herself for thinking it, therein lay the reason for the animation as Edwin read the letter aloud to her.

> *I'm in a terrible fix here, Edwin old man. I'm living in a dump and in a place that's wallowing in money I'm flat broke. The thing is, here, once you're down you're down for good. Amanda has left me. We never did get married; my luck changed just before we could and all my money went. It happened so quickly and I don't know how it did. One minute I was rolling in dough, the next – well, that's how it is, and now I haven't even enough to feed myself let alone get me home. If you can just forward enough for my flight home, Edwin, I'd be forever in your debt and grateful from the depths of my heart.*

There followed a page of explanation which Edwin glossed over. Helen determined to read it at leisure later, when he'd left for London. No doubt he would be too disgusted with what Hugh had written to take it with him.

When he'd gone, she opened the letter again and read slowly all that had happened to him – ending with the final words, "I'm sick, Edwin old man, not well, ill, Washed up."

> *I just have to get home somehow. All I need is enough to get home on. I'll be waiting to hear from you with a cheque. Meantime give my love to Helen and wish her and the children well. Hugh.*

Slowly she folded the letter, her eyes full of tears, the poignancy of his predicament striking her. He had faults, so many faults, but no man, however weak of character, should go through what he was suffering. In her mind's eye she saw him lying on a filthy bed in some filthy boarding house, hungry, unwashed, his clothing creased and hanging on him, maybe too frail even to get a job to sustain him. In his anger Edwin hadn't truly realised the plight his cousin was in. He couldn't just let him be, leave him out there. When he'd said he wouldn't help him out this time, he couldn't have meant it. It was true he had helped him many times and had received little thanks for it, but this time it was an emergency he couldn't ignore. What if Hugh were to die?

"You've got to help him," she told Edwin over the phone. "Maybe it is just one request too many, but this time you have to."

Edwin's voice on the line still grated with resentment. "How do I know he's not lying again? He's done it before. Given me a sob story then after a few months gone his own sweet way, cocking a snook at me, only to come crying back later with another tale of woe. No, Helen, this time, no."

"This time I'm sure it's genuine, Edwin. Look at the paper he's written on and all of it written in pencil. He can't even afford a pen. He's starving. Edwin, you're not thinking straight about this because you're so angry with him. But you can't let that blind you. For my sake at least, send him the air fare to get back home. *Then* you can make up your mind about him. But he's your cousin, your own blood, you have to—"

"Why for your sake?" queried Edwin, breaking into her diatribe.

Helen paused. It had just come out. Why should it be for her sake?

"You know what I mean – for all our sakes. We can't let him fall ill all those thousands of miles away. We've got to do something. If anything bad happened to him, your cousin, it'll always be on your conscience. I mean it, Edwin, you've got to do—"

"I've got to go, Helen," he broke in again. "I'm being called."

"But—"

"I'll think about it."

"No, don't think about it, Edwin. Do something!"

"I said, I'll think about it."

The phone was put down on her. He hadn't even said goodbye or that he loved her. Slowly she replaced her own receiver, her heart beating heavily from the angry things she'd said. They hadn't helped a bit and she'd almost incriminated herself into the bargain, or so it felt.

–

She had meant to fight Edwin on this one, but with her father falling ill just prior to Christmas, with his bronchitis returning so badly that he had to be taken into hospital, Helen's concern for Hugh had to give way to her concern for her father.

It was a miserable Christmas. Edwin arranged for a private ward for William but it didn't quicken his recovery. When in early February after a fortnight of convalescence he was finally declared well enough to go home – not fit, just "well" and, to Helen's mind, still in need of a certain amount of care – Edwin suggested finding a private nurse for him.

"I still need to be with him," she said as they drove out to Hertfordshire and the convalescent home to collect him. "He can't stay in London all on his own with just a nurse."

"I'll not be far away," said Edwin. "I can go in every day and see him."

Helen almost sneered. "Won't you be too busy for that?"

She wanted to say, "considering you don't come every day to see *me*!" but the tone of her voice conveyed well enough what she was thinking.

Edwin said nothing as she continued in a more placid vein, "I won't be able to stay in London indefinitely. The girls need me at home. But I should be on hand to look after him."

"So what do you suggest?" His tone had become as acid as hers had been a moment ago. She chose to ignore it.

"I think he should stay with us – until he feels capable of going back to living on his own. I know that's what he'd prefer."

It was indeed what William would have preferred. His whole life was wrapped up in his immediate community – he had a full social life there, with his Masonic colleagues and the Pensioners Club, where he was on the committee and helped organise events. He had friends all around him and although it would be beneath his dignity to allow them to come in and look after him, they would visit and keep him company.

He could see Helen insisting as time went on that he give up his flat here in London to become trapped out in the countryside. He hated the countryside, had never wanted anything to do with it, saw no reason to. He loved London, the noise of it, the hurry of it, the bustle, the ease of getting from one place to another. The underground, a short walk away, would take him anywhere he wanted to go. He could look in occasionally on Letts to be treated royally as Edwin acknowledged his presence. A host of cinemas awaited his pleasure, theatres and art galleries were but a short step away, and he could go along to a choice of pubs at lunchtimes so as to have no need to cook for himself. You didn't get that in the country.

Even so, his health forced him to submit, at least temporarily, to Helen's misguided sense of love and duty, and so he was installed in her home. His nurse, who Edwin insisted accompany him, was only too eager to see a bit of country, even if completely blanketed under snow.

It was an unsuspecting Helen, enjoying her father being in her home enough for her to overlook Edwin's dedication to his business rather than her, who opened a letter postmarked Las Vegas around the middle of March which sent a shockwave through her body and had her ringing Edwin demanding he come home at once to deal with it.

–

Hugh turned over on the dirty bed, coming out of a drunken stupor to stare up at the tiny square of window above him. Open a couple of inches because of stuck hinges and covered with broken netting, it didn't even help stir the heat in this airless room.

More a shack really, one of three similar ones, it measured twelve by eight and, but for an old wardrobe that was falling apart, there was nowhere for his belongings, if he'd had any. As far as he was concerned all he had was what he stood up in. For the past three weeks he'd only just managed to hold himself together doing menial jobs in the run-down garage and repair shop to which this room belonged. The pay was hardly worth the labour, with the garage owner taking a bit off his pay for the rent of the room, but better than nothing.

"And don' yuh go spending it on any more liquor," would come the advice as the couple of dollars, crumpled and oily, was slapped into his hand. "Get yourself a square meal fur once."

In the hope of turning a couple of dollars into maybe four and then eight, dreaming of recreating that fortune he'd once had, Hugh would find a crap game somewhere, mostly losing the little he had because he was no longer on the ball. Afterwards he'd have to beg the garage owner, Joe Wetzel, for a hand-out just to tide him over. He couldn't even beg on the streets – not that what little pride he had left would have let him. That could land him in jail, though at least he'd be fed there. But he didn't fancy a possible beating-up by some cellmate, or the police themselves, who didn't suffer beggars lightly in this town of flowing wealth.

But for the kindheartedness of Joe Wetzel, who gave him jobs that often didn't need doing to keep him going with an odd dollar here and there, he'd have gone under months ago, his body hauled on to a truck and driven outside town to be buried. But even Joe was getting fed up with being kind-hearted.

"You're a good-fur-nothin' bum," he'd said yesterday, or was it the day before that? Hugh couldn't remember – maybe it had been days ago.

"I used to be well off," Hugh had told him, his Englishness making the man grin. "My cousin owns a high-class London restaurant."

"Yeah, yeah," had been the caustic reply. "An' my sister's the Queen of England!"

Hugh had refused to be knocked back. "My cousin is a wealthy man."

"Then he can send some dough to get yuh home outta my goddamn hair!" The smile had vanished. "I'm givin' up givin' yuh money fur doin' nuthin'. Instead I'm gonna buy yuh breakfast now'n'agen, so's yuh can't buy cheap liquor or lose it in some two-cent crap game. How's that grab yuh?"

When Hugh could find nothing to say, he'd continued affably, "Yuh go on like this, yuh'll be dead in two weeks. Yuh're a dead-beat drunk, and it beats me why I go on financin' yuh. I should let yuh kill yourself, but I'm too much of a soft-hearted guy. Write to yuh so-called rich cousin and get him to pay fur yuh to go home."

He'd done that well over a month ago and had heard nothing. Edwin had no doubt washed his hands of him – and at a time when he had needed help, some friend or other, more than he had ever needed anything in his life. The only friends he now had were Joe and May, another lush like himself, a painted, fat, two-bit hooker of doubtful years who dressed like a teenager, making a ludicrous sight of herself while quite unaware of it.

She'd stagger into his room and, after dropping a kiss on his sweaty forehead, would make a play of tidying his room, though it still looked the same when she had finished. Not that he cared. But her company was most welcome as she sat on his sagging bed and showed her large breasts to him, perhaps to make herself feel more of a success, since very few customers were ever tempted by her. In his drunkenness he would fondle those breasts, feel the soft pliable mound of quivering flesh, and she would press her thick wet lips on his, but that was as far as it went for him. Moaning in ecstasy, she would fondle his limpness, drink having stolen all virility from him, and he would sigh and finally fall asleep.

--

The next morning at around eleven, with the heat already pounding in from the surrounding desert, May stole into Hugh's shabby room after a fruitless night trying to entice a customer or two. The room next to the garage was on the edge of town and was a trap for the windblown sand that about this time of day started to be swirled up into small dust devils by the hot breeze.

She would take a broom and stir up the invasive desert dust from the floor. It would settle back exactly where it had been before, but it made her look good. She would try the ramshackle cupboard as she always did when Hugh was dead to the world, knowing it would be locked. It always was. She had never seen him open it yet or even go to it. He probably had the key somewhere but she had never seen it, and she wondered what it was he needed to keep locked away – unless of course it was just jammed. Often she'd creep over and try to pick the lock with her fingers but all to no avail.

Far away the endless trucks of a freight train stretching from horizon to horizon and drawn by two, sometimes three engines whistled plaintively. This morning, as always, Hugh's silent room reeked of body odour and booze but a little fondling would make up for that, make her feel better, make her feel as though she could still do her stuff.

He was lying prone on the bed. She'd turn him over and then vent her lonely existence on him. She might even get that dick hard enough to ease it inside her. He'd hardly notice but she liked to feel that he had, and God knew she was in need of some comfort.

She plonked herself down beside him on the bed and shook him gently by the shoulder. "Wake up, honey. C'mon, wake up."

There was no response. She leaned over towards the bare floorboards and picked up an empty bottle of cheap bourbon.

"Ah, poor honey," she purred. "Had a skinful, ain't yuh? Well, come to Momma, then. And she'll give yuh a little love."

Lying over him, she took off her two huge, cheap and garish rings to reach around him down into the front of his pants and fondle him with plump, eager fingers.

"C'mon, honey. You like me doin' this to yuh, heh?"

She heard him mumble and was encouraged, but now noticed that his body was sweatier than it would normally be. Sitting upright, May eased him on to his back, an easy enough task with him being so thin and lightweight.

Hugh's face, putty-coloured and drenched in sweat, his half-open blue eyes staring at nothing, had her out of the room in seconds, hurrying across to the garage as fast as her plump legs could take her, breasts, stomach and butt bouncing like jelly.

"Joe! Joe! F'godsake – Hugh's sick. I think he's dyin'. Get a doctor."

Joe was about to say he had no money for doctors for bums like that, but one look at May's distraught face galvanised him into action. Dropping the wrench he was using on an ancient and banged-up automobile, he ran with her to the three-roomed shack he misleadingly called a motel, his narrow, weather-beaten frame arriving there before her.

"He's real sick," she moaned as they tried to revive him. "He's still breathing but he might not be much longer."

"I ain't payin' fur no doctor," Joe said, his kindliness not stretching that far. "He ain't worth it. We get him better, he'll only go tryin' to kill himself again."

With that he went off to make some strong coffee to force down the sick man's throat, the only thing he could think to do that wouldn't cost him a doctor's fee.

Meantime, May thrashed about the room searching in desperation for anything to assist the recumbent figure still gazing up into space. In doing so she discovered a key lying under the bed. She had never swept under there where the dust was out of sight. The key could be to the cupboard. Hurrying over, she tried it, wondering what she expected to be looking for.

Not only did the key fit, it turned. Dragging open the flimsy door she saw draped over a wire hanger a grey suit of the sort a man of means might wear, though it was now limp and dusty, as were a pair of black shoes and a once white, now yellowing shirt. Why hadn't he pawned them long ago? Amazed, she hastily felt in the jacket and trouser pockets. Nothing. But the clothes could bring in some cash.

A groan from behind her startled her mid-search and she swung round guiltily. Hugh's eyes were open, his hand to his temples.

"Jesus!" she burst out, thankful that he hadn't seemed to have noticed her rifling through the clothes. Quickly she closed the cupboard door and locked it, secreting the key in her podgy fist as she came over to him, angry now.

"You bastard! You scared the shit outta me! There ain't nothin' wrong with yuh, God damn it!"

But, going to him, she saw there was something very wrong with him. He had come to himself, yes, but there still seemed to be no life in his eyes. This man looked doomed to die, if not tomorrow, then this week.

Her large heart went out to him. She'd come to love him in a strange sort of way, this man with his limp dick and his worn clothes and his gaunt though still good-looking face. Now this man, with a good suit of clothes in that wardrobe which he had never pawned while he staggered from one hand-out to the next, lay next to death's door. She couldn't have that.

Hurriedly gathering up the clothes just as Joe came in with a steaming coffee pot, she waddled past him. "I'm gettin' some money on these things," she yelled at him over her shoulder by way of explanation. "You get that stuff down him. I'm goin' for a doctor."

Most of the money went on a casual medic to pull Hugh round. A bit she kept back – for her trouble, she told herself – the rest she spent on a letter sent to the address on a creased and greasy scrap of airmail paper she'd discovered during a more extensive search of the suit's breast pocket. What it said had shocked her rigid.

I know you are my cousin and I should respect that,
but I can't continue financing you. The restaurant
isn't there to sustain you forever and I can foresee
no hope of you continuing on in the business if you
continue to behave in this way. All I can say is you
are going to have to make your own way home.

There was no point reading any more. She had no family
that she knew of, yet May's heart went cold at the thought
of anyone being that mean to a relative. At the same time
she saw an easy way to get back something for her time
spent on caring for Hugh. And why not? She'd probably
never see him again and she had her own life to think
about. She wrote a hasty note telling this Edwin guy just
what she thought of him, and went on to say that his
cousin was at death's door and would surely die if Edwin
didn't do something for him. She added that it had cost
her bucks caring for him – the guy wouldn't know exactly
how much – and that she was broke because of it.

Eighteen

Hugh was back, a bedraggled ghost of his former self. It shocked Helen and wrung her heart.

"We have to look after him," she told Edwin, his cousin having gone straight to bed in his old room after his flight. "He can't look after himself."

Edwin too had been shocked by his cousin's appearance, but he still couldn't forgive Hugh for treating him the way he had after all that had been done for him in the past. "You'll have both your father and him to look after," he reminded her. "Don't you think you're taking on too much?"

"Dad will be going back home soon," Helen reminded him. "He's been chomping at the bit for weeks to get back to London. He misses it terribly, and he's quite well now. After all, it is July. He's fine in spring and summer."

It left Edwin with no argument. Helen was one of those women who always needed to be doing something, looking after people – the lame dogs, so to speak. If she was happy to have Hugh here taking up her time now that her father's illness was coming to an end, then he'd put up with it. So long as she didn't ask him to hold out the olive branch to Hugh. He'd done enough in bringing him home, and at far more expense to himself than paying out for a mere plane ticket.

A letter from some woman who said that she had been living with him – not the Amanda who had walked out on him the minute his money had run out, but someone named May – said, if her story was to be believed, that she had used up every bit of her savings caring for him. And because Hugh's health was purported to have been in such a bad way, he'd had to take her at her word, the letter in fact making her out to be a treasure indeed.

But he hadn't been in business this long to have the wool pulled over his eyes that easily. He'd sent her enough to get Hugh into hospital, then contacted a firm of solicitors in that area to make sure the woman did indeed use the money for that purpose.

A phone call from the American attorney had confirmed the woman's honesty, but Edwin would never be sure that she was really owed the seven hundred dollars she'd mentioned as out-of-pocket expenses. Feeling generous, however, being that she had written so poignantly about Hugh and how much he'd come to mean to her, and seeing as she was probably pining over never seeing him again, he sent her eight. As he mailed the money he visualised a blonde woman, the sort Hugh had always gone for, alone in the world. He hoped she would soon find herself another young man who might care for her as she had for Hugh.

Then there had been the fees for Hugh drying out in a clinic, and Edwin had had to forward the lawyer enough funds to kit Hugh out with some decent clothes, May having written that he only had what he stood up in. Edwin hadn't dared trust Hugh with the money to buy himself a decent outfit; he would more likely have gambled it away in hopes of making another fortune. There had been a hotel bill to pay following Hugh's recovery, then his flight home, coupled with the attorney's fees. By the time Hugh arrived home in early July, a sizeable hole had been made in Edwin's own funds.

But at least Hugh was back in England, where he could keep an eye on him, though he wondered what lessons Hugh had learned from it all, if any. And indeed what lessons he himself had learned.

"I just know," he told Helen dismally, "that once he's got over being penitent – and during the two days he's been here he's already flogged it to his very utmost, damned actor that he is – he'll be off again. But this is the very last time I'm ever going to bail him out. No matter what happens to him, in whatever part of the world, I'm not lifting another finger for him." He held up a forestalling hand as she made to protest. "It's not a warning, Helen, it's a promise, and you can tell him that from me. You'll be seeing more of him than I shall or shall wish to. Tell him he can come back to work alongside me but I want no more of his prima donna nonsense. He'll graft as hard as I do. I'm not jeopardising our business any more for him. If he can't stick to it then he's out and he can do what he damn well pleases with his life. I'm done with looking after him."

–

It seemed Hugh had indeed learned a lesson from his experience. Full of gratitude for Edwin's timely intervention and Helen's dedicated nursing, he finally regained his strength and began to go into London with Edwin as regularly as clockwork, staying with him late into the evening during the busiest times.

With Christmas coming up Helen found herself doubly lonely, missing not only Edwin but his cousin too.

As Hugh's gauntness faded and he regained his beauty she found herself watching his every movement as he'd once watched hers. It seemed to her, however, that Hugh no longer had any interest in her, was in fact intentionally avoiding her as much as possible.

Christmas was a lovely one with a good family gathering: he and Edwin; her father, who was keeping pretty well considering; the girls; Sheila and her family and Aunt Victoria. On New Year's Eve, however, just after twelve o'clock had struck and they had drunk the new year in, Hugh announced that he had found himself a flat in London – to be nearer the job, he said.

"I'm done with acting," he said cheerily. "Utter waste of time!"

Edwin was beaming, seeing his cousin as having turned over a complete new leaf, but Helen felt her heart sink. She immediately admonished herself, but the censure did little to make her feel any better.

"You'll be popping up to visit us, though?" she asked.

Hugh gave her a steady look. "Don't see much point really, being as I'm working with Edwin most of the week." A mischievous light crept into in his eyes. "I expect he'd have seen enough of my ugly mug. And you don't want me hanging around you, do you, Helen?"

Oh, I do. The words came into her heart, but she merely smiled at him and told him not to be so silly and that he was welcome any time.

"Then I'll give that some consideration," he quipped with such mock seriousness that Edwin burst out laughing in thorough approval of his cousin.

"You and I between us," he said, still chuckling, a little drunk from champagne on top of the spirits they had been consuming all evening, "are going to make

Letts synonymous with our names, just as our fathers did. Nothing can stop us. This will be a fortuitous year and I guarantee we'll still be around forty years from now, you and I, right into the twenty-first century. You know, I can't imagine what the world will be like in 2006. Sounds so strange, don't you think?"

"No stranger than me becoming a restaurateur," chuckled Hugh, "and not an actor. If you'd told me after my father died that this was what I'd be doing, I'd have laughed in your face."

Left out of the conversation, Helen stayed silent. Hugh had put her entirely out of his mind, and she didn't like the way it felt.

–

Her father's bronchitis had come back this winter, compelling her to spend more time with him, leaving the girls in Mrs Cotterell's care. After all, Angel was ten now and Gina eight; they were able to look after themselves to some extent, with Mrs Cotterell having offered to stay at night on the occasions that Helen elected to stay with her father.

When Edwin employed a nurse to look after William, Helen was free to return home, a little reluctantly because she had seen Hugh twice that week when he had rung her father's doorbell to see if she needed anything. He had asked her once to go out for a drink with him but she had refused. He hadn't asked again.

She had been mollified but her sole concern after all had to be for her father's welfare. His condition was a worry to her. The man who had returned to his flat in London last July had faded yet again. Then he had seemed so strong, his old self, concerned about her nursing Hugh. When she'd spoke of coming to London every Tuesday to look after him he had said, "You'll have enough on your plate looking after that cousin of Edwin's." Then the smile he'd given her had vanished and his face had grown serious. "But don't let that Hugh run rings around you, poppet. He's a manipulating sort and I worry about you. Don't let him get too near you. I don't entirely trust him."

Helen hadn't been certain as to what her father was getting at, except that he was probably irritated by the way Hugh had twisted her husband around his little finger, and more than once. She remembered thinking at the time that it was a good thing he had no notion of how she really felt about Hugh. He'd be so angry. He saw her marriage to Edwin as one of those made in heaven – of course with its odd ups and downs, but perfect for all that.

While her father had been staying with her, his company had taken the edge off Edwin's absences, and she had been able to put on a brave face about it all. It was as well that Will knew nothing of the loneliness she still suffered. Edwin was married to his job rather than her, was protector to his staff rather than his own children.

When he'd been well enough to go back home, she had been saved by having Hugh for company and had felt safe enough with him; he was so frail and in need of help that his nearest contact was to hold her hand and thank her for all the care she was lavishing on him.

"I don't deserve it," he'd say. "I brought all this on myself."

He had seemed genuinely penitent. Gone was the old joie de vivre, the self-opinionated lusting after her, and she came to feel much more at ease with him.

As much as his pitiful condition had wrung her heart, his return had lifted it. Under her care he had regained his health, strength, his good looks. He was still handsome, if in a pinched sort of way, as gaunt of cheek as Frank Sinatra – a heart-throb if ever there was one.

It didn't matter about Edwin's threats to cast him out; she'd vowed to see Hugh well cared for. She'd vowed also never to do Edwin down, even if the temptation ever arose again, though she cared for Hugh more than he would ever realise, her heart filling with love for him every time she looked at him. So he was weak-willed – it only made her want to care for him all the more.

Now it seemed that that temptation would never arise again as Hugh went gaily off to his new flat, seldom to come visiting. By September his visits could be numbered on the fingers of one hand.

In October, however, Helen found him on her door-step, Edwin having said he should have a break before the build-up to the Christmas rush.

Edwin himself hardly felt the need for holidays, meaning that Helen either didn't get one or else drove off taking the girls with her during summer or term breaks to the Lake District or some seaside town.

"They need their holidays even if you don't," she'd told Edwin sharply more than once. He'd contrive to look penitent but add that he never minded her taking them and that they were company for each other. To which she'd retort that it would be nice to have him with her as well just once in a while.

Hugh had surprised Helen by turning up at her home unannounced just prior to lunch.

"Thought I'd pop over for a visit," he said as he came in. "Hope you're pleased to see me, Helen."

She told him she was, asking him if he would like to stay for some lunch, an invitation which he readily accepted.

"In fact, I'm off to Malaga for a spot of relaxation for a week," he said as Muriel took his coat. "Long time since I've been abroad. Catching a plane tomorrow morning… That's what you should be doing," he continued as Helen poured him a drink. "Catching a plane to somewhere hot and sunny."

Helen laughed as she sipped her own, but Hugh remained serious, staring into the whisky he had requested.

"You're too cooped up in this place. Edwin should be ashamed of himself, never taking you anywhere, much less abroad. Your whole life is wrapped up here with you going nowhere."

"I've got the children – that's good enough for me." She dismissed the accusation with a wave of the hand.

But he was still teetering on the same subject by the time they sat down to the simple midday meal served by Mrs Cotterell of tomato soup, crusty bread, omelette, cherry cake and coffee, just for the two of them, since the girls were still at school.

His grin mischievous, he gazed at her across the small conservatory table. "Tell you what, Helen, how about coming with me?"

She stopped eating, "What? Oh, Hugh, don't be ridiculous."

"I could do with some company." He was still grinning but there was a meaningful light in his eyes even as he bantered, "You could stop me going off the rails with some unsavoury woman or other, or gambling again after all my vows never to gamble another penny as long as I'm working with Edwin. Come on, Helen, be my chaperone, eh?"

All she could do was brush aside his jocularity with a violent shake of her head. "I'm happy enough where I am," she lied and hurriedly waylaid the subject by asking how he was doing at the restaurant.

He told her he was doing fine – surely she could see that by the nice car he'd arrived in? – but she could see he had something on his mind that, though it was unspoken, made her feel uneasy with him as they sat with their coffee.

Despite his earlier contempt of the "catering trade," as he'd called it years ago, Hugh seemed totally taken up with his new life. Over lunch, when she had managed to steer him from his earlier course, he had spoken of those who could be seen in Letts from time to time, usually having a late meal with friends after having been somewhere else – mostly famous names: Vincent Price, Joan Crawford, Tab Hunter, Anthony Newley, Russ Conway – he even mentioned Judy Garland, though Helen wondered if he had not made up that one – and Benny Hill quite regularly. Helen listened to it all with patience and relief while still marvelling at Hugh's great change of heart about the reckless life he had previously enjoyed. Perhaps leopards did change their spots.

Hugh had come to sit in the garden while Helen dead-headed some clumps of Michaelmas daisies in an attempt to escape the waning conversation and the feeling that she should be keeping it going.

The late October sun was warm as any in September, though the clear skies indicated that tonight would be frosty, as it had been the previous evening. Autumn was pressing on. Totally at ease in a garden chair, taking in the rare warmth before the season really closed down around them, Hugh watched as she turned her attention to a couple of containers whose flagging plants needed lifting to make way for a few spring bulbs that her gardener had left over. Making no move to depart, he sat watching her as she bent to pull out the exhausted plants.

"We have a man come in several times a week to do the hard work," she explained, "but I enjoy getting my hand in as well." She didn't go so far as to say that gardening helped while away her days. It would have laid emphasis on her loneliness, and that was best avoided.

"It'll be Angel's eleventh birthday in a few weeks' time," she told him. "We're having a birthday party and I don't want the children's mothers looking out on a lot of messy old plant pots," she added with a laugh, awkwardly aware of him watching her all the time she was working. Ever since she had known him he had watched her. She should be used to it by now but somehow she never could be. She stood up suddenly.

"Stop it!" she scolded amiably.

He was smiling at her. "Stop what?"

"Staring at me. I can't move anywhere without your eyes on me."

"It's because I can't take them off you. You should know that by now."

She stood gazing back at him. They were alone. Mrs Cotterell had gone home. Muriel, married last March, only came in twice a week. The girls were being picked up from school by a friend's mother to have tea there. She'd take them and her daughter to dancing class and Helen would collect all three at seven, dropping off the friend. Edwin was in London, and would come home as and when he felt like it. She was used to it by now, but his absences had never lost their edge.

"You'd best start thinking of leaving," Helen retorted, "if you want to pack for your holiday."

He was still smiling. "That won't take long. I prefer to stay here and drink you in."

"Don't be silly!" She made to resume pulling out the dead plants.

"It's not silly to be in love with you."

Helen felt her heart leap. She kept her head bent over her work, unable to speak for the tight feeling in her chest and that awful sense of excitement threatening to suffocate her.

She heard Hugh get out of his chair. She stood quite still as he came towards her. She didn't move as his body touched hers and his hands came around to cup her breasts. It felt as though her loins were about to explode. It was a job to breathe.

"Hugh…" It was part protest, part longing. She let the hand fork she'd been using fall from her grasp, heard it drop softly on to the soil. Now her breath returned, panting. His hands were like fire on her breasts.

Her body was being borne without protest down on to the patio, Hugh beside her, easing her skirt up past her thighs, slipping aside all that would restrict him. Seconds later he was inside her, her resolve, those vows of loyalty, that last brave vestige of self-will gone as her hips rose to meet him with a hunger that a long-standing sense of neglect had slowly and unconsciously built up bursting out of her. And all the time she heard his voice close to her ear: "I love you, Helen. I've always loved you. Always and always…"

It was over so quickly. As she stumbled up and away from him into the house, she was already sobbing. Her whole body shaking, she staggered on through the conservatory, the kitchen area, into the hall and up the stairs as fast as she could. Once in her bedroom she slammed the door behind her, locked it and threw herself on to her bed. It was a single bed these days; when Edwin was home it was at such odd times, he found it simpler not to disturb her. So often she'd told herself she had become used to that, that they had been married long enough for it not to matter any more and that first passion died as married life went on. Was it that deception that had promoted the moment of madness just gone by?

Sickened by what she'd allowed to happen, she lay rigid on the bed, face down, ears keened for the slightest sound of Hugh coming upstairs after her. Her whole body trembled in case he tapped on her door pleading to be let in. She couldn't let him in. She loathed herself. How could she have let him seduce her? It was awful.

For a while there was nothing. Was he at this moment tiptoeing up the stairs? Would she hear his voice any minute now whispering that he was sorry, he didn't know how it had happened and could she ever forgive him? But there was only total silence. Birds could be heard singing in the garden but that was all. Where was he? What was he doing?

There came the sound of a car. Scrambling up, Helen ran to the window in time to see Hugh's vehicle belting off down the driveway, turning left, obviously back to London, the squeal from its tyres virtually advertising to her the anger he was feeling. Was it directed at himself or her? Was he too suffering remorse at what had happened? Perhaps she would find out eventually, now that he was gone. She recalled the need she'd had to succumb to him even as she feared any repetition of it.

Nineteen

Hugh's holiday in southern Spain had been weeks ago.

He was back with Edwin, and obviously still pleasing him, but for her there was only silence. He hadn't even put in an appearance for Angel's eleventh birthday nor sent any word of apology for his absence. Was it that he felt too ashamed?

"Will Hugh be coming?" she had casually asked Edwin and he had shaken his head in all innocence.

"You know him," he'd said. "Never comfortable with kids. I expect he's off somewhere enjoying himself for the day." Edwin had made a point of coming home this Tuesday, leaving Letts in the capable hands of his staff. "So long as he's not gambling away all he's made this year and provided he's sober by the weekend."

It was obvious that Hugh still liked his drink, but Helen had wanted to keep the conversation going. "Does he still gamble a lot?"

Edwin took a sip of the non-alcoholic punch provided for the young guests. "Afraid so," he'd said ruefully. "As for drink, there are times when he's had too much to be of any real help to me. I knew all those good intentions of his would go out of the window after a while. But with Christmas three weeks off, I need him to be there – need his help, such as it is. He's like my father, can charm birds off a bush."

How true, she'd thought, but Edwin had continued bemoaning his lot.

"The customers like him and that goes a long way to making Letts a place to come to. The trouble is I never feel I can trust him. At any time I expect him to come in dead drunk or come begging me to pay some gambling debt, or even to flit off to try his hand at acting again, bloody idiot!"

To all this, she'd said nothing. She had her suspicions as to why Hugh was drinking. Perhaps like her he hadn't been able to get that episode in October in the garden out of his mind. Sometimes it seemed like a dream, as though it had never taken place or had happened to someone else. Other times she recalled it so clearly that her insides cringed, her nerves crawling like tiny beetles under her skin at the thought of herself allowing such a thing to happen.

Hugh hadn't even bothered to see her since. Even if he had come back begging her to renew that moment of passion she might have been able to face it better, have had the opportunity to right a wrong by rejecting him. But the fact that he'd not even come near her made her feel cheap, used, wounded and humiliated.

"I've always loved you, always," he had said, but it was a funny way of showing it. No, not funny – it was a wicked lie a casual lover would tell any of his conquests. Did he know, or even care how wretched he had left her?

–

Sunday evening Hugh let himself out of his small but well-appointed Mayfair flat and went down one flight of stairs to the flat below. Edwin could do without him tonight.

At least a couple of evenings a week he'd pop down to his neighbours, Julian and Jacqueline Hampton, who with half a dozen other friends would hold a quiet little party talking theatre and art and philosophy. There in a haze of well-being, smoking pot, he'd forget the troubles of the world. It wasn't easy to gloss over the failure he was. To everyone he was hail-fellow-well-met but inside he ached. He ached for the theatre, the great name he would never have, money of his own – lots of it in unlimited supply rather than what came from that bloody restaurant business, paltry and always feeling to him like a hand-out rather than his due. He ached to have been wealthy enough to be able to sweep Helen off her feet, away from Edwin who'd pinched her from him in the first place.

At the same time he wanted to forget the way she'd willingly let him have her only to look at him when they'd finished as though he'd sickened her to her very core, as though she saw herself as having been raped, even though she had done it with as much pleasure as he had.

The prig. He would never forget nor forgive her that look. Way back in October last year that had been, yet five months later it was still there in his mind. So he hadn't gone near her since. Let her stew, came the resolve, let her long for it until it screwed up her loins. But it didn't stop him thinking about her, wanting more of her.

Pleasantly foggy with all that grass he would tell his friends all about her and how he felt towards her, and they commiserated with him, said they understood his feelings. That was nice. He enjoyed their company. They were the best friends he'd ever had. And there was a certain Ursula there, and in a sweet, tender, hash-invoked haze she and he would make love, she making up for Helen. Yet even as he took his fill he knew the time would come when he'd have to see Helen again no matter how much he enjoyed this new flame.

–

Christmas and New Year had come and gone with not a peep from Hugh. She wasn't going to demean herself by asking after him or sending a message. That way if he did turn up she could have the luxury of giving him his marching orders.

It was now March and still she felt unclean – would often look at Edwin and wonder how he'd react if he knew about what she and Hugh had done. Even after all this time, guilt and remorse, like all things locked away, begged for release until they threatened to consume her.

"You're not looking at all well these days," taxed Edwin. "All that driving up to London every other day this winter to take care of your father has taken it out of you."

Dad had gone down with bronchitis yet again, each winter helping to bring him a little lower in health. This year there had been another threat of bronchial pneumonia, though this time his doctor had helped him evade going into hospital. But Helen had still wanted to be with her father as much as possible. There was little to keep her at home, and the girls were quite old enough now to be left with Mrs Cotterell or Muriel.

Besides, it took her mind off other things, helped stop her wondering what Hugh was doing at that precise moment, helped keep at bay the self-loathing that had become her constant companion, the knowledge that at any time Hugh could pop up out of the blue to turn her insides to jelly and sweep aside her brave vows to send him packing. Deny it though she might, that sunny October afternoon had been the most wonderful moment of her life. Five months later she could still feel his hands on her, the way he'd borne her to the ground, the way he'd taken her, and despite herself her stomach would chum and she would long to experience it all over again. The thought consumed her constantly. Would she be able to resist him a next time?

These past months she had striven to bury such intro-spections in merciless rounds of activity, visiting her father more than she need, seeing more of her friend, Carolyn, taking an intense interest in church and village events – it didn't eradicate it as much as she'd have liked, but it helped.

Today she was keeping the thoughts at bay with the usual conducting of Angel and Gina to their local twice-a-week dance classes. They were presently taking part in rehearsals for a show for Easter.

The girls having changed into their leotards, Helen lingered as they took their places in the group lined up in rows before their tutor, Jeannette Sellers, a gifted ex-dancer of around thirty-five who seemed able to work miracles with the most reluctant or podgy pupil. This was the older group, which included a couple of boys. The rest were girls ranging from nine to seventeen, and a second group of tots were in the care of a girl of around eighteen.

The hall was alive with chatter as youngsters changed into leotards, attentive but superfluous mothers clutching items of outdoor clothing, collecting up bits and pieces and trying to be helpful but really getting in the way. They were ignored by their offspring, who were only too eager to be free of them for the next two hours while they dedicated themselves to their teacher, her word now law.

The mothers began to leave, one by one, Miss Sellers tending to frown upon those who insisted on remaining. She turned now to Helen.

"Are you intending to stay, Mrs Lett?"

Helen came to herself, realising herself guilty of daydreaming again. "I'm just going," she responded and let herself out through the glass swing doors of the hall, pausing momentarily to gaze back.

The groups had formed properly, the last stragglers hurrying to their places. The piano had struck up, its tinny notes echoing from high ceilings and bare walls. One wall supported climbing apparatus, the one opposite was dissected by a stage littered with unused chairs and stage paraphernalia with dusty crimson curtains drawn haphazardly to each side. The far wall had two small doors and high windows while the scuffed floor was marked out in white lines for indoor football, handball and such sports. The wall through whose glass doors Helen gazed was ranged with chairs and wooden boxes of sports gear. The very air emanating through the ill-fitting doors smelled of sweaty sports shirts as well as dust and floor polish.

Continuing to watch, unnoticed by Miss Sellers, Helen surveyed her daughters. To her eyes they stood out proudly from the rest: the tiny, fairylike tots; the chubby eight-year-olds; the gawky teenagers with budding breasts and skinny limbs yet to develop but full of promise. As were her girls.

The groups comprised all sorts, some attentive, some aggressive, with their eyes on the main goal, others apathetic, there only to please doting parents, torn between clock-watching and avoiding their tutor's gaze, dreading being picked out whilst others clamoured to be. All of them expected to be cajoled and bullied into difficult steps and impossible stances, their tears of frustration ignored, good results praised. But Helen could rest content that her girls always came through with flying colours, eager to be back for the next lesson, endlessly practicing in their bedrooms.

They were natural performers, Gina the quicksilver one, Angel methodical, afflicted by her hearing yet still the one who led. Together they complemented one another rather than clashed.

Helen turned away, making her way back to her car. On the way home she applied her thoughts to her daughters, loving them equally if differently. Gina she adored for her vivacity, her energy, even her mercurial temper, but secretly Angel was the one she always felt a need to defend, her defective hearing making her seem vulnerable, her pretty face with its intent expression endearing her to all who spoke to her, her lovely grey eyes taking them in. Angel maintained that she could hear perfectly well, but she'd never known what perfect hearing was and relied on following a speaker's lips.

Despite her impairment she was at one with the rhythm as it surged through her body, quite accustomed to what others might hear as distorted music. She was gifted, as was Gina: they were as well matched as though they'd been twins – the perfect pair. How wonderful it would be if one day they put their dancing and their promising voices to good use. She could see them in a few years making a successful career out of all they were learning. Angel and Gina Lett. Was the call of the stage in them as it was in Hugh? But she didn't want to think of Hugh. At this moment she felt happy and his name wasn't going to spoil it.

Helen arrived home to the phone ringing in the hall. She took it before Muriel or Mrs Cotterell could get there, calling out, 'All right!' to them and seeing them retrace their steps. Maybe it was Edwin. She could tell him how well the girls were doing today.

The voice in her ear said, "Helen?"

"Yes." Not Edwin. Already her heart seemed to miss a beat.

"Hugh," the voice confirmed.

Helen strove to quiet a now racing heart. He had phoned her up after all this time. Perhaps a message from Edwin. "What's wrong?"

"Nothing's wrong. Just thought I'd give you a tinkle, see how you are."

"Hugh, you gave me a fright. I thought something had happened at the restaurant. What do you want?"

"I've just told you, I just wanted to see how you are."

Anger took the place of alarm. "Thanks, but I'm fine!" Seething, she slammed down the receiver.

After all this time, how dare he? All she heard of him these days was the snippets of information Edwin passed on to her, mostly to do with work matters, though he would sometimes comment disparagingly on Hugh's unsteadiness after a night out or his non-appearance when most needed. She would listen with a growing sickness in the pit of her stomach while presenting a bland face to whatever tale Edwin had to relate.

Almost immediately the phone rang again. She snatched it up, her heart racing now, breathing as though she were suffocating.

"Hugh, leave me alone," she cried. "All this time and you think you can telephone me out of the blue as and when you feel like it?"

"I'm sorry," came the voice. "I've tried to stay away. I know you didn't want me pestering you and I've tried to respect that. It's not been easy for me, darling. But I can't take it any more." So bloody dramatic – ever the actor.

"So what is it, Hugh?" She was shaking. "Has some girlfriend let you down and you thought I'd come handy to soothe your broken heart? Is that it, Hugh?"

"No, that's not it. I've thought of no one but you all this time. God help me, Helen, I've tried to keep away, but it's so hard."

"And you've not looked at another girl in all that time?"

There was a pause. "I'm not made of stone, Helen."

"No, I guess you're not." There was a fluttering inside her, that old longing. This time she must not give way. "I'm sorry, Hugh, but it's over. It was over the minute we made love. I don't want to go back to that."

"Don't say that, darling." His tone had grown seductive in her ear. "I've thought of no one but you, all this time, my love. It's nearly killed me. How I've managed to hold off for so long, God only knows. I have to come and see you, Helen. Please."

"No."

"You love me, Helen. You must do, the way you let me make love to you. I know you were appalled, but not at me, at the fact that you're married to my cousin. But you've not loved him, not in that way, for years. I could see that in the way you rose up to me, so full of hunger. Helen, I have to come and see you. This thing has to be thrashed out. I want you to divorce him. Yours hasn't been a real marriage for years. I know that. We can get married. I can support you now and—"

"For Christ's sake, Hugh!" She burst through the tirade at last. "Don't you ever give up?"

"Not with you, my love. I'll pursue you to the ends of the earth – to my life's end."

"Stop it, Hugh! No more. It's over. I don't even want to think about it. I want you to leave me alone."

"I can't do that, darling. I love you."

"You're going to have to stop loving me."

She doubted he'd ever loved her. He'd merely used her, and she'd been the fool who'd succumbed to it. But he could be so charming. His touch, the mere sound of his voice, was enough to melt her like warmed jelly.

With an effort Helen pulled herself together. Making each word slow and positive, she said, "Get this through your head, Hugh. I don't love you. Now there's an end to it."

"There'll never be an end to it, Helen." His own voice too had grown hard, assertive, almost menacing. His next words frightened her. "I don't know how I've managed all this while to keep what we did to myself. I've had to stop myself time and time again from confessing to Edwin. Only knowing how wonderful it was when we made love, and how you responded so willingly, kept me from saying anything. I've honoured our secret, Helen, but I don't know how much longer I can contain myself. It haunts me that one day I might let Edwin know how much I love you and tell him about the way you showed me how much you loved me."

"That's not true!" she burst out. "I don't – not at all."

"But you wanted me. You made that plain enough that day. And by the sound of it, you still do. I could ask Edwin if he'd give you a divorce, and—"

"No! No!" she found herself yelling in panic down the telephone. "Hugh, you mustn't say anything to him. Promise me you won't."

"Darling," came the reply. "I don't see how I can stop myself. I need you and I know you need me. I'm coming over. We can go somewhere quiet, where no one knows us, and we can talk about it, and then—"

"No!" she shouted again, slamming the phone down a second time.

This time she waited, fear gripping her. He obviously intended to blackmail her into submission. But the phone remained silent. He was already on his way. If she didn't give in to him he'd go straight to Edwin.

Mrs Cotterell's voice right behind her made her jump. "Is everything all right, Mrs Lett? Is there some bad news?"

Helen tried to pull herself together. "No, no trouble."

"Only, the way you were talking, I thought it might be your poor father taking a sudden bad turn."

"No, he's fine now." Helen managed to control her voice. "He's well recovered from the winter." An idea came to her. "But there is something. I have to go to see him this evening. The girls are still at dancing classes. I was wondering if you could…"

"Pick them up?" Mrs Cotterell finished for her, her smile motherly and understanding. "Of course. No trouble. My Muriel could go in her car. No trouble at all."

"Thank you so much," breathed Helen in deep gratitude. "I'll be back around eight, if you could…"

"Stay with them? Of course. I've no one to rush home to, and I wasn't going out tonight. My weekly social's on Wednesdays."

"Thank you," Helen breathed again and, giving the woman no time to chatter on, turned and hurried out of the house, making for her car.

She mustn't be here when Hugh arrived. Getting advice, help, had become a matter of urgency and the only person she felt she could trust was her father. Having to admit to him that she had been unfaithful to Edwin was more than she could bear, but there was no one else to turn to and now, with blackmail staring her in the face, she had to swallow her pride and ask for his help.

An hour later, having driven against the commuter traffic coming out of London that in 1966 was beginning to reach alarming proportions, Helen sat in her father's flat, he with a blanket over his knees for all the warming fire and hot cup of tea he'd made on her arrival.

"Dad." She leaned forward, gripping her teacup. "There's something I need to tell you."

It had taken ages to get around to what she had come here to say – the hardest thing she had ever needed to do in her life.

"What I have to tell you has been gnawing away at me for months. I can't tell anyone but you. I certainly can't tell Edwin. But I've got to tell someone."

His loving smile expressed willingness to help her with any problem she might have, she who so seldom piled her troubles on anyone. He had taught her well, using a maxim of his own – "If you want a helping hand, look no further than the end of your own arm."

"Fire away," he said now.

Helen took a deep breath "I don't know if you've realised but Edwin and I haven't had a proper marital relationship for almost a year. We have separate bedrooms now. He says he doesn't want to disturb me when he comes home late after the restaurant and that he's too tired and I can't bring myself to go into his room disturbing him. We've just got into a habit, I suppose."

Her father had begun to frown, and now she had to force herself to plough on. "But last autumn I did something terrible. At least, I allowed something to happen."

He was looking at her intently, almost as though he guessed what she was going to say. What would his reaction really be? Would he be appalled, saddened? Would he understand? There was no other way to lighten the burden. Having embarked on it there was no going back. She found herself telling her story to a blank face, finally ending with some desperation, "I had no idea it was going to happen. Afterwards I was so ashamed."

There was such a strange look in his eyes that Helen, who was about to add that it had been eating into her all this time, stopped to stare at him.

"Dad, I know I did something wrong, but don't look at me like that, please."

She saw him wince as though he had been struck.

–

There was a tightness in William's chest that didn't come from his bronchial affliction. His heart seemed to be beating in his ears with a thumping roar.

"My God, Helen!" he burst out.

Her face had gone white with apprehension. Words burst from her lips in a torrent.

"I know what you're thinking, Dad, but it wasn't like that. It was just that once, not even an affair. I was so lonely. I felt ignored. Edwin thinks of nothing but that restaurant. I'm sure he loves me but he never shows it. He never tells me he does. We've not led a proper married life for years, and when Hugh came that day with his loving words and his—"

"That has nothing to do with it, girl!" he burst through her tirade.

William fought with his conscience. It was he who was wrong, not her, not her marriage, threatening to go sour from neglect, not some brief and illicit moment of adultery. He had been too much of a coward to speak the truth long, long ago and all this was his fault.

He knew his face was working, causing Helen to stare at him in alarm. He strove to compose himself. How could he have been such a fool to think that the truth could be concealed forever?

"Helen, my child…" His voice trembled and faltered. She wasn't his child – she was another's. And she must be told before any more harm could be done.

He tried to reach out for the table to put his teacup on it, but missed. Cup and saucer crashed to the floor. Helen leapt up to assist.

"No!" He too was on his feet. "Leave it! Sit down. I need to talk to you and you must listen without interrupting to what I have to say to you. Sit down, my dear."

Mystified, she did as he'd asked. She was gazing up at him, her hazel eyes bewildered but full of trust. There was nothing of her father in her. William began walking about the room, desperately searching for a way to tell her his secret so that it would not slay her. After all these years of being locked away it was now too crippled to walk forth – yet walk it must. "I've tried to be a good father to you, Helen—"

Half rising, she broke in, "Of course you have, Dad. I've never—"

He saw her surprised face as he rounded on her angrily. "I said be quiet, Helen. Let me say what I have to."

He waited until she sank down again, hands gripped in apprehension in her lap. This had to be got over with as soon as possible whether he hurt her or not.

"As I said, I've tried to be a good father to you, but things are not always what they seem. I was never your true father, your natural father... No, don't interrupt!" he snapped as she again made to do so. "I married your mother when she was pregnant with you. I'd loved her for years before that. At one time we were going out together, but she married another man. That man was Geoffrey Lett, but he soon divorced her. He saw your mother as not being good enough for him. He'd fallen in love with her but she was working-class. Back in the twenties people saw class as important, and your mother held him back. He'd met someone else."

He stopped abruptly, hearing Helen's intake of breath. "No, my dear," he hurried on, his face turned away from her in fear of being confronted by the expression he might see on hers. "Geoffrey Lett wasn't your father. They divorced long before she had you. I'd no idea how alone she was. Had I known I'd have married her. I never looked at anyone else after she chose Geoffrey Lett, blinded by his good looks and his charm, and maybe his money, though she never was a gold-digger. It was when she was on her own and ill that Henry Lett, Hugh's father, came on the scene. He too always admired her. She was a beauty and turned both brothers' heads. She was in the depths of despair, forsaken by Geoffrey, when Henry came to comfort her. He was already married but that didn't stop him taking advantage of her and she fell pregnant. He couldn't marry her so he came to me, as a bachelor and at one time her sweetheart. He asked me to do him a great favour and I agreed. I married her and gave the baby my name. It didn't matter that I was promoted because of it. I did it for her."

Letting his voice die away, there was only silence in the room. On impulse he turned. Helen was sitting in her chair like a statue, her wide eyes unfathomable, registering neither shock nor horror nor even disbelief, but staring ahead as though transfixed on some immovable object.

"Helen," he pleaded. "Do you understand what I am trying to say?"

Now she moved, slowly. Not looking at him she bent to pick up her handbag from the floor beside her and stood up. He watched as she took her coat, thrown so lightly and carelessly over the back of a chair earlier, and put it on, all without looking at him.

"Helen, I had to tell you – because of Hugh. Helen, don't go yet."

But he couldn't touch her or stop her as she went to the door and let herself out like someone sleepwalking, closing it without a word.

Twenty

There was no recollection whatsoever of driving home, her actions automatic while her mind remained like dry cotton wool. Yet there was a sensation there somewhere in that confused fuzz. Disbelief? Grief?

When she finally pulled into the drive of her own home she had no idea that as she got out and made for the house the car door had been left open, the engine running, the brake off.

A bewildered Muriel Cotterell answered the thumping on the door, started to ask if she had forgotten her key but broke off to cry, "Whatever's the matter?" receiving no reply as Helen stumbled past her, along the hall and into the lounge to collapse in an armchair.

Muriel followed her, frightened by the chalk-white face, by the vacantly staring eyes, by the grip of Helen's fingers on the chair arms, her knuckles white.

"Mrs Lett, have you taken bad? Is there something I can do? Shall I ring Mr Lett? Shall I ring your doctor? Have you been in an accident?"

The barrage of questions drifted over Helen's head. She felt incapable of replying to any of them. Rather she seemed somehow to be floating in mid-air, unable to think or speak or move. The cotton-wool feel in her head was slowly being replaced now by a sense of betrayal from all sides. The man she had always known as her father was not her father; she was just a bastard, taken on as a favour to someone else, not loved, not truly wanted, but a chance for her adoptive father to better himself and gain promotion. She was a thing, nothing more. Edwin must know he was in truth her own cousin, but he had married her. Then his love for her had gone stale – because she was what she now knew she was? Hugh, her own half-brother, sick and depraved in his pursuit of her body – did it give him a kick, making love to *this*! She wanted to vomit.

There were voices, Muriel calling for her mother to come quick, and a man's deep voice in her ear, offended and accusing.

"What's goin' on? Mrs Lett, you left your brake off and your engine runnin'. I 'ad to turn it off. Ran right into one of me flowerbeds, made a right mess – me lovely daffs and wallflowers and primroses all flattened."

A stupid thought sped through Helen's head. At least she'd had the presence of mind to put the car into neutral otherwise it would have stalled. Left to itself it had followed the slope of the driveway into one of poor Arthur Brain's lovingly tended flowerbeds and he was livid.

From deep down inside her a giggle began to erupt, a giggle growing out of control until it burst from her in shrieks of laughter, maniacal and uncontrollable. What was the matter with her? Laughter? She should be sobbing her heart out yet here she was laughing her head off.

Someone was shaking her, someone yelling, "Get the doctor! She's ill!" The laughter finally dissolved into wracking sobs and as she felt herself lifted, carried upwards, laid on something soft, her body was already letting go of consciousness.

–

Helen opened her eyes to the low light beside her bed and the familiar surroundings of her bedroom. For a moment she felt fine. Then she saw Edwin sitting beside her on a chair, and it all came flooding back like a fist ramming down on the top of her head. She shot bolt upright, felt a resultant painful thump deep in her brain.

Edwin's calming voice broke through it. "We had to call the doctor, sweetheart. He gave you a sedative. How are you feeling?"

He was going to ask her what exactly had happened to make her behave as she had, but as he leaned forward to touch her something inside Helen snapped and she found herself shrinking from him, struggling out of bed to back away. Her head reeling from the sudden exertion after being sedated, she staggered and almost fell. Edwin was off his chair immediately and coming round the bed to catch her, holding her elbows to steady her.

"Keep away from me!" Shrieking at him, she struggled to free herself. One arm released, she reached for his face with clawed fingers. "Don't come near me – ever again! I want a divorce. As soon as possible."

She was crying. Exhausted, her strength failing her, despite herself Helen collapsed in his arms. "How could you marry me, knowing what you knew, that the man I'd always thought of as my father is not my father? No one ever told me. You, him, Hugh – all of you – lying to me."

"Darling, it's all right. No one has lied. Try to stay calm." Edwin's voice, sounding so stupidly lost, brought a surge of rage.

"All of you deceived me. Why didn't you ever tell me we were cousins? Why keep me in the dark?"

"It doesn't matter, Helen."

So he did know. "It does! It makes Hugh my brother, half-brother – and I let him…"

Even in hysteria, there remained a grain of sanity warning her against coming out with something she might regret for the rest of her life.

"Darling, why should it matter?" Edwin queried, his round but handsome face puckered in bafflement. "I should have told you. But your father… William… was afraid. He wanted to tell you but could never bring himself to, and as time went on it became harder for him. He asked me not to say anything until he could bring himself to tell you personally. I honoured that. And as more time passed, our marriage was so happy that it didn't seem to matter that much any more. I know I should have told you, my darling."

With an effort she tried to push away from him, but felt so weak that she had to bear the indignity of having him hold her firmly to him.

"It didn't seem to matter?" she echoed hollowly. Bitter though her very soul felt at being deceived her whole life, uppermost was the knowledge of what she and Hugh had done.

It was the last thing Edwin must find out. Her affair with Hugh, no matter how brief, must be kept out of all this horrid business, though the thought of his vileness, of him getting his kicks out of touching her, making love to her, sickened her beyond measure. She wanted to wash the memory of him from her body, from her mind. Wash and wash until the skin melted, leaving only bare untouched bone. How could he have been so evil?

"How could you all have been so wicked?" she moaned. "No one's been wicked," Edwin soothed, trying to lead her back to bed while she resisted with weak ineffectual movements so that he let her be where she was for the time being.

"I feel dirty," she moaned. "All of you have made me feel dirty and used and degraded, as though I am nothing."

"Helen, you are not *nothing*! You're everything to me." There was a trace of impatience in his tone. 'There's no law against cousins marrying.'

"I know that," she whispered wretchedly.

"Then that's all that matters," he said against her ear. "In a little while you'll come to terms with the rest."

She would never come to terms with Hugh.

"Your father," Edwin was saying, but paused to rephrase as her body stiffened. "William – he brought you up when your real father rejected you. He loved you and you loved him. Isn't that all that should matter in all of this?"

How could she tell him of the harm her so-called father's secrecy had done her? He should have told her just a few years earlier, that was all. Even if she would have found it hard to accept being told that she'd have been born a bastard but for someone taking on her unmarried mother, she would have been saved from Hugh. That was the worst, the most disgusting thing, her mind harmed, her body defiled because others had lacked the courage to tell her the truth. What if Hugh had got her pregnant? A deep shudder of revulsion passed through her.

Edwin mistook the shudder. "My darling, you're cold. Get back into bed. I'll help you."

Still she resisted. "I don't want your help! I don't want anything to do with you, none of you, after what you've all done to me."

Now anger really was distorting his voice. The hands still gripping her arms tightened. "For God's sake, Helen!"

She glared up at him, hatred for them all flaring in her gaze. "Now I know where that trust money I came into when I was twenty-five came from. I always thought it was a rather substantial amount for my so-called father to have put aside for me on what he must have been earning when I was small. But I never queried it. I was only too glad some of it went to help us when you were struggling to make something of Letts. Now I know where it really came from – my real father. And yet none of you ever had the courage to tell me the truth. Even then." Why was she saying all this? It had no bearing on the most terrible truth of all. "And on top of it all, Hugh—"

She broke off in panic, knowing how dangerously close she was to revealing her own secret. Battling to compose herself, she ended lamely, "I had to wait until now to be told. Can you imagine how I feel? I feel unclean. I want to rub all this out of my mind, but I can't."

What little strength was left to her was ebbing fast. She could feel it. So could Edwin. Quickly he gathered her up in his arms and lifted her into the bed, tucking the covers gently about her.

"Stay there, darling," he whispered. "Until I get back. I need to have another word with your father. I don't want to phone him, I want to have a good talk with him, face to face, about how you feel. I don't think he truly realises it."

Lying there without energy, she watched him stride from the room.

She would have lain where he'd left her, had it not been for Angel and Gina being tentatively ushered in by Hilda Cotterell, who explained that the girls had been worried and she couldn't keep them away any longer.

Standing awkwardly, they looked down at her after Mrs Cotterell had left, not knowing what was wrong with her and how to cope. Their two young faces wrenched at her heart.

"I had a very nasty shock yesterday," Helen explained as best she could. "It made me feel very unwell and the doctor says I must rest. I'll be fine by tomorrow. You'll hardly know I've not been well. It's just a passing thing."

It was hard to smile at them, to behave reassuringly, but they smiled back, their young lips twitching tremulously, still uncertain. She held their hands, soothed them with bright words which didn't reach her own heart, making her wonder if they indeed reached her daughter's bewildered ones.

"You're not going to die, are you, Mummy?" asked Gina, seeing how pasty and drawn her face was.

But before she could say, "Good Lord, no!" eleven-year-old Angel rounded on her sister.

"Gina, people don't die of unhappiness. Mummy said she's had a bit of a shock over something and just doesn't feel well. She'll be well again tomorrow, won't you, Mummy?"

This last was couched as an abject plea, making Helen summon up her brightest smile. "To tell the truth, my sweets, I'm beginning to feel a lot better now, enough to get up, and I think I will."

They must never know how heavy her heart was, that, but for them, she could willingly let go of life if that were possible. But as Angel had so rightly said, people did not die of unhappiness. Unless it was by their own hand — and Hugh was not going to have that satisfaction. She hated him with all her heart now. Any recollection of ever having felt anything for him conjured up instant nausea.

Pushing him from her mind, Helen sat up to prove to her daughters that she was fully recovered, was well and strong again.

"You two go downstairs," she commanded. "I shall get dressed and put on some make-up and come down in a few minutes. Then we'll all have something to eat. You go and tell Mrs Cotterell to make us something really nice."

Edwin returned home to find her up. The girls were laughing as they watched a comedy show on the TV but, aware of her drawn and pale looks and seeing that she wasn't laughing along with them, he came over to reach for her hand. As though she'd been stung, Helen withdrew it. She saw his arm fall to his side as he moved away to sit down in the armchair opposite hers, making no attempt to look at her.

"I've spoken to William," he began. "We had a long chat."

Helen felt her heart give a start. "A long chat" must mean that he knew of her affair with Hugh. His expression was serious, almost grim. To realise that she and her own half-brother… If he could ever forgive her infidelity, could he stomach incest? The way she was feeling, did she even care?

She found herself caring very much. "Edwin, I'm sorry," she began.

He sat there just looking at her. "What's there for you to be sorry about?"

Was that a statement or a challenge? But his expression had softened.

"It's he who should apologise – to you, to me, for trusting me to wait for him to tell you himself. It wasn't fair on you. I've told him that. I should have known better and broken that trust years ago. I'm at fault too. I never realised the effect it would have on you. I should have known better. I had no idea of the harm it would cause you."

Was he referring to Hugh? How could he take it so calmly that not only had she been unfaithful to him but that it had been with her own brother?

Bile rose up into her throat and she turned her eyes on the two girls, still riveted by the television screen, taking no notice of the conversation. Even so, young ears heard everything.

"Angel, Gina," she rasped. "Go upstairs and play, will you?"

"Mummy!" began Gina, indignant. "I'm watching—"

"I said go upstairs!" Helen heard her voice rise and fought to control it. "Daddy and I have something serious to discuss." How she managed to steady her tone, she couldn't imagine, for inside she was shaking. "We need to be on our own. Now, please, do as I say, go upstairs to one of your rooms. You've plenty of jigsaw puzzles to keep you busy. Just for a while."

Angel gave her a look. She struck Helen at that moment as being far older than her years.

"Come on, Gina," she said promptly, taking her sister by the arm, "Come and see how far I've got with mine – it's ever so complicated."

There was something about Angel that always gave Helen pause to reflect – something almost too adult for a mere eleven-year-old. Perhaps it was her slight deafness that made her more perceptive to the feelings and expressions of others. By merely looking into their eyes, she saw into their souls.

The girls trooped upstairs, and she turned to Edwin. What she had done had to be explained. "Edwin, about Hugh. It happened so—"

"I can't begin to imagine what all this has done to you," Edwin burst in. "Hearing it from him like that. No wonder you came home with half your mind gone."

Relief flooded through her. He'd been told nothing about her and Hugh. The man who had brought her up, who had professed to be guarding her against harm, was a liar, but he wasn't a fool.

There welled up inside her such anger against the silence that had caused her such anguish that she burst out in a welter of venom. "I can't forgive him! What he's done to me – I'll never forgive him!"

Edwin put out a hand to her. "No! You mustn't be like that, darling. He thought he was doing the right thing. And it's never worried me. Believe me, it doesn't. It hasn't changed anything."

"He has no idea of the harm he's done, keeping me in the dark," she wailed, breaking down as Hugh's face and the burden she must carry for the rest of her life hovered over her. One of these days what they had done would come out. Hugh had never been known to keep his mouth shut about anything.

Another thought raced through her head. She'd taken it for granted that he knew of their relationship. Why should he? Now she wasn't sure. But if he was ignorant of it she was going to have to see him one last time – put him straight, put the fear of God into him about what they'd done. Not even he would be so low as to boast about that. As for trying his hand at blackmail for his own ends, surely even he would be as sickened as she was by all this.

Edwin had risen from his seat, was coming towards her to offer comfort. In a moment of idiotic panic she heard herself cry, 'Don't!' and, leaping up, hardly knowing what she was doing, ran from the room before he could stop her. Racing up the stairs and practically falling into her bedroom, she flung the door to, turning the key against intrusion.

For a while all was quiet from downstairs. Her ears keened for any sound, she heard Edwin coming upstairs. Listening, hardly daring to breathe, she heard him go into Angel's room, perhaps to tell the girls that there was nothing to be upset about, that their mother was a little overwrought at the moment and would be fine later. Then she heard his tread coming towards her own room, his light tap on her door. His voice was soft and imploring.

"Helen, I know how you feel. But please, don't stay in your room, nursing this all on your own. We need to share it. Please let me in so we can talk."

"Go away!"

"Helen…"

"Go away, Edwin."

He must have taken notice of the entreaty in her voice for he didn't speak again and finally, quietly and prudently, departed to his own room leaving her to herself.

It was a miserable night. She was unable to sleep for the turmoil going on in her head. After the girls had gone to bed, Edwin tapped on her door again, inviting her to go into his room.

"Nothing untoward, darling, just that it might be better for me to be on hand to comfort you. We have to share this. I can't bear to think of you facing all this alone."

But when she refused he went back to his own room, leaving her to lie awake, caught between wondering if he too lay awake worrying over her half the night and deciding that she must have misjudged Hugh. Surely he was unaware of their blood ties. If it was so, then she had to make contact with him. The thought was not a pleasant one.

Next morning after Edwin left for London – reluctantly, though she assured him that she was quite all right – and the girls were safely at school, she dialled Hugh's number, which she had found in Edwin's address book. Sitting by the telephone, she listened as the ringing at the other end went on, seemingly forever.

He had to be in. Edwin's reply to her carefully couched query as to whether Hugh would be at the restaurant today had been that he didn't expect him until early evening.

"Not much going on," he'd said, "and I'd rather not have him under my feet until later."

Maybe he was still in bed this early in the morning. Unless he had spent the night at a friend's home, or maybe with a girl. Helen felt a small shudder of revulsion run through her, mixed with an uninvited stab of anger. Hugh was a foul creature, taking his pleasures just as and when he wanted, even from his sister, if it did turn out that he'd known of their relationship all along. Though surely he wouldn't stoop so low, she thought for the hundredth time as the ringing at the other end continued.

–

Hugh let himself into his flat, his thoughts miles away. It had been a great night. This morning he would ring Margherita and tell her so. Later he would send her roses.

She loved roses – yellow ones. Yellow went well with her long, sleek, dark hair and her smooth, Mediterranean skin. Her sultry, deep brown eyes had captivated him from the start, several weeks ago, when he had met her in a bar. She'd given him a look that had brought him hurrying over and, with pouting lips and moist eyes, had told him all about how her boyfriend had thrown her over and how lonely and forsaken she was feeling. Then in her open Italian way she had leant towards him, linked an arm through his and said how very handsome she thought him. He had bought her a drink and it had started from there. That was weeks ago and it looked like continuing. He'd slept with her nearly every night since last week. Before then it had been a tentative affair, but now it was progressing rapidly. She would murmur how fast she was falling in love with him, prompting him to reciprocate. She had intimated a longing to settle down, and his heart had responded. It was about time he did, too. With any luck…

The telephone was ringing as he opened the door to his flat and he raced to snatch it up.

"Hullo!"

"Hugh? It's Helen."

Hugh's heart took a drop. Damn! A good job he hadn't blurted out Margherita's name. It would have made for awkward explanations.

Helen's voice was toneless, almost commanding. "Hugh, I need to see you. Come here tomorrow morning when Edwin's in London. I've something of great seriousness to tell you and I don't want him around. Come about eleven. The girls will be at school and Mrs Cotterell and Muriel will not be here either. They're usually back here around twelve thirty – an hour and a half's time enough for what I need to see you about."

Hugh tried to make his tone lively. "Funny, I was thinking it was time I saw you," he lied. That had been true up until meeting Margherita. Helen had always had the ability to turn him on, but now... "You're never much out of my mind, you know," he gushed. He didn't want to hurt her. Best to let her down lightly. "And despite..."

"Don't start jumping to the wrong conclusion, Hugh," she cut him short. "What I have to say, I need to say to your face. But I warn you now – you're not going to like what I have to say. What we did was wrong. I'm banking on the fact that you don't yet know how wrong it was. That's what I intend to talk to you about. Don't let me down, Hugh. Be here!"

The phone went dead, leaving him staring at it in bewilderment. What on earth was she talking about? Whatever it was, it sounded important. He'd better go. He had something to tell her too, though he'd need to butter her up to start with.

It was annoying yet in a way pleasant how the mere thought brought with it that old excitement. Well, perhaps this one last time; then he really must put those sort of thoughts from him now that there was a better fish in the sea. His new love had shown that she could match Helen's power to turn him on. Better still, in her case there were no complications of a husband in the wings.

Slowly he put the receiver down then, picking it up again, began dialing Margherita's number.

Twenty-One

It was obvious that William hadn't spoken to him yet — playing the coward yet again, Helen thought bitterly. After what she had confessed, surely it was Hugh he should be telling above all else. Instead he was leaving it for her — the contemptible bastard!

Again hatred rose against the man she'd once so lovingly called father. To think that, knowing what he had, he'd stood by, even encouraged she and Edwin when they'd first met. When they'd spoken of marriage and the day of their wedding dawned, he'd still withheld the truth about her real father. To her mind, that silence was as much a lie as any verbal denial. She wanted nothing more to do with him. When she'd told Edwin that she never wanted to see or speak to William ever again, she'd meant every word of it.

Helen paced the house waiting for Hugh to arrive. She was smartly dressed in an appropriately dark suit, her short fair hair neatly backcombed, a minimal amount of make-up on. Would he come? It was eleven o'clock already. Still no sign of him.

In a ferment of foreboding, she rehearsed what she needed to say to him, still with no idea how to embark on it. Would it be better to come right out with it, cruelly but honestly, or creep up on it slowly? The thought that had continued to plague her since finding out the truth resurfaced – what if Hugh had known for ages? No, that possibility was too awful to contemplate; it made her feel physically sick to do so.

Eleven fifteen. If he didn't come soon, Hilda Cotterell would be here before she could tell him anything. It felt like hours since she had last looked at her watch. Her insides, churned up ever since she had made the phone call early this morning, were feeling worse by the second as she paced the floor, looking at the telephone each time she passed it.

Perhaps she should phone him again. Perhaps he'd decided not to bother coming, shrugging off her demand to see him, laughing at it. If only this nausea would go away. If only William had found courage enough himself to shoulder this burden. It was his burden, after all. If he was still getting round to it, he was too late. Again hatred consumed her at his lack of grit.

She was about to lift the phone in desperation when the sound of car tyres crunching on the shingle drive arrested her. Hugh was here. She heard the solid click of a car door.

Quickly smoothing down her dress in nervous reaction, Helen went out into the hall and stood waiting for the doorbell to ring. She let the double chime die away before opening the door. Hugh stood before the wide portal, framed by the twin columns of the portico. He looked so sure of himself, debonair in dark, well-cut trousers, a grey roll-neck jumper, his fair hair professionally tousled, his features handsome to a fault. In days gone by her heart would have leaped in response. Today it merely lay like a lump of coal inside her.

He was smiling, a stupid, self-assured smile. Perhaps even now he was planning to seduce her again. Nausea rose up in her throat and she turned abruptly away, marching ahead, leaving him to close the door.

In the living-room, she turned to face him. His smile vanished leaving him frowning at her bleak expression.

It took all her will power to try to compose herself. She must not give way to the quaking that had begun the moment she turned to face him. But it was no good. The word burst from her lips with a scream. "Incest!"

Hugh was staring at her, his blue eyes like saucers, his expression ludicrous, like a clown.

"What?"

"I said…" No, she couldn't repeat that word. Trembling, fighting to calm herself down, to find controlled words, her hands curling into fists, her lips tightening, she swung away from him so that he wouldn't have to see her face, nor she look at him. She began pacing the floor.

"I take it that my…" – her voice shook – "that William Goodridge hasn't spoken to you."

"Why should he?" came Hugh's voice. "What was it you said just now? Incest? What incest? What're you talking about? Look, come here and sit down."

He'd sat himself on the sofa, was patting the place beside him, his voice taking on a purring, persuasive tone. "Come on, darling, come and tell me what's upset you. Something you've been watching on television?"

Television? Helen's mind reeled with anger and frustration at his idiotic response. Her head was feeling swimmy. What she had to say to this fool, this evil fool, had to be said quickly or she might break down altogether. Hugh, sitting there in front of her, patting the place beside him, still imagining himself capable of seduction, made her want to be sick.

In a rush, before her courage could give out, she burst out with what she'd learned, not pausing to imagine what it must sound like.

"Your father and mine are the same person," she finished, at last turning to look at him.

Horror registered on his face, yet there was disbelief too. He plainly thought he was listening to the ravings of a maniac.

"It's all true," she cried. Her words caught in her throat as tears threatened to engulf her. "Don't you understand what I'm trying to say?" She hiccuped. It was obvious to her now that Hugh had had no idea of this and was utterly stunned.

Standing in the centre of the room, her body bent towards him in entreaty. "Don't you understand? We've the same father. Ask Edwin. Ask my stepfather."

"He's lying!" Hugh shot up from his seat, made towards her, but she backed hastily away.

"Helen, don't believe what he tells you," he continued, reaching out to her. "I think he suspects about our affair and he's using any—"

"It's the truth!" she yelled at him, backing even further away from the outstretched hand. "He took on my mother when she was carrying your father's baby. He told me himself. He doesn't lie. Whatever else he is, he isn't—"

She stopped. But he had lied. All these years he'd lived that lie. She was weeping now, hardly able to get her words out.

"And you and I, we...we made love. That's what I mean. Brother and sister — we made... I can't bear to think what we did — what *you* did. It's... it's disgusting. It's despicable."

She was striding frantically about the room in new anguish. "I want to scrub it out of my mind, but what you did can never be washed away."

"What *I* did?" he cut in, but she hardly heard him.

"I've tried. Ever since I found out, I've tried." Convulsed with weeping, her body bent over, she let herself sink on to a chair. She leaned forward, hugging herself.

Hugh was standing before her in stunned silence. Then his voice, self-protective and sharp, broke through her misery.

"Don't blame me, Helen. You were as much in the wrong as me. You didn't stop me."

"I didn't know."

"I can't believe this." Despite what he was saying, when she glanced up at him through the mist before her eyes, she saw that his face had grown pasty as reality forced itself upon him.

"I'd better go," he said in a low, chastened voice – but she wasn't done with him yet. He wasn't going to get away that easily, leave this house and, driving back to London, beginning to cheer up, cast this morning off as he did everything that didn't quite sit right with him. So he'd made love to his half-sister. But he'd been unaware of their relationship at the time. So he'd put it all behind him. What had he to lose?

The thought hit Helen with the weight of a water-logged sandbag. Up out of her chair, she threw herself at him, shrieking, hands reaching out, fingers curled like talons. Before he knew what had hit him, she'd clawed both his cheeks, leaving deep weals that slowly began to ooze little beads of crimson.

"You bastard!" she screamed. "You bloody selfish, uncaring bastard!"

Fighting to hold her off, his face suffused with rage almost as great as hers, he blasted back at her: "You're the bastard, Helen. You're the one born out of wedlock. Your mother was a whore and my father was a fool, but what you are is nothing to do with me!"

Catching her wrists, he flung her from him with unexpected strength. As she fell, he turned and made for the door.

"And you can keep well away from me," he yelled as he went. "As far as you possibly can!"

–

His mood as he drove back to London he couldn't describe accurately even to himself. Black, yes. Horrified. Stunned, disbelief hovering even now. But more than that – his whole being revolted against the injustice of it all, the blow dealt to his peace of mind, his self esteem. To be made a fool of like this, that was the worst thing of all. All the way back to London he drove like a maniac, doing seventy mph in some places. He was lucky not to encounter and be pulled up by police.

Now what? The best thing would be to check the truth of all this. What if Helen had gone off her rocker, gibbering, talking a load of rubbish to get back at him for that brief affair they'd had? If it hadn't been over before this morning's demand to see him, then it was now! But he had to double-check her babblings. She'd said ask William Goodridge, ask Edwin. That he would do. Edwin, he thought. He didn't know Goodridge particularly well.

Better to confront Edwin. Then go home, pack, and disappear, putting miles between him and the mad Helen.

Italy, Rome, take Margherita with him – she'd love to go back home. In Rome they could live it up and he could forget all about this sordid business. In Rome they would get married and live in luxury for the rest of their lives. It was time he settled down.

–

"I'm going abroad," he announced to Edwin, taking him by surprise. "I've had about enough of this family, of being tied to this damned restaurant business. I need to get away, far, far away – from you, from all this, from Helen."

Edwin stared at him, taken aback by his cousin's venom. So he had seen her this morning and she had told him about her true parentage. It had possibly come as a bolt from the blue finding out his real relationship to her, but why should that make him so uptight?

"So Helen and I are cousins," he said evenly. "It's not against the law for cousins to marry."

"She's also my half-sister."

"Why should that make you so angry? You can hardly be ashamed of her. I'd have thought it would have been pleasant to find you had a sister, even if it did come as a bit of a shock."

He'd been about to laugh but was arrested by the look on Hugh's face. He could only have described it as stricken. It was then that an inkling of the truth dawned on him. He wanted to cast it aside as utterly ludicrous but couldn't.

He stood horror-struck as Hugh turned on his heel and made towards the door of the penthouse, calling over his shoulder, "I have to get as far away from her as I possibly can. I'll let you know where I am when I get there and you can send my cheques on to me. I shan't be coming back, not this time, not even if I'm down to my last quid!"

The door closed sharply behind him, and Edwin heard the sound of Hugh's feet racing down the stairs, fading quickly. He almost made to run after his cousin, to question him, but he knew he didn't want to hear the confession he'd get. He felt sickened by what now bombarded his brain, knowing that in those few minutes of Hugh's visit, his life had been turned upside down.

–

Helen wasn't well. He tried to be home as much as possible to be with her, but he might as well not have bothered for what notice she took of him, brooding up in her room, hardly leaving it despite the lovely summer.

He had never taxed her about her and Hugh. Refraining from doing so helped him to some extent to still not believe it. Yet the questions were always present. How often had they made love? Did she still love him? Obviously, for him, love was ever superficial – that was Hugh all over, loving them and leaving them. Love meant little to him. Though knowing he'd made love to his own half-sister had shaken him to his boots, Edwin had seen that clearly enough that afternoon in his penthouse. Even Hugh wouldn't knowingly stoop to such depths.

Another question – did she love him, her own husband, at all? She seldom spoke to him, replied briefly and in monosyllables to all his efforts to converse. Her whole mien cried of betrayal – by him, by Hugh, by the man who had led her to believe that he was her real father – and rather than anger or bitterness at what had transpired between her and Hugh, he felt deep sadness and sympathy for her. She'd been led up the garden path, and now he realised he'd been to blame, neglecting her for his love of work and sending her into the apparently sympathetic arms of his cousin. There was nothing he could do now to rectify things; he was unable to approach her about it so long as she remained distant with him.

Only when he mentioned William, the instigator of this tragedy, did she become eloquent.

"I don't want to talk about him!"

"If you were just to go and see him," he ventured as summer faded to autumn, "you might not feel so bitter against him. I'm sure he meant well."

Her smile was twisted as she sat gazing sightlessly out at the last roses, their leaves mottling to old-age yellow. "They say the road to hell is paved with people who *meant well*."

"I don't mean just that," he coaxed carefully. She could easily leap up and leave the room. "I'm thinking of you, not him. You can't go on nursing this grudge forever. It'll eat into you until you'll never be able to get rid of it."

Still she stared through the window, her voice flat. "I don't want to talk about it," was all she said, and in the face of her refusal to reply to any more entreaties, Edwin gave up, hoping that perhaps another day he might persuade her more successfully to see his point of view.

He saw William as often as he could, mostly to soften the edges of Helen's silence towards him. The man wasn't looking at all well. He looked frail, thin. Once tall and upright, he now stooped, his cheeks drawn into hollows beneath his cheekbones, his eyes dull and a little sunken, his teeth seeming too large for his mouth. Bronchitis every winter and spring had taken its toll. Even now, in autumn, he was troubled by a nasty cough. The whole thing worried Edwin. He had to coax Helen with all his might to see her stepfather before something happened for, by the look of him, William's body might not take another year of illness.

"You've got to see him," he told Helen after telling her how ill William was looking. "Before it's too late."

But she merely shook her head and refused to reply.

–

Hugh's letter was cheerful. He'd obviously put his trauma behind him, maybe even forgotten it. He had married the girl he'd taken out to Rome with him. Margherita was her name; she was an Italian girl he'd met in London.

They were gloriously happy, said his letter. Italy was doing him good and he'd been exceedingly lucky since settling there – with some money Margherita's family had given him he had opened up a cafe, and he had an excellent Italian cook who not only pulled in the locals but the growing tourist trade as well, German, Dutch and English. He was doing well; also, Margherita was pregnant with their first child, her family having taken him to their bosom.

There was not one mention of Helen. To Edwin, sensitive to the slightest nuance, that omission in itself spoke volumes. Not once had Helen ever mentioned Hugh, either, not even when Edwin tentatively referred to where he had ended up.

"Seems he's given up the acting lark," he said, forcing cheerfulness. "Opened up a cafe in Rome. I expect he still gambles, though now he's married an Italian girl he might have given that up."

It seemed best to give up on any further news as Helen, her face a mask, sat staring at virtually nothing, picking sparingly at their Sunday dinner. She had hardly eaten all summer. She was thin as a rake these days. It seemed she only came alive when the girls were about. She would laugh and chat with them, but the moment they went off somewhere, the old haunted look of a betrayed soul returned, sometimes frightening him, though he should have grown used to it by now.

A few minutes later he was startled by hearing her speak, something she hardly ever did without first being addressed and then only when forced into a reply.

"The dance school is putting on a show next Easter," she said now. "They wanted it at Christmas but it's coming up so quickly they won't do it justice. They want to do a really big show so it'll have to be Easter."

"That's nice." He made himself look attentive. There was still hope. He was about to say more, to encourage her to make normal conversation, but she seemed not to need his assistance.

"They've said they want Angel and Gina both to take lead dance parts as they're doing so well, and to do a solo spot as well. Their tutor said that as they both have good voices she was thinking of a song and dance duo, something modem, perhaps from one of the West End shows. She's going to combine the show with the annual prize-giving and Angel and Gina's special spot will be included as part of their exam. That's good, don't you think?"

Edwin couldn't recall her speaking at such length since Hugh's departure. For a moment he wondered if it would be an appropriate moment to bring up her seeing her stepfather, maybe suggest that he come here for Christmas or they go to see him? But then perhaps not. Best not to ruin this unexpected and heart-raising moment. He'd wait until nearer Christmas. Now wasn't the time to pull her down with talk of William, not when she was showing this first sign of a return to normal. Better he bide his time until a more appropriate moment cropped up.

It did, one morning two weeks before Christmas, in the form of a phone call. He still hadn't spoken to her about asking William here, though since it looked as though the man was beginning another bout of bronchitis, rather early this winter, Edwin wondered if it would be best for them to go and see him for a short visit so as not to tax him too much – that was if he could get Helen to comply. It was going to be hard, but if he could persuade her, perhaps the sight of William's plight might melt her bitter heart.

Edwin, about to leave for London, answered the phone. He intended coming home again early that evening; he was afraid to leave Helen alone for too long these days. But with Christmas coming up it was getting difficult.

Not that it was busy in the same way as it had once been. Things had changed, times had changed, and not for the better to his mind. Today he no longer went to work with the light-hearted anticipation of talking to those regulars he'd once known. Today Letts was showing signs of becoming out of date, as it had when Uncle Henry had died, before he'd taken it over, modernising and pulling it up by its boot straps.

Once again it was falling by the wayside, subtly, the change at first not being noticed. Swinging London with its brash vitality, its skinny, mini-skirted girls and pink-trousered, long-haired young men, its raucous guitar music and even more raucous behaviour from groups like the Rolling Stones, was putting places like Letts at risk.

His own daughters had their bedroom walls plastered with pictures of them and other groups – the Kinks, Pink Floyd, the Beatles – and played all their records over and over again.

Today, instead of going out to dinner, nice people stayed in to watch TV and entertain at home, while the children of the Swinging Sixties, with hip, pot, the pill and "Freedom", roamed London, high on drugs and music. Even the Stones, up in court on drug charges, were still feted as idols.

On occasion a group of better-off hippies whose parents would have frequented Letts in earlier times would invade the restaurant looking for a laugh. So long as they behaved and spent good money he couldn't refuse them entry, even if his regulars were disturbed by their presence. Fortunately they didn't come around too often, but Edwin was at his wits' end about how to attract his old customers yet keep up with the times. He refused to stoop to hiring rock groups, even the more famous ones; Letts would stick to their sedate four-piece band. With this on his mind, he picked up the phone.

"Yes?" he enquired casually.

Twenty-Two

The woman's voice at the other end was crisp and direct. "Am I speaking to Mr Lett?"

"Yes," he replied.

"The husband of Helen Lett?"

"That's right."

"Is your wife at home, Mr Lett?"

"Yes. Who wants her?"

"Mr Lett, this is St Bartholomew's Hospital. Your wife's father, Mr William Goodridge, was brought in to Accident and Emergency this morning, apparently having lain all night on a cold floor with a serious pulmonary condition. His cleaner found him this morning and called an ambulance. He has since suffered cardiac arrest which we have been able to stabilise to some extent, but in the circumstances we feel his daughter might like to be on hand, here at the hospital if possible."

"It's serious, then," was all he could say, his mind running ahead of him.

"Could your wife travel up to the hospital this morning?"

"Yes, of course. We'll leave straight away."

"We will expect you as soon as possible," came the voice, which went on to inform him of the enquiries desk's location and then rang off.

Edwin found Helen in the kitchen speaking to Mrs Cotterell. She was beginning to be fractionally more talkative these days. He'd hoped she was at last starting to put the bad times behind her. As for him, he still couldn't forget what she and Hugh had done behind his back. That it had been incest, if unknowingly, was oddly unimportant next to the fact that she'd deceived him, been unfaithful. Though he might forgive, for he loved her and didn't want to lose her, he'd never forget. But the phone call had knocked everything for six. Panic consumed him. This would bring it all up again.

"Helen, I need to speak with you," he burst into her conversation. "It's your father."

She turned, her hazel eyes wide with instant anger, but he hurried on, not sparing her.

"I've just had a phone call. From Barts Hospital. Your father was taken in early this morning. They said it was a heart attack."

The anger faded to obduracy. "What's it to do with me?" she grated.

Edwin was stunned. The man who'd raised her so carefully, selflessly, who had loved her like a true daughter, was dying, and this was her reaction?

"How can you ask that? He did everything for you."

"Except be truthful with me."

"That's all over now. Helen, we must go to him."

"You can. I'll stay here. You can let me know how he is when you get back."

How could she be so hard? He suddenly saw how deeply she must have been injured if she was unable to forgive the man she'd once loved, once called father, even now he was close to death. But if she refused to see him now, unable to forgive, and he were to die, she'd never

293

have another moment's peace remembering how she'd allowed him to go unforgiven. For her own sake, she must go to him now.

"Whether you like it or not you're coming with me, Helen. That's my last word. Go and get your things. We're leaving."

"No."

She made to brush past him to escape to her bedroom, perhaps to lock herself in, but he grabbed her arm, propelling her from the kitchen.

"No you don't, Helen! Mrs Cotterell, will you please call a taxi to take the girls to their school this morning," he called over his shoulder to the woman following them out to the hall in bewildered concern.

"I always take them," protested Helen, but he ignored her, conducting her along the hall to where their everyday outdoor clothes hung in the cloak cupboard, yanking open the door and lifting one of her coats from its hook. Luckily she was wearing shoes ready to drive the girls to their private school five miles away. The coat didn't match the shoes, it being brown, they being blue, but that was too bad.

"Mrs Cotterell," he ordered again. "Get Mrs Lett's handbag from her room, will you? Whatever one is in use."

The woman scurried upstairs as fast as her ample frame would allow, came back down seconds later with a large tan one.

"It's what she was using yesterday," she declared, "but it don't go with anything."

"It doesn't matter," he said tersely, passing it to Helen, now too dumbfounded to argue. "Come on, let's get going!"

Helen said nothing the whole way to London. Whether she was chastened, angered and refusing to speak to him, or silenced by fear of what she would find at the hospital, he wasn't allowed to discover. He tried to make some attempt at small talk, asking if she was warm enough, if she was worried and if he should have allowed her time to visit the bathroom before leaving, but his questions were met with no response. It was a long, long, silent journey.

Having negotiated the London traffic with Helen sitting like a stone beside him, Edwin was glad to reach Barts. She was still failing to respond to anything he said as, following directions from the enquiries desk, they found their way to the ward. She seemed hardly to listen as he spoke with the ward sister and the doctor and were finally conducted to the screen-surrounded bed. The nurse checking a heart monitor screen looked up and left as they entered.

The ward sister, picking up the notes at the foot of the bed to consult them, nodded. "He appears to be stable at the moment but we need to keep a close eye on him. As things stand I would advise staying here at least for tonight."

"You do think it's bad, then?" queried Edwin when Helen still said nothing.

The woman nodded again. "You may stay as long as you like. There is a canteen if you want tea or coffee or something to eat. But it might be best to be on hand in case of any change. We have facilities for visitors needing to stay overnight. I'll leave you with him for a few minutes. We will come back from time to time to check on him."

Edwin glanced at Helen. She was gazing down at the thin face, its skin parchment-like against the white pillow.

A spaghetti tangle of wires and tubes surrounded the patient, linking him to drips and instruments; tiny lights on monitors blinked on and off; a transparent oxygen mask covered nose and mouth. He lay quite still. Helen's expression was one of granite.

"Don't you feel anything for him?" Edwin queried in awe, but when she looked up at him in reply, her eyes were arid.

"I shall never forgive him," came the harsh whisper.

–

Given pillows and blankets they tried to make themselves as comfortable as possible in the room that allowed a partial view of the ward William was in.

Helen had said very little all day since that last statement at William's bedside, merely shaking or nodding her head when Edwin enquired if she wanted a coffee or tea, something to eat or to go outside to stretch her legs.

They'd had a meal around lunchtime and another around seven, bland, uninteresting hospital food – not that either of them felt inclined to go outside to find more acceptable food. Edwin thought of his restaurant, how it was faring in his absence. He'd phoned and been told all was well. But it was Friday and busy and he'd most likely be missed by whatever regulars might be there. Perhaps, informed of the reason, they'd be concerned for the maître d' that some of them would remember with fondness.

He had also phoned home to tell Mrs Cotterell that they'd not be home that night.

"Oh dear," came Hilda Cotterell's motherly tones. "I do so hope poor Mr Goodridge pulls through. I feel for poor Mrs Lett. She must be beside herself. Of course

I'll stay tonight, give an eye to the girls. A good job tomorrow's Saturday – they don't have to go to school. But I will get them a taxi to their dance class, there and back, as you say. They should be kept busy at a time like this. And I'll give them yours and Mrs Lett's love. They'll understand; they're both old enough to know."

Helen had eaten without interest, as though merely to order; had walked beside him along the roads around the hospital, stretching her legs, but in silence. He had suggested going for a decent lunch at a restaurant but she had shaken her head without speaking. He wanted to urge her to bend towards her stepfather but hadn't the courage to voice the words.

Around one thirty in the morning, while doing their best with hard chairs, blankets, thin pillows and a kindly offered cup of cocoa, they were alerted by sudden activity from the darkened ward. Medical staff bustled down the ward and there was an urgent hurrying to and from the screened area through which a light glowed eerily.

Helen started up with a look of fear on her face, and Edwin got up to enquire what was going on, but already a nurse was coming towards them.

"Would you both come with me," she requested in a whisper and together they followed her starched progress from the side room to the ward and the glow through the screens.

The oxygen mask still covered William Goodridge's face as they gained his bedside. His eyes were still closed and what could be seen of his nose and mouth was like a pale mask itself. The main monitor was bleeping feebly, the white line moving erratically, a doctor watching it closely. He looked up at the visitors but made no attempt to leave.

"William?" Edwin whispered, bending close to the still figure. Getting no response, he felt for Helen's arm. "Speak to him," he ordered. "Call his name."

She stood rigid, unmoving. Looking up at her Edwin saw her staring blank-faced at the man she had once loved so dearly.

"Did you hear me?" he asked.

Still there was no response. "Helen, did you hear me?" he asked again and, again receiving no response, his whisper came harshly, urgent and unforgiving – a taste of her own medicine.

"If you don't, Helen, we're finished, our marriage, everything. D'you understand? I've gone along with your bitterness all these months. I've done nothing about the way you and Hugh deceived me. But this, I draw a line at."

He gave her arm a vicious tug. "The man is dying. Your father, the only one you've ever known – is dying. Your own father, my uncle, put you from him, but this man took you in, gave you the love of a real father. And you stand there and condemn him because he was fearful of breaking your heart. Even if you don't mean it, *say his name*!"

Helen was staring at him, realisation of her situation dawning. Stonily she obeyed, an automaton. "William—"

"No, what you would normally call him," prompted Edwin viciously.

"Father."

"I said what you'd normally call him."

She hesitated, glanced up at him, then looked back at her father.

"Dad?"

Something magical happened with the uttering of that word. Edwin saw her body bend towards the man, heard her repeat more softly, "Dad?"

And then in a kind of entreaty, "Oh, Dad. It's Helen." Then, with even more pleading, "Dad, don't go. Please don't go. I love you, Dad. Please, stay. I love you."

In the light of the cold glow above the man's head, Edwin saw the brief sparkle of something falling from the lowered face, the short fair hair half concealing it. The sparkle came from a tear.

He moved forward, put an arm about his wife's shoulders as she remained bowed over her father and, looking at the bent head, saw that Helen's cheeks were wet with tears. Under his comforting hold, he could feel her shoulders beginning to tremble.

"He'll be all right," he whispered inadequately.

"He mustn't die," she sobbed. And again, softly, "Dad, please don't go. I love you so much."

The face on the pillow seemed to crease a little. The eyelids fluttered open, the mouth beneath the mask formed a faint smile, then, as quickly, the expression dwindled and the eyelids became fixed. The feeble bleat of the monitor became one single tone. All about them the staff broke out in urgent movements. Edwin and Helen were hustled away, the doctors moving in, ignoring them.

Edwin was holding Helen tightly to him, watching the silhouettes of those working to retain the last threads of life. Then all seemed to slow. One by one nurses came from behind the screen. Helen, clutching Edwin, flinched as the ward sister reached out to touch her arm.

"I'm sorry," came the sister's voice. "We did all we could but there is nothing more we can do. He's gone. Do you want to see him?"

Helen turned away, pulled herself from Edwin's grasp, away from the sympathetic eyes of the sister. He hurried down the dark ward after her, but when he reached the side room, she was already picking up her coat and handbag.

"Darling!" He was shocked. But though her voice trembled with grief she was able to speak.

"No point going back to look at him," she said very slowly. "I saw him smile. His eyes were full of love and he knew I loved him, that there was nothing that needed forgiveness. We both knew. No point going back."

–

In the large hall the babble from the audience of families and friends faded as the lights were dimmed.

There was a stir of anticipation as the music began then, as the curtains were drawn back in a series of small erratic jerks, there was a concerted intake of breath at the tableau of eight tiny tots dressed as elves and fairies in a woodland scene. One or two children were a little unsteady maybe, the hand-painted flats and wings were slightly flimsy, the cut-out shrubbery and trees not quite to scale while behind them the large, early morning sun rose somewhat unevenly, but the lighting, growing in strength with the sunrise, was perfection itself.

Amid a bevy of oohs and aahs, Helen straightened up in her seat next to Edwin. "When do Angel and Gina make their entrance?"

Edwin consulted the typewritten programme. "After this, with the older girls. They don't do their own spot until just before the interval."

"I'd have thought—" Helen began but stopped abruptly as someone behind them, no doubt a parent of one of the little ones, shushed her. Sitting back to endure the scenes that didn't include her girls, she forced herself to concentrate on what was going on up there on the stage. She needed to concentrate to take away the bad images. Three months since losing Dad – that she had known him as Dad as far back as she could remember must count for something. The memory of that day when she had finally been able once again to call him by that name still brought tears.

If only she hadn't been so ready to lay blame at his feet. If only she'd had enough generosity to realise how much her refusal to see him must have hurt. Her heart ached, thinking how he must have felt. She had been so wrapped up in selfishness that she had only seen her error at the very last moment. That their reconciliation had come moments before his end was little consolation to her. It was said that every death lays a burden of guilt on the bereaved to some degree, and her guilt in leaving it so long before telling him that she at last understood and accepted was something she'd carry with her forever.

This evening was no exception. To push it from her, Helen trained all her attention on the little dancers. Seeing one or two occasionally get out of step, she hoped her own girls would enjoy a faultless routine, and for a while forgot about guilt.

Angel and Gina were her life, her sole escape from those things she'd rather not recall. Their future was her all. They were so talented. Would they one day make a profession of that talent, maybe be like Hugh, looking for the limelight? At Hugh's name, she cringed inwardly, forcing her mind back to the present.

The fairy dell scene had ended. The audience applauded and the chubby little ones bowed awkwardly and unevenly before running off stage to their tutor in the wings.

Older girls were taking the little ones' places. The woodland scenery was hurriedly and visibly manoeuvred aside to accommodate a city scene; one of the curtains had proved hard to close, and the pair had been drawn back again to stay unclosed for the rest of the show.

"There they are!" Edwin pointed out and with all else swept from her mind Helen trained her eyes on them for the rest of that scene, willing them not to make any mistakes. Her reward was to glory in their perfect steps, their lithe movements, the rest of the dancers dimmed by comparison.

But it was their solo spot that enthralled her as they went through the routine put together by their tutor, Miss Sellers, to the lively song "It's A Lovely Day Today", singing it through the once before going into a tap routine then slowing with the music to more elegant ballet steps and finally reverting to lyrics once more.

As the applause rose, necessitating a curtain call, Helen grabbed Edwin's arm in excitement. She felt his hand cover hers, the first time he'd properly responded to her touch since learning about her and Hugh, and an unexpected thrill of relief ran through her veins as she recalled that past wilderness.

These days he made a point of being home more often, yet he'd remained distant for all that. Sometimes she would catch him looking at her as though at a loss about what to say or do, but perhaps it had been her own ongoing moodiness that had kept him at a distance. So many times she had prayed for them to get back to the way they had once been, when the children were small. They'd been growing apart for years and maybe that was the way of married life, but this business with Hugh – she'd begun to wonder if that would ever go away. Edwin behaved kindly enough, as though he had put it behind him, but could he ever truly do that? Would it always be there at the back of his mind? Nothing she could do would mend that.

At the touch of his hand, she looked at him and, as the auditorium lights began to come on, saw that he was looking back at her and that his regard was tender.

Her pleasure at her daughter's achievement faded, replaced by wonder that after all that had happened, he could still look at her with tenderness.

"Everything is going to be all right?" she whispered hopefully.

Edwin's hand tightened on hers.

"Of course it is," he whispered back. "For our girls' sake, for all our sakes." And to confirm it he bent and touched her lips lightly with his own in full view of the audience now moving off to enjoy the interval.

That was all it needed. She must put it all behind her – Hugh, her stepfather, her real father – none of it must matter if she wanted to save this marriage. It was a good marriage, its only fault that perhaps she had expected too much of it. So now she would not expect heaven, just a little lightness and contentment. And there were always her girls to lighten her days when Edwin was working, their future to fill her with anticipation. And really she did love Edwin, always had, despite everything.